Lots of Love

AVIDE

[signature]

FRION FARRELL

Enjoy!

TINOBAR BOOKS

ISBN: 9798339784449

Cover design by: Conor Watson and Matthew Duncan
Library of Congress Control Number: 2018675309
Printed in the United States of America

*IN MEMORY OF AUDREY AND THE EVERLASTING
LEGACY OF GENTLE KINDNESS*

Chapter One

Sand, gritty and sharp, fell from my eyelids, as they quivered open to face the stinging glare of a milk-white sky. Images of the night before were imprinted over the damp sand and the long-vanished tide. I lay naked on a beach in Lindisfarne, Northern England. A pile of clothes lay neatly stacked by a piece of driftwood. The garments looked vaguely familiar, winter greys and blacks. Mine. Stones stabbed at legs that felt heavy and useless as I crawled towards them and pulled on the pants and socks of a man who wore sturdy walking gear. Trembling arms pushed gratefully into a jumper designed to defend against the worst heating malfunctions in a host of student digs. Before, and that is how it would always be from this moment, before this time. I had heard many say it in intense shock, how the world had somehow stopped and restarted, even when they could not. Standing, I staggered further away from the shore, where the ground was covered with sharp blades of marram grass. Salt and earth spiked my wet face to remind me I was truly still alive. Footprints from the night before still patterned the sand. When I had been simply Joseph, in a tunnel of pain, vanquished.

How distant the sound of her tread had seemed, though she was only a mere matter of steps away. Shuffling her feet to let me know she had arrived. The tide, with its rhythmic wash of sound pulled in a little closer.
"Do you have to leave?" She was breathless, having run from the village. Her words carried on the wind, tinged with fear.
"I can't stay," I told her, focusing on the flecks of white in the darkness before me.
"You really resigned from your job?"
"Yes." I had been a hospital chaplain in Manchester.
"Your folks are devastated Joseph."
I turned towards her to gauge the depth of her statement and saw that her face was pressed into luminous sadness by the moonlight. My own remained unmoved. A spreading numbness across my chest. I could not summon compassion, either for myself or for her.

"They don't see me. They don't hear me. What they know of me is just a reflection of their need."

My words came out wooden and matter of fact.

"But," she began, her hand reaching out, "I need you."

Her blonde hair was an intricate spider web, blown back in the breeze from the pale, earnest face. There was no desire to touch her. The pain of her betrayal with Daniel had long since eaten its way into the hollow space where despair had established its own dark kingdom, overwhelming every other emotion.

"You don't need me Louise," I told her with pinched lips.

Her head bowed, turning away, processing defeat. She sighed, facing me again. "Where will you go?"

"As far as I can." I barely heard her words, for only the sea held any purpose now.

She moved in nearer until the fresh scent of eco-friendly apple shampoo, a sensation that used to thrill, was now a transitory, wind-blown moment of no significance.

"Joseph," she choked, one shoulder slumped, face dropping. Her sigh was swallowed in the wash of the incoming tide. Louise mirrored my stance astride the sand. I felt the moment of her surrender, the long breath of goodbye as she turned and left. I did not watch her go.

Stiff-backed, despairing, I sat and rested my head against a large stump of driftwood. Bereft of the sweetness of my lost faith and overwhelmed by bitterness, I felt as much adrift as this dislocated skeleton of some far distant tree, that had trailed the ocean and cast upon an unfamiliar land. My mind was blank as gradually the water crept closer to my feet. I undressed easily, for it seemed fitting that I go out naked, the way I had entered this world. Slowly and deliberately I stepped into the beckoning sea. Cold, so much colder than I had thought, but I embraced its bite. Almost submerged, I lifted my head as a charcoal sky split into strobes of white light casting lustrous silver fingers upon dark waves. A strong breeze stirred across my skin and through my hair, as a spiralling cylinder of light enfolded itself around me. Lifted in a fold of wind, my feet dangled above the tumultuous ocean. Some part of my consciousness reasoned that I had drowned. But this was not death, not the end of my human condition, but a strange and new beginning that was old and yet familiar. Colours in the distance, golds and reds, flashing greens and those I had no words for in this time. Tanamaarin. Joyful and poignant came the memory of the dimension I once inhabited. I willed my body towards where my heart longed to be. But no. Nesu, standing on a dazzling disc was there in front of me. Grey flecks in tawny fur, tufts of hair above his ears. Eyes the colour of a wind-blown leaf, liquid green. Feline limbs, staunch and dangerous, barred my way. When Nesu spoke it was as if everything that mattered was nothing and nothing that mattered was everything. "It is time, Osweald." the lynx told me.

I plunged back into the water, where a rogue current caught my foot, driving me further out to sea. Frantic seconds of thrashing until I saw Nesu still above me, calmly watching. The moon lighted a shining track back to shore. Like a drummer answering to a beat, I began my dance of the arinokra, knowing I was born to it. I let the sea shape me. Forward, my shoulders dipped, arms reaching, a diving curve of torso. I continued the moves that my muscles knew so well. A rolling dip of forehead and neck, eyes raising towards the stars, nostrils breathing in the air, the earth, the sky. The water fountained in a springing dance, a circle of moonlit jets opened beside me, a whirlpool of rushing water at its centre. In seconds a roaring geyser sprang upwards with Nesu riding atop, until he plunged into the ocean beside me. I clung onto his back, fingers entwining his strong wet fur, the power of his presence bringing a lightening shock of physical change. Dark became light, the clear sounds of night creatures hunting on the shore, individual scents of living creatures, his powerful muscles combatting fatigue. The stench of one that did not belong.

A seductive whisper of doom snaked around my ears. In the distance I could see what had previously been hidden; an inhuman figure waiting on the beach. A shadowy rawdin, invisible to almost all human eyes, stalking its prey of human despair. A flat grey face, pinched nostrils, long body covered in distorted symbols, that crawled spider-like across its surface. Mercury eyes gleamed with the madness of the world from which it sprang. When and where I had last seen one of these poisonous creatures I did not know, yet the recognition was instant. My feet found solid ground and I released the lynx, who soared above me in a powerful spring. Too late, the rawdin saw his danger. Nesu landed directly upon the unseen imposter, even as it clawed savagely for escape, of which there was none. As a species, the Rawdin do not swim well, but this one was already dead as the lynx cast the creature adrift. Still wading towards the shore, I pushed away the distorted figure as it floated towards me. The extinguished predator disintegrated to nothing, as his own dimension claimed him. I spent some time cleansing the clawing touch of twisted limbs, the choke of ashen breath, in a familiar ritual that I had yet to understand. Stumbling, I finally reached the shore and felt my face hit the sand in utter exhaustion. Nesu had gone, but I knew he would come again at my bidding.

Joseph, the young man I had been, had ended his lonely vigil, only to find that he had never been alone, even in his most secret places. Only to know that at the moment when he was so sure that no sense of purpose could ever again fill his heart, it had leapt from the sky, the sea and the earth to reveal itself in utter clarity. I had come to find Avide. Having stripped away everything I knew, this is the sum of all I know.

Lindisfarne, a place of saints and history, the remains of an old priory, where shops speak of art and reading, St Cuthbert's story. All so familiar. The house in the village was immaculate, quaint and blessedly empty. The old stone building had been refurbished by the church community for visitors. I passed shelves filled with biblical interpretations as I crawled to my room. My parents ran a retreat here, for those who wanted to explore their Christianity. I had no quarrel with any religion, sincerely felt, least of all one that had given me so much. Values of service, a living, the music of spiritual love. But I had seen the roof crash in on my church of many colours and many doctrines. I now understood that the identity hidden within, could not have revealed itself, until that moment. Stripped naked, dowsed by the ocean, that which had been hidden for twenty-eight years had made itself known. Joseph would always be there, but Osweald, who was beyond the imagining of the tragic hospital chaplain, had stepped from the past to carve out the future.

I sat down on the bed, retrieving a small bag from on top of the patchwork quilt. My parents were good people; it was with horror that I remembered the blow I had so nearly dealt them. I tore up the note that I had written the evening before, tossing the pieces into my bag. With new insight I saw clearly that my parents would be as considerate as possible. In their minds, allowing me time to find my way back to the religious path, that was their direction and inspiration. I wrote a note thanking them for all they had done and asking for some time off the grid; trusting that they would let me be alone. Recalling the love I felt for them both, I said I would be travelling for a while. As an old measure of gratitude, I left my priestly blessing. I wandered over to the window and ran a hand over the old oak, as if each small pane were part of my jigsaw. Vision blurred as I gazed towards the priory, befogged in a strange haze of soft light. Without warning came the first memory from a time long forgotten and little known, when I had lived as Osweald, in seventh century England, fourteen hundred years ago.

I was alone on the river path. At my back stood the tall arches of the Monastery of the Folded Wind. Senses awash with summer. Air filled with sweet honeysuckle, bees humming. Vast swathes of undergrowth to my right, from which sprung tall oaks and beeches. Below, the river formed a blue satin ribbon that curled around our sanctuary. The calls of wild creatures far outweighed the distant chanting of my fellow monks. Amongst them I could clearly hear Nesu's rasping growl and rumbling breath. His presence disturbed my brothers, but he would come to my side later. To the north was a quiet garden, missing the ministrations given to those on the south. Here, Nesu favoured an outcrop of rocks, beside the long branches of a rowan tree. I had taken to spending my time in this place every evening after prayer.

Lindisfarne was a day's ride from our own less important monastery. I knew Avide would have left at sunrise and not have broken fast. He never named himself abbot, always Avide. Always our dear lord, who would brook no outward acknowledgement of his work, content to remain in the shadow of his more illustrious companions. I saw him above, on the high track that ran through the thick of the forest, and that most would not use. He sat tall and lean, long hair loose down his back, for he did not follow the ways of dress used by Cuthbert and our fellows of Lindisfarne. Avide patted his horse in thanks, as he gave the mare's care over to Aelred, skilled in horse-lore. I expected him to make his way to the refectory but instead my lord called me over.

"You are troubled," I said, drawing towards him.

It was rare that he did not smile when he returned from travel. The look he gave me sent a shiver through my bones. To my surprise he walked towards my small, empty garden as the sun began to dip in the sky. Nesu prowled above us and dropped from the rocks to our feet. Avide was the only other he would allow to touch him, rolling his head beneath his outstretched hand. The lynx gave a discomforting cry, as if he sensed the solemnity of our master. Avide removed a sealed parchment from his pack and placed his hand upon a boulder nearby. To my amazement, the stone began to emit light. Lines of fire criss-crossed the surface until I could clearly see the bright outline of a turtle. I gasped as the top half of the boulder slid to one side and once again fire appeared, this time from within the stone, scoring out a bowl in the lower half before it abated.

I placed my hand in the bowl, which was surprisingly cool and smooth. I turned to my master, speechless. He placed the parchment and another package into the stone bowl and made a slight gesture with his right hand. The top half of the boulder slid into place, the turtle engraving disappeared from its surface. It was not the first time I had seen my lord perform what were clearly miracles. All those who knew him closely were aware that these events were to go unvoiced to the world, though we often remained reluctantly tight-lipped as others won praise. For the first time, I did not want to hear Avide's words. Already the air had changed. The sky was dark. Without doubt I knew our time of sanctuary would soon be ended.

"Osweald." He waited until I turned my eyes to his and, as always, their compassion pierced my soul. "Many years ago, you were forced to come to this place. It was not of your intention. Now I ask you, in free will, if you will stay with me to fight the darkness beyond this end, which is merely another beginning?"

I little understood his meaning but I did not hesitate to give my allegiance for as long as he wanted it, whatever the cost.

"Of my own free will I do so pledge."

At last a smile to lighten the doom-filled night, but there was sadness as he turned to Nesu.

"If the time comes, this boulder contains my Mark and the way to find me." Nesu circled the stone, his nose close to the ground.

" Guide him to find it," Avide whispered to my beloved companion. "Wherever it may be."

I shivered in the March cold as the memory vanished. It's hard to explain how certain I was that this was no daydream. No imaginative projection of my own making. With every fibre of my being I knew that I had lived and breathed as Osweald the monk centuries ago. That I had walked the earth beside Avide, though he is unmarked and unrecorded in history, a rare and precious Solar of Tanamaarin.

Chapter Two

In Budapest, the Danube was lower than usual for this time of year. The man, for he was still a man, sat in a heated, private pool on the roof of a huge old building, that had survived occupation by the Nazis. Reminded of those times, now known as the Second World War, he remembered the bite of power, the taste of manipulation, the elevation of sadistic cruelty. The shadow of Jarinbissar, the malign dimension which had long ago claimed him, hung low over the world in that prolific twentieth century period. Of necessity he had become even more hidden. So often invisible in plain sight, he and his kind still held a powerful hold on the world, their dark intent screened behind a thousand public manipulations. The building had a unique view of the city's two distinct parts, split by the river. The cruising riverboats were now eerily absent, but a trickle of locals crossed the green bracelet, Liberty Bridge. He savoured the scent of fear, his delicacy, as it crept through empty shops, unused hotels and closed cafés. He adjusted his position, suddenly uncomfortable; a change in the energy distribution network he named the Bissarat.

He snapped his fingers for Price, his bodyguard and manservant, who emerged from the shadows, immaculate in a suit of Harris Tweed. The man pulled himself easily from the pool and accepted the towelling robe, letting it hang easily on his shoulders, as he took a seat by the edge of the roof. In more recent years he had sat in the same place, satisfied to observe the fruits of destructive energy in the Middle East, when Europe had once again become a hot bed of fear and moral contradiction. Refugees from Syria and Africa had flooded the borders. Hungary was, as always, at the centre of it all. His people worked hard to fuel tightly gripped prejudice within the masses - hidden bombers, rapists, and fundamentalists. What he had not predicted was that those safe within their fences of relative prosperity - a job, a home, warless - were torn between strong compassion and the fear that he was so determined to sustain. Europe had touched and seen that those of the Middle East were essentially the same as those of the West. They would no longer turn their backs on the families who presented traumatized and desperate in their own backyard. Latterly the pandemic too had fostered connections across the world that he had never seen before. This awareness and compassion were dangerous; it threatened the very fabric of Jarinbissar. And now this change.

It was his purpose to ensure the world turned to those who ensured that power remained in the hands of those who were best prepared to use it. Long fingers swept over dark hair. A face that had changed little in the sixteen hundred years it had served him. He was the centre of darkness, the human core of Jarinbissar on the planet. Scenes from the rawdin's mottled mind had passed along the connections of consciousness through the Bissarat. Like an old Saxon arrow they found their target, revealing a male figure emerging from the sea and the lethal spring of a lynx. The sky darkened. He raised his eyes, as lightening flashed and thunder growled. Price held the door from the roof open. Slowly his master walked towards the open door issuing his instruction. "Find Marcus."

Chapter Three

Dawn was merely an hour old and I was determined to be gone before my mother and father headed for church. I filled a bag with a few clothes and supplies from the kitchen and stepped out into eerie quiet. Behind me, I heard the picture-book wooden door close, arched and surrounded by an established rose bush. Lindisfarne was a place of charm and historical charisma. Fleeting glimpses of the Priory, now in ruins, flitted through my mind. Behind these thoughts were images of a complete stone monastery, filled with the comings and goings of a time long ago. A flurry in the bush behind made me turn, ready to fight, but it was just a cotton-wool cloud of linnets, dispersing the frost. Joseph would not have recognised the speed of reaction, the instinct to challenge, the animal prowess in that small instant. And yet, I was still Joseph; but I had always been Osweald.

The old Nissan splayed a winged cascade of water as it picked up speed across the tidal path. It rattled in protest as I reached the other side, minutes before the sea covered the causeway behind. The small settlement would remain separated from the mainland until the tide retreated again.

The snow-topped highlands of Northumbria gleamed in the sunlight, as I drove across the moors. Winter still played its game of hide and seek with spring, as the deadly grip of the viral pandemic began to loosen its hold on the planet. Covid had appeared over a year before in the East and spread into every corner of human life. The skies were swept clean, footfall echoed in empty streets, the thrum of human interaction had become silent. Mass graves had appeared in New York; Spain had sent graphic images of its struggle against the onslaught. All over the planet, military style hospitals sprung up in anticipation of unremitting demand. I saw inside the closed doors of many care units, where exhausted health workers cried in their frustration and grief. There was so little we could do in those early months. Yet Italian song sent hope from window to window, and communities came together to protect their vulnerable. Most of us still lived in a masked world, bounded behind screens, touching no strangers, divided to defend against the invisible virus. A counter-intuitive expression of love.

I left the moors and dropped to the motorway, pressing down hard on the accelerator to go round rumbling trucks, clogging the inside lanes. I tried to summon other memories of those long-ago times but, like existence in Tanamaarin, they completely eluded me. I felt as if I was standing underneath a fresh, overflowing and spectacular waterfall with a test tube. I could hold only a tiny sample of the precious force above and around where I stood. There was a distant sorrow as I headed back to Manchester. I was still Joseph, still the minister who had lost his faith, the betrayed lover, the despairing son. In the space of a day, what had been enough to end a life was now virtually irrelevant. I had rented a flat in the city centre, where Louise and I were to live. I don't think, truly, she had any intention of leaving Lindisfarne. She had been in love with the idea of being the wife of a hospital chaplain, working amidst those in need, extending her benign attributes to a wider audience. Perhaps I do her a disservice, for it was obvious to us both that I no longer shared the aspirations of our families, or her doctrinal certainties.

Emotion had come crashing down amidst the burnt-out fire of too many days where the world was out of sync with itself; rabid with disease and stricken with loss. Too many times I had found myself ill at ease in the constraints of religious rigidity. Yet to reach beyond those confines, meant the destruction of a culture that had nurtured every tenet of my belief and self-concept. It was through the disassembling of everything I thought I knew that I found my real nature. Osweald had been released, never to return again to his hiding place in the consciousness of Joseph.

The flat was located in Ludgate Hill in the Northern Quarter. The place was functional, but in fact I had hardly lived there at all. There were many staff from the hospital who had rooms allocated in unused hotels in the city during the pandemic. We slept, we worked, we Facetimed those we cared about. A number with vulnerable family members, dared not go home. Now, with most of us vaccinated and deaths falling, restrictions were beginning to lift and those who could had returned to our families. As Joseph, I returned to mine, only to find I had nowhere at all that felt remotely like home. I parked in the space allocated for residents beneath the building and made my way to the top floor that looked out over Angel Meadow. The parkland was now occupied by a smattering of local schoolchildren who came there for supervised play, hesitantly trying to re-establish routines. Their youth and diversity rained a new vision upon this old ground. In the nineteenth century this area was filled with back-to-back homes, mostly housing impoverished Irish immigrants. Beneath the parkland, underneath St Michael's flags, lay the remains of forty thousand souls, whose lives had been picked clean by wont and disease. I had been involved in the nearby drop-in centres for the homeless. These charities had evolved from institutions founded over a hundred years previously, in a different age. Dickens, at that time, had called the place a 'Hell on Earth'. Engels had been driven to write about the appalling poverty of industrial England. The well-off lived a few miles, and another universe, away from the savage semblance of civilisation within the heart of this city. One of the reasons we had picked this spot was because it was a place of hope and renewal. There were gardens within gardens, offering messages of redemption and peace. I now felt the force of the tangled history beneath and wished the project well.

The sky was heavily laden with grey-tinged cloud. The city felt bleak and empty as I made my way down High Street in Manchester city centre. The carved stone and intricate iron gates of the old fish market, engraved with the year 1873, now only enclosed an empty plot. Bright yellow umbrellas, canopies of pretend sun, would give little protection from the rain to the empty tables beneath. They dotted the alleyways of the Northern Quarter, where my younger days had been filled with long nights, thriving clubs and wine bars. I decided to eat out. Indoor hospitality remained forbidden in the restaurants and pubs and tables had been quickly erected on the pavements, between alleyways. Anywhere, in fact, that the mandatory two metres space between customers would allow. A year and a half ago this part of the city was thronged with customers, huge halls needed to provide capacity for a bustling city. Now I sat in a cold street surrounded by empty buildings in thundering silence. I reached for the hot sandwich and cup of coffee, nodding to others around me. A smattering of hardy Mancunians, determined to find some company and a diminished return to past freedoms.

At this point I acknowledged that there was still choice. After all, my friends and family would tell me that what was going on in my head was really a symptom of an emotionally disturbed mind. There was no historical record to evidence my belief that the Monastery of The Folded Wind had ever existed. Nor was there any knowledge of a monk known as Avide. Sense and logic began to demand that I file away this aberrant chain of thought and return to the track I had now abandoned. A low growl beside my chair. Screams and shouts from those around me as Nesu nudged my side. The flimsy tables were upturned as my fellow guests, screaming at me in fear, ran to avoid the lynx. "Peace, Nesu," I whispered, standing up from the table. Nesu followed at my side, licking his lips and turning his eyes on the retreating figures heading away from the tight space. I turned a corner into an empty street as Nesu disappeared from external reality. Avide's Mark. Was it real? Yes. As Nesu was real. As the memory was real. As Avide was real. I could not find Avide until I found the Mark. I could not find the Mark until I knew the location of the monastery. My ecclesiastical knowledge told me that there were no records of its existence, of which I was aware.

I decided I would step in what I felt was the right direction and trust that the memories would unfold in their own time.

Chapter Four

"Euair, you are disturbed," Marcus observed.

It was strange, even to him who had arranged it so, that the name Ellan had given to him so long ago, was the title still used by those nearest to him. It was an old word from an old language. A poisoned tree. Sometimes he was entertained by his own perversities. No one however, had quite pronounced it the way she had done, a voice that could call to the leaves and bring the earth to whispering.

"Come, eat with me Marcus." A half smile, laughter had long ago dropped from his palate of expression.

As ever, his protege looked in need of a good meal. The man took his pristine, white napkin and shook it, before placing it carefully over the knee of his younger companion who, to others around him, was not young at all. Price clicked his fingers to bring an elegant, Slavonic waitress to the table. Silently they waited until she had set out extra silver cutlery and baccarat crystal.

"Wiener schnitzel for our last evening in Vienna. You were always fond of spring in this house."

Marcus looked around at the sumptuous, glittering dining room. Chandeliers sparkled from the ceiling. Long, lavishly curtained windows gave a view of dazzling lights, now more sparsely scattered in the still recovering city. Live opera once again provided the background hum for its revived international community. Restrictions were still in place and Marcus understood the covid figures were rising again. Like his host, he never considered that those restrictions applied to him.

"There have been some irregularities in the North of England."

His companion, expression clouded as ever, nodded as he lifted a wine glass.

"The rawdin are restless. One was dispatched by a wild cat at

Lindisfarne."

Marcus gripped his glass more tightly to stop it slipping. "After all this time."

He replaced his wine on the table. "A lynx once again in Lindisfarne?"

The man beside him, his eyes hooded, turned away. "Perhaps," he allowed.

The food was delicious. Marcus ate because he knew it would displease the other if he did not, wiping his mouth carefully, modulating his breathing before he spoke. "And Sereka?"

A long pause. "I do not know, yet."

Marcus was aware he would pay in some way for forcing that admission. Still, he continued.

"The Bissarat quivered with her return some years ago. Another life, another face. And yet she has not come to us."

The man pushed his plate away, standing up abruptly and ending their dinner. Marcus was prepared for a vicious strike, but instead he saw that his companion was more excited than he had ever before witnessed.

"At last they are showing their hand. Avide's hand. Sereka is out there; she does not know herself or she would have found me by now. If he has truly returned, find Osweald. He will lead us to Sereka."

"Even Avide perhaps?"

The other man turned empty eyes towards the magnificent view of Vienna's Ringstrasse. Marcus saw that he was lost, as he had been on other occasions, in some distant reflection of another time. He waited.

"I sometimes wonder if he ever really existed," commented the other.

Despite himself, Marcus felt a thrill of intimacy at this insight of the other's mind. His guardian, as his companion was legally termed, did not continue to explain. Before Marcus could elicit anything further, he found himself alone with Price. Pushing his unfinished plate to one side, he held his hand out for the A4 envelope that the manservant proffered. Attached to several sheets outlining contacts and addresses, was the time his private flight would leave for Manchester, England. Three hours. Without haste he finished the wine and left the table.

Chapter Five

Amy Rowan had come looking for Os Ryland. His driving licence said Joseph Ryland, (she was responsible for checking ID) but he told her he preferred to be known as Os. Some nickname from school maybe? Skinny jeggings caught against the wall as she made her way down the narrow passage to the vestry. The bulb was out in the corridor, she hugged her jacket closer, remembering the heating had yet to be switched on. May had been a mixed bag of weather but that morning she felt distinctly cold. There was enough light disseminating through the stained-glass windows to soften the heavy stone. The old masonry was wreathed in gentle golds and rich reds. The church reached back in time, with fortress-like old stone and heavy studded wooden doors. There was a high altar that Paul informed her was at least twelfth century. It was a long time since she'd been a part of organised religion. In the past she had found herself wandering into various places of worship, here and abroad, of many different faiths, to spend some time alone. There were huge, ornate cathedrals that she found cold and sometimes even cruel in their essence. Others left her with a profound sense of awe and belonging.

The church in which she now found herself, St Michael and All Angels, spoke to her of ancient mystery, a link to simple fundamentals of kindness and worship. She felt respect for every sincere effort to connect with whatever spirituality spoke to the human individual. For herself, Amy acknowledged her main driving force was that she would not be bound by tradition, culture or imposed obligation. Coming from a strong Catholic upbringing, this had not gone down well with her parents, who had moved back to Ireland three years previously. Prior to the last few weeks, she had not known Croston existed.

This small village had a kind of middle-earth feel. St Michael's itself added to the sense that she was in the midst of the arcane and magical. Working with Os, she had come to love the peace she found in this building.

"Amy." Paul's broad Lancashire accent drummed out the two syllables, His lanky form filled the doorway to the side entrance. Closing her eyes she stopped, hiding a sigh as he caught up. He squinted to see her in the dark passage.

"There are bulbs in the vestry," he remembered.

Paul hustled past her and placed a key into the lock. Amy was startled by the hanging vestments reflected in a full-sized mirror as the door opened. The disembodied robes seemed to signal a sense of loss, of emptiness. She made herself breathe. Amy had no doubt Os had gone and she had no clear understanding why some disembodied clerical robes should speak to her with such intuitive certainty.

Had it only been a fortnight since he first entered her life? She and a few fellow nurses had started collecting for families left homeless and devastated by the war in Ukraine, when Russia had struck its terrible blow the year before. As the only childless team member, and therefore presumed to have time, she'd been drafted to link up with the voluntary sectors. In March that year they had collected again, this time for the local homeless. The GP practice storeroom had been filled with donations for the growing numbers of those without shelter. Even before covid, she knew first hand that changes to the benefit system, trying to weed out those who abused it, had mainly caused devastation to those who needed it most. Now, after the pandemic, and a year of war in Ukraine, destitution had become rife. Again, she had been asked to liaise with local voluntary services and charities to ensure the best use of donations, often given by people who could least afford to do so. It had been over three years since the pandemic had first stopped the world in its tracks. 'A marathon, not a sprint,' she remembered the words of her manager in that first month. She, like many others, had risen every day, digging deep for some resilience to meet the unexpected, to hold on to those colleagues and patients who clung tenuously to their painful edges. She had felt for her friends in Intensive Care, who had borne the harsh brunt of those first terrible few months. Most people who worked in the NHS and other essential services were still battling overwhelming exhaustion, trying to catch up the routine care that had virtually come to a standstill. It had been a time of vast change and unpredictable outcomes and no one she knew had come out of it unscathed.

St Michael's in Croston was thirty-five miles from the practice in Lancaster, where she had been working as a part-time locum Practice nurse for the last three years. The pandemic had struck just as she was preparing to leave to work with the medical team on a cruise ship sailing to Scandinavia. Instead she stayed with the practice through covid, doing extra hours with the community respiratory team. She had changed roles, becoming familiar with online consultation, the massive vaccination effort and as a member of one of the few teams who carried out home visits in the early days. Amy had resisted several permanent job offers, looking, as always, to move on. However, it was true that this time she had been tempted to stay. The weekend charity work had quickly become a weekly highlight. So much so that when her nursing contract ended, she decided to spend two weeks full time finishing her work at St Michael's. The church had provided a room to use for sorting and storing. Amy had gone there each Saturday for the last few weeks, stunned by the need and distress of families unable to feed themselves. Paul was a paid member of a charity providing shelter for the homeless and he co-ordinated the distribution of donations and worked with the food banks. He was rummaging in the drawers by the vestments. In the mirror she watched his pale, thin face fixed in concentration. The pointed, unshaven jawline was set in determination, always keen to take charge. Amy stood to one side as he came back towards her, holding the replacement bulb. She blinked as the electric light brought the charity worker into full glare.

"Amy," he began. She winced at the earnest tone, involuntarily stepping back.

"You'd best lock up the vestry again," she quickly interrupted. She waited for him to nod his agreement and head back along the corridor, leaving her free to move into the broad nave of the church. Feeling the need to place a physical barrier between herself and Paul, she slid towards the recess in which stood the altar, and around which the existing church had been built.

Something had changed. On the south side of the chancel there was a carved stone, beneath which, she knew, were two stone bowls. These, Os had explained, had been used for washing communion cups. It had given her chills when he had revealed them a couple of days ago; strange to think they had been there for several hundred years. On the floor beneath was a substantial stone block, that had clearly been removed from underneath the bowls. The top half of the stone block had slid to one side revealing a shallow recess inside. Drawing closer, she noticed a shape wrapped in what appeared to be old linen cloth. As she began to unfold the material, it dropped away to reveal a red silken layer covered in white symbols, none of which looked familiar. With great care Amy unwrapped the silk, finding herself transfixed by a golden cross, inlaid with rich red stones. Unpolished, with the gravitas of true age, she found her fingers stroking the flaming jewels.

Another silk cloth lay within the stone recess; it had the faint marks of being wrapped around something for a long period. It too, was covered with white, unfamiliar symbols. Os. The thought flitted across her mind, it had to be something to do with him. Unsure why, she picked up the spare cloth and placed it in her pocket. Just as she straightened up Paul's noisy breathing could be heard as he entered the nave. "Amy, I think it'd be best if we..."

She turned and saw his mouth form a silent circle. His eyes moved between the stone block, surrounded by the dust of removal, and what she held in her hands. Amy moved towards the altar, placing the cross upright to show him. At that moment, the sun broke fully through the huge stained-glass window above the altar. Coruscating strobes of light penetrated the ancient jewels, causing great flashes of red and gold to stream through the chapel. Amy felt as if she had been lifted out of time to some other world, as her flesh tingled in a sea of sparkling colour that pulled strongly at some long forgotten buried memory. Paul was physically shaken, placing his hand on the altar to steady himself. Amy's own hand trembled as she carefully laid it down.

Paul gasped. "Where did it come from?"

He walked towards her without removing his gaze from the object. Shaking herself, shrugging off the sense of something she would not yet describe, Amy thought all they needed was some angelic background music to underline the awe in Paul's expression.

"It came from down there." She pointed towards the gaping hole in the stone wall.

"I don't get it," she continued. "Why would someone break in, go straight for where this lay hidden, then leave it behind?"

Paul picked up the cross, his eyes catching fire as his fingers stroked the ruby inlays. Carefully he took the cloth that Amy had placed on the altar and wrapped the golden cross within it. He raised his head, alarmed. "Perhaps we disturbed them!"

Amy hugged her arms close, listening for movement, as Paul pocketed the cross and exited the room, giving hoarse instruction for Amy to stay put. She raised her eyebrows but stood silently by the ancient altar. She felt in her pocket for the precious cloth she had removed, confirming the tell-tale assumption something else had indeed been removed from inside the stone. There was no way she could allow Paul to have any idea that Os had been involved in removing an artefact from the church. In fact she really had no evidence that the event had anything to do with her friend. And yet....

Yesterday she had watched as Paul explained to Os that he needed to pack the donation boxes in such a way the storage space was efficiently used. His deceptively mild tone had not hidden the dislike in his face as he spoke to Os' broad shoulders.

The younger man, hardly listening, was examining the altar area. Just before Paul was about to repeat his instruction, the new recruit had turned, eyebrows raised in an untroubled question. The charity worker had dropped his head and eased back towards the storage room. Amy had understood with her usual instinctive appraisal. Everything that Paul found hard, Os made easy. She had witnessed those people that Paul had tried to persuade for weeks to come in off the street, succumb to the gentle voice of a man they had only just met. The most hardened user halted in their relentless self-destruction to hear what Os had to say. He had practically taken over the team in terms of loyalty, always managing to have care for the carer as well as for those on the streets. She suspected Paul himself was drawn to the man but couldn't admit it. And then there had been her own relationship with Os. It wasn't just his unusual face, his insight, his young-old smile. She was drawn to the quirky way he had of ignoring convention, drawing his own lines while somehow never crossing yours. She had fielded several offers to date Paul; he had not been slow to recognise her enjoyment in Os' company.

The fact that Os should have been there that morning to work, and was not, would itself bring suspicion. She let her fingers wrap around the old fabric, suddenly unsure if it would disintegrate. A tactile exploration reassured her that the silk cloth seemed to be fairly sturdy for its age. What else then had been taken from the secreted chamber? She moved back, towards where the relic had been hidden. The stone block was too heavy for her to replace. Her eyes squinted at what seemed to be a trick of the light. Flecks of colour appeared above the surface of the stone in a mesmerising dance. When she moved closer, fascinated by the shifting shapes, Amy now saw what appeared to be an engraving in the stone, previously unnoticed. The engraving, she looked closer to make sure, was indeed a turtle. What the....? She stepped back for something profound had formed itself into a heavy, heart stopping thump in her chest. She could not catch her breath and turned away, choking, falling to her knees, pulling at her jacket in desperation. A cry for help emitted as a wheezing, desperate exhalation.

"All clear," Paul called from the entrance hall.

To Amy's relief she gasped in air, though her chest still heaved. By the time he had made his way down the aisle and back to the altar, she had forced herself to straighten up.

Paul didn't notice Amy's distress. He was now in serious taking-charge mode.

"Have you seen Os?" he demanded, with a sharp edge of interrogation.

"He messaged to say he'd been called away on a family matter." Uncertain why she had just lied, and hoping Os wouldn't come walking through the entrance, Amy's level gaze met Paul's quizzical, suspicious eyes. Finally, he turned, mumbling about making some calls.

The place was in turmoil for the rest of the morning. The minister had been summoned and there were serious murmurings from the vestry. There was no doubt the discovery of the cross would change things for the church. Amy anticipated a flood of interest from the local media. The police were called and she was thankful that the cloth strip was zipped firmly into her jacket as she gave a statement. The strange thing was there seemed to be no crime. This was a gift, finding what was thought lost for several hundred years. Someone had already called it 'St Aidan's Cross', probably Paul, although from what she had read Aiden's was once a stone cross in the village centre. Supposedly it had been placed there to mark a gathering place for worship, as no church was available when the revered saint had first arrived in Croston, hundreds of years previously. Hence the name – Cross Town. As the day went on its return was said to herald everything from Preston North End winning the cup, to the demise of evil in the world. A miracle in Croston. She said her goodbyes to the team, relieved that Paul was so pre-occupied the fact it was her last day had completely escaped him. Amy let her fist fold in the centre of the cloth inside her pocket and quietly exited through the side door.

Chapter Six

Venice. The city that rose from the sea. A mere pastel reflection of those fleshy years, ripe with intrigue, redolent of blood and power. Here, in those early centuries, he had built the foundations of the vast wealth he now controlled. They came and went. He and Sereka, who paraded her dark beauty in the Palazzo Ducale. She delighted in political manipulation, twists and turns more numerous than the many bridges that crossed the dark lagoon. The man sat on a terrace, overlooking the Grand Canal. San Marco, as always, overstuffed with tourists who inevitably spilled their excited chatter into the vaporetti and gondolas beneath. He sipped his espresso and waited. It was unlike Marcus to be late.

The bells rang from the Campanile. He turned towards the distinctive domes and spires of the Basilica di San Marco, inescapable and undoubtedly magnificent, yet a building he had never entered. In the November tide of 1845 Sereka had become trapped in the Church. She emerged wide eyed and fearful, all her sophistication reduced to the level of a hunted doe. Unlike him, she was not yet enmeshed in Jarinbissar, but instrumental in increasing its power. After that evening, she began to lose interest in the games she delighted in playing with those who frequented her sumptuous palazzo. She left quietly, on her own, a few weeks later. He had considered it another whim of her imperial temperament until, some months later, the unthinkable news reached him along the Bissarat. Dead. With all her power, for she was more skilled even than he with the delnome, she had allowed herself to be murdered on a lonely track in Ireland at sunrise. Arriving a few days later, to his astonishment, he found her heralded as a heroine. She had led an uprising to oppose the English Lord who let his people die of famine whilst he shipped grain across the sea. He could only think that she had been caught in the intricate web of her own long games.

A chill in the summer sun as Marcus entered breathlessly behind him.

"Forgive me Euair," he came beside his guardian, apprehensive to see a delnome coil wrapped around the other's wrist. "The flight was delayed."

The coil tightened.

"I have news." And loosened.

The man nodded towards the seat opposite.

"The Cross of the Folded Wind has been discovered."

The other leaned forward.

"Where and when?"

"Just a few days ago. A church in a small town in Northern England. I spoke to the self-important youth who found it and he claimed there was nothing else besides."

Marcus continued to recount his visit to Croston, adding no further significant information. He had long years of practice in setting his mind in such a way that the other was unable to penetrate it without the use of the delnome, which his guardian had now slipped back into the gold box he always carried. In fact, it had soon become obvious to Marcus that there had been someone else involved in the find and he had been shocked to hear the familiar name of Amy Rowan.

"You verified the Cross?"

"Oh yes. The artefact has been moved but this youth, Paul, was more than willing to show me photographs." He passed his phone across the table. Carefully his guardian examined the picture of the gold artefact.

"My understanding is it was buried with Avide's Mark." It had taken him years to elicit that information.

Marcus nodded his agreement. "The stone in which the cross was hidden was left exposed. There has been no investigation as nothing was taken."

"You made your own enquires?"

"They are ongoing. I wanted to give you the news personally."

"And so you have," said the other in dismissal.

◆ ◆ ◆

Amy pulled a light raincoat over her T-shirt and jeans. She tried to stop thinking of the soft wool jumper she had rejected that morning, totally underestimating the unseasonal cold. 'Can you believe this weather?' she asked herself out loud, pulling the hood across her face. It seemed ironic, all those hot days incarcerated in PPE during the pandemic. What she would have given then for some cool rain! Amy's mouth tightened, remembering the convincing conspiracy theories that had abounded. Some believed that the vaccination was chip implanted and bore a whole host of other evils. Manipulative media, deliberately aimed at the young, declared there was no virus. Come and spend the day with me, she told old school friends, who saw no reason to give up their freedoms, when they were given a case not to. All unsubstantiated by anyone, other than those seeking their fifteen minutes of mischievously concocted fame on social media.

As a locum, she didn't have planned annual leave. There seemed to be a continual need during the pandemic to cover for sick colleagues, those self-isolating, those caring for family members. As a result she had taken very little time off work. The agency still contacted her daily with job offers, but she had decided to take a full month off. Perhaps she was just burnt out, seeing things that didn't exist. Maybe she had got everything wrong after all. Four days had gone by since finding the old cross in Croston, with the fleeting turtle impression in old stone. Afterwards the markings had become less distinct and no one else had commented on seeing the shape of an animal. In her jeans pocket she still carried the slip of fabric she had found, but doubted it was as relevant as she had first assumed. Amy reflected that she had been hesitant to commit to any post for too long. Driven by a sense of unknown purpose, she had scoured European cities, explored the Andaman sea, worked her way to Australia and back. The only valid direction she felt, was the need to be available when the time came. For what? As more and more of her friends settled down to domestic life, Amy felt no wish to join them. And then Os had walked into the old church in Croston. It was like finding a raft in the ocean, one that had, even as she reached towards it, disappeared into the sea.

The light waterproof was woefully insufficient to stop the onslaught of cold rain that hammered down. The hood pulled forward, obscuring her view. Lifting her chin, she could see the 'egg-slice' outline that was the huge CO-OP building. It was in a part of the city she rarely visited. The NOMA development project had been widely advertised, centred around the building in Angel Square. She had briefly read about the innovative, eco-friendly design of this iconic development and other similar buildings surrounding it in North Manchester. There were old, refurbished buildings and brand-new glassy frontages casting a general, positive light upon the city's future. Still, she loved the old house where she lived in Urmston, bequeathed by her aunt after her untimely death in a road accident. Amy's own sense of estrangement in the world found a safe and accepting home in the quirky terraced house. It had been hard at first, staying there without Maria. Her aunt had been a force of nature, eccentric and clever. She was also very secretive about her work and had been little understood by her family as a whole. In the immediate period before her death, Maria had intimated that some aspects of her esoteric pursuits might interest her niece and so, always open to exploring new ideas, Amy had agreed to shadow her at work the following week. Maria was fatally struck in a hit and run the next day. Sadly, the only way she could now try to understand her aunt's life and work, would be to pore through the copious notebooks in the attic. Amy, through a mixture of grief and genuine lack of time, had yet to do so.

Amy halted on a path that cut through the parkland area. Leaves rustled to each other on the breeze in haunted, sorrowful whispers. Her hood dropped unnoticed as she moved

down the path. Her mother called her 'fae', for Amy had always
been able to sense the energy of the past. Before she learned
to keep her thoughts silent she would elicit slight fear in her
parents, picking up on some earlier battle or past tragedy in
places of which she could have no knowledge. It was only with
her aunt, who received similar disapprobation, that Amy felt
she could be fully herself. As she walked through an area of
carefully arranged greenery, she felt history calling out to be
heard. The tumult of lives crushed together, forlornly lived in
a chaotic world of violence and desperation. Short lives for so
many, and some young ones barely taking breath in a fog of
filth and disarray. A shrill whistle, eerie in the empty park. The
rain clouds coalesced into a darker, threatening mass. Amy's
eyes widened as a shadowy figure stalked a woman heading
away from Angel Meadow towards the undeveloped part of the
northern sector.

Dressed in a thin shirt and jeans, the woman's emaciated
figure was outlined in her wet clothes. Rivulets of rainwater ran
between sharply accentuated shoulder blades. Amy suspected
that she was younger than the impression given by her slow
movement and a bowed head. Her hair hung straight black and
long. It was hard to make out more than an outline of the one
who followed, for his image faded in and out of focus. The face
was marked with tattoos, that failed to hide an unhealthy pallor
beneath. She shivered as long thin arms reached towards the
woman. Impulsively Amy shouted, running across the green, as
both stalked and stalker vanished behind the trees. She reached
the park's edge, running breathlessly downhill and saw that the
woman was about to make her way beneath an old road bridge.
Filled with discarded cans and rubbish, the smell of stale urine
and beer oozed from the wide mouth of the enclosed tunnel.
Amy quickly searched for the strange, shadowy figure she could
no longer see. Her stomach relaxed, as it seemed her cry had
scared him off.

The thin figure in front turned, the first time she had
shown any awareness of someone behind her. Amy, about to

offer a smile, stepped back in shock. The skeleton was more prominent than skin, as sharp bony edges lifted in a snarling, ravaged face. The eyes had the painted-on look of the near dead and at that moment, were wild with hate and fear. The desperate girl, for girl she still was, pulled a blade from her hip pocket and thrust it towards Amy who hardly moved. There was no physical capacity for real threat, the blood stains on her shirt confirmed what Amy had already surmised. She was physically wrecked by drug use and God knew what other abuses in her relatively short life. Hatred was projected out towards Amy, but the jaws and teeth of the emotion were hidden within. It tore pieces from its host, devoured dreams and aspirations, leaving only the malignant poison of self-destruction. Whatever the girl saw in Amy's face brought a howl of fear. She waved the knife, speaking in slurred, unintelligible snatches, and turned back to the descending path.

The shadowy figure returned, now walking hand in hand with the woman, turning for a moment to show Amy an inhuman face, silvery eyes gleaming in the darkness ahead. Fear pierced through Amy's immobility, as she heard an eerie whistle sounding behind her. She turned, this time seeing clearly the long thin limbs, assaulted by its fetid stench. Though it was day it seemed as if no light could be absorbed by the misshapen figure, who seemed to breathe only the shadowy miasma that surrounded him. Covered in the same asymmetrical symbols she had already witnessed; the distorted creature strode towards her like a giant blade. The familiar sense of leaving enveloped Amy. Surrounded by stars in a daytime sky, driven by a cloud of propulsion, she surrendered to the element by which she had been so profoundly overtaken. It carried her body beyond the present moment to a place of immense beauty and peace. A black stallion looked up from its grazing on the green field, nudging towards her. Amy placed her hand on his muzzle before he assumed his usual position of guardianship, bringing her head beneath his to rest against a powerful chest. Where she stayed, as she always did, in quiet rest, until he lifted his graceful neck and released her back.

Chapter Seven

"Amy."
Os, sleek and calm, was beside the bench on which she was sitting. She looked up, nervously checking around and beyond him. The park was empty but for the two of them. "You're getting very wet!"
She swallowed her fear, centred herself, smiled her surprise.
"What are you doing here?" He asked gently.
She shook her head. The space washed emerald green by rain, was a benevolent mixture of trees and grass.
"I don't really know. I came in for a walk round town and just ended up here I suppose."
It seemed his beautiful, dangerous grey eyes were watching her with a look that she had often seen in her childhood. One she had worked hard to avoid by developing practical knowledge and skills. An unspoken speculation that there may be something amiss going on in her head.
"Do you want a coffee? My flat's only there." He nodded towards a refurbished red brick building above the park. The wind shifted, hurling the rain towards them. She jumped up.
"Good idea." She replaced her hood over soddened hair and ran up the slope. Os' unhurried tread followed behind.
The red brick building had been the Old Tobacco Factory, retaining the name in chalk white letters above rows of old mill-style windows. Light poured into the central stairwell from the high, glass vaults above a geometrical network of black steel fixings. The modern urban transformation celebrated the about-turn of the building's place in the industrial history of this quintessentially northern city. Os ignored Amy's lingering gaze towards the lift. Of course, he would live on the top floor. She felt the weight of the building's history with every echo of her squelching steps as she climbed behind her companion.

His easy grace of movement always gave her the impression of understated capability. The flat was refurbished and modern, clean lines, shiny floors. Functional, revealing little of the man who lived here. He handed her a towel, as he hung the dripping raincoat in the kitchen, where she watched it create pools of water on the floor. She grimaced in apology and he laughed, throwing a smaller towel onto the floor beneath the soaked waterproof. Apart from her head, and where the rain had skirted down her back, she felt fairly dry.

"I think you need a hot drink," she heard him say, nodding a towel covered head in reply. Running fingers through her short hair, she caught him watching her thoughtfully. She turned into the living room, uncharacteristically uncomfortable with his examination. The space was light and airy, big windows giving a good, corner view of the parkland, though now greyed-out with rain. She sank into a large, black leather sofa. He handed her a flat white, that tasted as perfect as it looked.

"Great coffee. And this is very impressive," Amy nodded to the oversized cup and saucer often found in coffee shops.

"It came with the machine my parents bought us."

"Us?" She tried to make it sound as conversational as possible.

He was equally level toned. "My ex-fiancé, Louise. We split."

"I'm sorry," she said sincerely, exploring his face in return. The disturbing eyes, a wintry grey that spoke of impassable places, inaccessible landscapes. Dark hair that drifted across his forehead, as if it was always caught in the wind. A jaw of jutting bone, enough to define a man who was wholly and firmly himself. Os sat opposite on an identical soft black settee, coffee table in the middle. The seating took up most of the space in the living room.

"So what were you doing in Angel Meadow?"

She ignored his question to ask one of her own. "What did you take from the church and how did you know it was there?"

Amy pulled out the silk strip, seemingly no worse for its dampness, and laid it on the table. The strange whorls and geometric patterns remained clear on its surface.

"You left it in the stone compartment, in the wooden box, next to the cross."

He put his own coffee cup down and met her eyes. There was something feral in his demeanour that she had never noticed before. She registered quietly, somewhere in the back of her mind, that she was on her own with a man she barely knew.

"You came looking for me?"

He hadn't moved from his seat, but it was as if his voice had reached over and sat too close.

She firmly shook her head. "No, I'd no idea you were here."

He considered this.

"I was really glad to see you," she added quietly, keeping her gaze level. Waiting.

Os nodded as if he had come to a decision, then was gone from the room in one lithe movement. He returned quickly, holding an object in his outstretched palm. He handed her a scroll wrapped in red linen. Perhaps this was why he had left behind the second silken cloth?

"Hidden with a cross in a secret compartment in a church from the thirteenth century?"

He looked amused. "Guilty," he said softly, without the slightest trace of guilt. "I forgot about the other cloth in the excitement of finding this."

There was a single sheet of old parchment. Nervously Amy unrolled the scroll. The page was filled by one symbol, written in a charcoal-like substance, an X.

Confused she looked up at him. "Really? This is what you found?"

"Yep."

She leaned forward enthusiastically. "Maybe there's some microdot film around the edges?" She peered closely at the lines, without finding anything useful.

"In the seventh century?"

Amy snatched her hands away.

"Oh my God! How is it not disintegrated?"

"Well for a start that's not paper it's written on."

She looked carefully, finding a slightly yellow hue to the surface; it completely looked like paper.

"Mysterious. What is it made from?"

Os shook his head. " I'm not really sure. Maybe a type of vellum."

"There seems to be something more in the centre though," she commented, after further examination. In the middle of the X there seemed to be an unwarranted heaviness, as if someone had overlaid the central point again and again. Suddenly there was a moment of disorientation, when her vision blurred and the centre of the symbol seemed to move.

"Yes, I saw that too."

She detected a slight disappointment in his tone, as if he had expected her to know more. Os wandered back to the bedroom to replace the scroll and from there he continued his conversational tone. "Almost as mysterious as you appearing from thin air in Angel Meadow! I saw you materialise onto the bench. One minute it was empty, the next you were there."

Startled by his discovery, Amy stood up thoughtfully and went to replace the bowl-like cup in the kitchen. Perhaps it was time to leave. His voice came again from the bedroom.

"You don't have to go Amy. But I understand if you're afraid."

Os appeared, filling the bedroom doorway, leaning against the wood with his hands in his pockets. She eyed her coat on the hook, the door that led to escape, confronting the calm grey eyes that invited her to stay. She gave a slight shrug of her shoulders before returning to the sofa.

Chapter Eight

Os switched on the heating. A colourful flame lit up a panel to Amy's left. She hadn't previously noticed how wet her jeans had become, nor the fact that she was shivering. He handed over some clothes and retreated to the kitchen, noisily heating a can of soup.

"I'm okay now," she informed him. Swamped by a fisherman jumper and sweatpants, she finished rolling up the sleeves, reaching for a large mug of tomato soup. He placed what looked like half a loaf on the table.

"Aren't you having any?"

"I've eaten," he stated conversationally, leaving her to finish.

Amy could hear him in the bedroom; he was giving her space to gather her thoughts. However, she hadn't managed much of that by the time he returned, changed into a sweatshirt and pants. He sat opposite looking completely relaxed, long limbs stretched out beneath the coffee table. All in all, Amy found that she felt very cosy in this living room, with this man.

He smiled, trailing his fingers over the top of his mouth. "You have a red moustache."

She laughed and wiped the soup from her top lip, laying down the mug on the table between them. In good hospital chaplain style, Os waited for her to begin. Which she did.

"You were there when I..?" She stumbled.

"Appeared from nowhere."

She nodded, her eyes glued to the untroubled expression in his.

"Oh yes." He waited again.

" It's funny but I've only ever," he waited as she searched for the words, "er, returned, when no one else is there." Again, she hesitated to gauge his reaction, but he remained still, allowing her time.

"Return from where I get taken, when I'm in danger. It happens sometimes."

"Tell me about the times it has happened before." His voice was softly directive.

"Why?" She countered.

He looked at her gently, "I think I can help you to understand."

Amy tried to stop the overwhelming surge of relief that flooded through her, but it was too strong.

"Who are you Os? Really, who are you? I didn't think anyone could help me with this...." She didn't know what to call it, having never previously described the experience to anyone.

"Well, whatever it is."

"You have found your arinokra," Os told her.

"Arin what?"

"Tell me about the times before."

In the folds of the thick woollen jumper, curled safely on the sofa, she had never felt more exposed.

"I was very little the first time. I remember reaching for the handle on the front door. I was so excited. I remember the sound of my own giggling, as I toddled into the street, straight into the path of a car going too fast on the quiet road. Afterwards, they said I had crawled through underneath the body of the vehicle as it screeched to a halt, missing the wheels by centimetres. My first near miss."

"And what really happened?"

"I found myself in a green field with a beautiful black pony. I put my head against his leg and wrapped my arms around him. He nuzzled my neck and when he stopped I knew I should go back."

"Go on Amy," Os said quietly. Uncertain, she hesitated.

" It was the first time he spoke to me."

"He?"

She nodded. "Not so much in words as in feeling. I struggle to remember what he says, a bit like when you talked to someone in a dream. I just knew, even at that tiny stage, that this had to be hidden. I've been hiding most of my life since, in one way or another."

"How often has it happened ?" Os asked.

She stared at the floor, it was so hard to get these things out. Again he waited quietly.

"Only a couple of times involuntarily- in extreme danger. I was going to take a short cut through a graveyard one Sunday morning, after an early shift. I was on the path for just five minutes when I knew it was a mistake. There was a man following me. Trying to get away, I walked into a secluded courtyard between the church and a high wall. I saw the shock in his face as I felt myself leave and ended up with Choriscuro"

"Who?"

"My horse." She hesitated. "Well, the one in my....er.."

"Private space?"

She swallowed and nodded appreciatively.

"And then I slipped on a cliff edge in Peru, to find myself in the green field again. Choriscuro stopped me trembling. I came back to find that I was sitting with my legs dangling over a chasm."

Amy was definitely babbling now, but she couldn't stop. "Sounds pretty daft and unbelievable doesn't it?" Os' face remained neutral.

"But it gets worse. I can do it whenever I want to now." She took a breath, it was finally out there. The surreal life that she lived had finally become the reality.

"No, it doesn't," he told her seriously, "sound daft, I mean." The sincerity in his face brought chills down her spine. "So was this one of those times or were you in danger?"

Amy described what had happened by the bridge and the creatures she had encountered.

Os moved towards the window. The rain had now stopped and the afternoon was bright. He peered out across the park, coming back to sit on the sofa. He leaned towards her, serious, alarmed.

"Amy, these creatures are called rawdin and they're not normally visible except to a very few."

"Rawdin," she took in the name, wanting to spit it back out. "They were foul. What do you mean not visible?"

He sighed. "They're from another dimension."

Amy, despite herself, started giggling. "Yeah, right!"

Only he didn't return her laughter. "How real is Choriscuro? Where do you travel when you meet him?"

Quickly, she found her laughter disappear in a choking sigh. Travel seemed a difficult concept to associate with those episodes. They were so personal and hidden that she had never asked herself or Choriscuro proper questions. Or perhaps she had hidden them away, somewhere in the back of her mind. "Do they have names, these dimensions?"

"The place where you meet Choriscuro is called Tanamaarin. The rawdin is a product of Jarinbissar," explained Os.

" I don't understand."

" They have their reflections in our mythology. Think Mount Olympus and Hades, the toing and froing that seemed to happen in those times. Think about the descriptions of multi-dimensional connection. Quantum mechanics."

"Erm... I don't really get all that stuff." He opened his mouth to explain, but she held up her hand.

"It's okay. I can trust the feeling of it all, without having to know the science."

It was his turn to look puzzled.

"I think some part of me may understand the science, which, by the way, must be really out there."

Os nodded and again started to elaborate. She interrupted.

"But it's okay that on a day-to-day basis I can't explain it to someone else in scientific terms. I will definitely not understand what you are trying to tell me. But I do feel the truth of it. Do you get what I'm trying to say Os?"

He looked at her appreciatively and smiled. "I do," he said softly.

"So Tanamaarin and Jarinbissar are like opposite dimensions. Light and dark?"

He hesitated, taking time to frame his answer. "I suppose it's fair enough to think of it like that, though it's not so black and white. The interaction between the dimensions, and our life here on earth, is very complex. Human beings do not inhabit these dimensions as a rule. Very few even have any knowledge that they exist at all."

"Are there others?"

"Yes, but Jarinbissar and Tanamaarin are specifically entangled with this planet's energy. There's a kind of reciprocal influence between each dimension and the earth." Amy frowned, unable to take it all in, yet what he said resonated with what she felt she already knew.

"Human actions and intent," he continued, "have the potential to become directly involved with either dimension. You saw the rawdin because you have already crossed the bridge to Tanamaarin, making you an inter-dimensional being."

Amy was open-mouthed as he spoke, but her lips came together and her frown deepened in confusion at this last statement. "So that means you've been there too? To know all this?"

"I only found my arinokra in Lindisfarne two years ago. Since then I've been studying in a way I've never done before. A little like following a trail without a map, but just trying to decipher the clues along the path."

She found herself abashed, noting the intense emotion in his expression, the hoarseness of his voice.

"I was in a bad way two years ago. I worked in specific places in this country to find out more and spent a bit of time abroad last year. It eventually led me to Croston. And to you."

"To me?"

Os nodded seriously. "I don't think it was any accident that we were both brought to Croston. There's somewhere else I'd like to take you." He looked for her reaction.

Amy fell quiet, unsure how to respond. Seemingly encouraged by the lack of protestation, he continued. "It's an isolated cottage in the Yorkshire Dales. It's very high up, a place called Greenhow."

Somehow the strange proposal helped her lighten a little.

" Os, you sound like a cross between a really bad internet dater and a psychotic murderer."

He smiled, letting his head dip to one side: his eyes flashed blue amongst the chilly grey.

"I've heard of Greenhow," she surprised him by saying. " Four years ago I picked up a book, written in the early twentieth century, from a shop in Shude Hill. It was a strange shop, y'know. Almost as if time hadn't really made an impact."

"I remember it," he replied.

It was Amy's turn to feel surprised. The shop seemed to go out of its way not to attract customers and she had always found herself browsing the shelves alone. Her friends had never noticed it or been interested in visiting.

"On the edge of the road, it's windows stacked with paper manuscripts." His description was exact. "Looked disorganised and untidy from the outside and meticulous within. Noisy and busy by the doorstep, but always so quiet inside. "

Amy nodded her agreement. "Yeah, a bit spooky I suppose."

She thought of the owner who was in his fifties. He either couldn't speak or didn't, but it never really mattered. A small maze of shelves, neat and geometrical, filled the floor space. He'd nod and point towards a particular book, which she inevitably found resonated with whatever was going on in her life. After the first visit, when he completely ignored her attempt to chat, she conducted every encounter in complete silence. Somehow she never felt snubbed, quite the opposite really. Because they never talked she relied on sensing in other ways. The smell of polished wood, musty old books. The presence of a hundred minds sharing their thoughts on paper seemed to hum like an orchestra tuning up in her mind. When she had returned from her last trip abroad, Amy had been disappointed to find that he was no longer trading.

"I bought an old book with a chapter in it describing Greenhow Hill."

She had loved the weight and age of the pages in the green hardback. Even the round stain on the front, from someone's cup or mug, gave it a sense of authenticity. Inside, the original owner had pencilled in the date of their own purchase as 1929, for the princely sum of fifteen old English shillings. The same year it had been published and likely a first edition. It proudly announced its 'twelve plates in colour'. These were pastel-coloured paintings, each preceded by a soft, empty, almost transparent page. It reminded her of the tissue paper that surrounded precious gifts. The chapter on Greenhow had captured her imagination. A drive over to the area found a village, high and remote in the Yorkshire Dales. There was a sense of great age, great earth about the place. Beyond that, she had no idea why the chapter had claimed her attention.

"Will you come?" Os asked. Amy sat back and adjusted her posture, feet on the floor, examining the face opposite. A dangerous face, not quite handsome. Not a chaplain's face at all, though she could see the soft adjustments he could make when he was inclined.

"I'll come."

He stood up. "I'll go make a call."

The sound of Os making small talk on the phone in the kitchen seemed so much in contrast with her quiet desperation. Her attachment to cultural norms left her feeling marked as a target for ridicule and disempowerment. She was no longer hidden, and she could no longer pretend that the intermittent aberrations did not exist. She had been exposed to this man, this strange enigmatic character of whom she knew very little, but with whom she felt more herself than with any other person she had ever met.

Chapter Nine

On the first day of June the sun finally made an impressive appearance. Os had picked up Amy in an old Nissan, that looked ready to be scrapped anytime soon.

"Are you sure you can get us there?" She placed her case in the boot and shouldered a cotton bag.

" Have faith," he looked relaxed, laughing, tapping the roof as they both reached the front of the car. "She's been everywhere with me."

"Hmm, I can tell."

"Amy, meet Ena!"

"The last three letters of the numberplate? Ok!"

He looked impressed. "You noticed."

"I thought I might need if for identification when I have to phone for help!"

Plus, if she felt threatened, she could send it to her friend Alfie, who worked for the police in Manchester. She may have been through a hundred emotions since that afternoon in his flat. It didn't mean she'd grown stupid. Careful was good.

Amy's mood lifted as they drove through the Yorkshire Dales. The sun shone over sumptuous views, rolling hills and blue skies. The car was too old for air-con and the passenger window only rolled halfway down before sticking, but it was enough. For the first time in a very long while she let herself sink into the pure joy of being alive. They stopped in Grassington, a small market town in Wharfedale. She had travelled the world but would have been happy to stay right there, absorbing the feel of community, quirky shops and cobbled paths. There was so much beauty right here on the doorstep, a morning's drive away. Os bought her coffee at a small café at the top of a hill, taking an outside table overlooking the cobbled market square.

"So, how far are we away from Greenhow?" Amy took a sip of a perfectly made latte.

"Hardly anything at all. Maybe twenty minutes."

They had settled for sandwiches and soup, homemade and delicious. Os went to pay the bill, giving her another chance to consider what was going to happen at Greenhow. Her companion had chatted lightly on the way and she had followed his lead. To all intents they were enjoying a wonderful day in a beautiful place. Still, she could not prevent the feeling of dread that lurked in a corner of her awareness as she looked around at colourful hanging baskets, amidst the compelling backdrop of the Yorkshire Dales.

Os smiled as he returned with baked goodies in a brown paper bag. Placidly, she followed him back down through the village and into the National Trust car park. They travelled in silence until, shortly after leaving Grassington, he pulled into a stone building, at what seemed the highest point of an enormous hill. The old-world interior was delightful. The eye was guided to the lamplit bedroom, sumptuous with carefully chosen fixtures, beautiful carvings and pictures. The bed was lavished with rich linen bedding, scented with lavender and eucalyptus, overrun by a wealth of cushions. One bedroom with one double bed. Amy swallowed her protest, for now, suppressing the misgivings she had warred with as soon as she had agreed to come. The kitchen was compact; the owners had left a basket containing homemade jams, bread and essentials. Slate flooring covered the two levels of the main living area. A dining table on the upper level and a cosy sitting room on the lower. A log burner was ready for use. The most spectacular thing about the cottage, however, was the view. Two large patio doors framed a magnificent green moorland vista. A stone patio, lined with small curved walls, provided the perfect setting from which to look out towards the distant hills.

Amy came back in from examining the patio and the external building, to find that Os had moved her things into the bedroom. "Os, really? I mean it's gorgeous but it could be someone's honeymoon destination!"

He put up both hands to stop her.

"It's owned by family friends. They rent it out as an Airbnb. I just get mate's rates."

She looked unimpressed.

"I won't be sleeping here, you're on your own," Os continued.

"Where are you going?" Suddenly alarmed at the thought of being in such an isolated spot by herself. Damn!

"I have somewhere else I can stay at night. We'll be working together during the day."

"Working?"

He nodded. "Starting in about ten minutes."

"It's a scoured land Amy."

They stood at the top of Simon's Seat, a popular climb from the lush fields of Bolton Abbey. Grit stone boulders formed the craggy summit. Gratefully Amy and Os leaned against the trig point to share a lunch of cheese sandwiches and water. The view was spectacular, spanning over Wharfedale to the higher fells beyond. Barden Fell provided a riot of colour, where outcrops of gritstone contrasted with rich heather and acres of moorland. They had come through a patch of land known locally as the 'valley of desolation'. In 1826, Os informed her, a huge storm had caused flash floods, devastating the area and uprooting the original great oak trees. It reminded her a little of Angel Meadow, picturesque and heart-warming, the original damage no longer evident; young trees now matured to majesty. Yet the imprint of that time had been strong enough to remain fixed to this day in the consciousness of the humans who inhabited this part of the world.

"Where we are staying gives a wide view of the landscape, this is wider still. I wanted you to get a feel for the whole area."

"What do you mean, a scoured land?"

He nodded towards the great expanse before them. A bird of prey flew out across the landscape at eye level.

"Light and shadow. In terms of humanity this area speaks of survival, toil and the rooted validity of long experience. So many lives birthed from this soil, a way of living intermingled so closely with the voice and history of the land. Like the orchids and trefoils that peep out from an unforgiving terrain, humanity has held on here; clinging to what it loves - open space, the wild and uncompromising nearness of the earth. This land has relinquished some portion of its secrets during years of lead mining, amid harsh British winters. Miners and the folk who have long dwelt in the area, created hollows and intricate tunnels beneath these green carpeted hills. But there are still places that have lain undisturbed for long ages."

Amy took his proffered hand to pull up from the boulders.

"Let's head back to Greenhow and I'll show you."

On the descent she had difficulty keeping up with Os' long stride. She wasn't used to fell walking, with its hard to navigate nooks and crannies, hidden drops and unlooked for edges. It was with relief that she saw the riverside car park where they had left Ena. Dusk was starting to fall, the restaurant and shops, full of tourists when they arrived, were now empty and closed. Ena stood quite forlornly alone in the huge car park.

"At least the loos are open," she told him, heading off in that direction. Looking at herself in the steel panel, it was evident how thin she had become. She wouldn't have been sorry to call it a day, but Os clearly had something else in mind. He pulled up by a narrow track, a little way from the cottage. She reached for her rucksack but Os told her that she wouldn't need it. He gave her a small torch to wear around her head.

"Okay," she said hesitantly.

Amy followed Os down the track until they reached a barely visible path. She panicked for a moment as he disappeared between the erratically positioned boulders on the rise. She followed, but he was nowhere to be seen. Her heart began beating wildly as she looked around, relieved to see him signal from the top of another path. Dropping after him she found herself in an arched tunnel, invisible from above. She felt the history of the men who had worked the mines as she made her way through the hard-won passage. Life had been tough and demanding for those who had worked these tunnels. It was getting dark as she reluctantly followed him downwards into what was clearly an old mineshaft. Slats in the roof, grey walls, worn piping. cold damp walls came under the glare of their head torches. The stone was pockmarked with indentations, where picks had pounded the walls, leaving scarred and knotted patterns in the rock. In some places, there were long stripes where material had sheared away. Old machinery parts were left abandoned, torch lit skeletons of carts and metal tracks. Amy followed him inwards, underneath the hill, until they reached the end of the tunnel, where a natural fissure branched to the side and led to a wider cave. Os moved around the cave, jumping easily on jutting edges. "It'll do," he told her.

"What exactly will it do for?"

He smiled ruefully. "Our purpose. We can head back now."

Amy was thoughtful as she followed Os out of the old mine. A terrible sadness had begun to gnaw at her abdomen, as if she had found an old tragedy that had been deeply buried, unbearable to touch. On reaching the road Os picked up his rucksack from the car and handed her the keys to the Nissan and the cottage.

"It's not far and you're insured. Just turn right when you hit the road."

Amy was really jumpy now. "What about you?"

"I'll see you for breakfast. About 8am?"

It took her a minute to realise what he was saying. "But where will you stay? Should I drop you off?" She hadn't seen another place for miles.

"I'll be fine. See you tomorrow."

Amy was too tired to argue further. Exhausted, she made the short drive to the cottage, shunning the loneliness reinforced by the isolated building and the brooding presence of the fells around it. She could barely make herself a drink, settling instead for water. After a couple of sips she placed the glass carefully on the bedside table and fell asleep, fully dressed on the beautiful linen bed.

A few hours later she opened her eyes to dark stillness. Blackout blinds enclosed the space absent of any electronic devices. No clock-light to give her an idea of the time. Her phone was still on the kitchen counter. She strained her ears to catch the sound that had awakened her. Stones stirred on the gravel path surrounding the cottage. Quietly, she reached for the bedroom door, gasping as the outside light sensor came on, momentarily flooding the living room and then returning to the meagre visibility afforded by the clouded moon.

Amy edged herself towards the kitchen, peering out at the darkness beyond the uncurtained glass. A fox perhaps? Or some other animal? A low growl emitted from beyond the patio doors. She grasped for the poker beside the log burner. The noise was not a fox, or any small creature that she knew. Standing behind the armchair she concentrated on the courtyard, seeing a flicker of movement. A deep guttural snarl came, just as she approached the glass doors to check if they were locked. She jumped backwards, her breath coming in stuttering gasps as a large shape, catlike, crossed the patio. Amy began to call to Choriscuro, but the transition wouldn't happen. For another ten minutes she waited, frozen, looking for movement outside. Nothing. She wasn't willing to risk the light with bare windows. Feeling her way to the sink Amy splashed water on her face and headed back to the bedroom, pushing a chair underneath the doorknob. For a long time she sat listening, hands around her knees. Eventually, in the absence of any further sound, she climbed into bed, curled into a foetal position, until, overtaken by exhaustion, she drifted back to sleep.

Chapter Ten

Light crept under the door. Amy could hear someone moving in the kitchen, the clatter and clink of pans and dishes. Carefully she removed the chair and stuck her head round the door.

"Morning." Os greeted her cheerfully.

Looking through strands of hair and with eyes still unsure how to open, she noted that he seemed as fresh as if he had been staying in a five-star hotel. Disgustingly exhilarated in fact! What was intended to be 'good morning', came out as an unintelligible grunt.

"How'd you get in?" she asked.

"The spare key," he replied, nodding to the table where he had thrown it.

"Hmm," she mumbled.

Half an hour later, showered and dressed in walking pants and T-shirt, she joined him for coffee and scrambled eggs. As Os showered, she took the opportunity to check outside on the patio. There was no sign of any overnight intruder or mysterious animal. It was a glorious day and she could see distant hills across a series of green pastures, even with the one on which she was now standing.

"Everything okay?" He was putting his boots on in the living area. The blue vest and track suit bottoms showed a powerful leanness. His hair and skin glistened with moisture. Amy caught her breath at the sheer unconventional beauty of him. It took her a moment to realise he was waiting for an answer. "Err, yep. Just thought I saw something out here in the middle of the night. Must have been dreaming."

It was only later that she remembered that he hadn't asked her what kind of thing she'd seen.

"We need to go," was his clipped response. It unsettled her, the sense of urgency, his serious face.

They were back at the cave in half an hour. Amy followed him in, bringing her arms about her, as they left the hot sun outside and found the dank tunnel.

"Watch your head," he told her, as they continued to walk past the old mining area. It surprised her how far in they had come yesterday to reach the fissure in the back wall. She had been too tired to take it all in last night. Once again, they reached the cave and once again Amy found herself deeply affected, afraid, as if something intangible was closing in around her. It was with relief that she turned off her head torch. Natural light streamed in from a number of gaps in the roof of the cave.

"I can hear water." It was quite distinct and seemed to be coming from behind the wall.

"There's an opening up there." He pointed to the roof, where she could just make out a ledge .

Os cupped his hands to help her up.

"It's too late now," Amy ruefully whispered to herself. She put her foot in his hands and felt herself levered upwards, level with an opening that seemed to have just enough room for a person. She reached forward and clambered into the space, glad for her long trousers, as she pulled herself over the flat ledge. It extended out, like a cliff into a hidden cavern. Carefully she brought herself upright. The ledge sloped downward to the floor of a natural space, filled with stalagmites and stalactites. A number of them had grown together in the middle of the roof and floor to form pillars of grey calcite. Water trickled down eroded grooves in the back wall of the cavern, where a light source above created a beaded curtain of captured luminosity. Down the road Stump Cross Cavern was visited by tourists from all over the world. Amy had seen the booklet in the cottage. Unique shapes had been given names according to what they looked like. Stories and legends were magnified and careful lighting used to increase the sense of magic. Yet here they were, just a few miles away, stood in what she was certain, was a previously undiscovered chamber. There was no artificial light at all, but still a feast of reflected colour abounded.

"Glow-worms," Os told her, pointing to a number of globular shapes in the higher crevices.

The water sparkled with flecks of gold and silver. The effect was stunning, far more magical than any show cave she had previously seen. Os disturbed some small stones as he followed her down the slope.

"Quite something," she commented. "How did you know it was here?"

"I found it last year, coming at it from another direction."

He pointed to a pool of water in the far side of the cave. "They've had a bit of rain since then. I guessed there was another entrance, but I had to widen the way through."

She saw the fresh pile of stones at the edge of the slope. "Quite a night's work!"

It made her uncomfortable to think of him being here alone in the dark, risking injury to find the cavern. "It doesn't look as if it's been touched before."

"No," he agreed. "But I didn't bring you here to look at an old cave, however stunning."

He paused, sighing. This man possessed a quality that frightened her, even as it drew her towards him.

"Amy, it's time."

"What do you mean?" The words came out startled and defensive. She was assailed by a sense of being trapped. It had been a mistake to go there with him. Her eyes scanned the cave, the ledge, wondering how fast she could run.

"It's okay Amy," he took a step back. "Leave if you don't want me to explain further. You're free to go." Another step back, his hands behind him. "I promise you I have no intention of harm in my heart or mind towards any human being."

A funny way to put it, she thought. Almost like a mission statement, going beyond this moment when she was desperately trying to decide if she should go or stay.

"Why did you bring me here?" She found the need to know had grown bigger than fear.

"Because it's very private, surrounded by acres of remote

pastureland and contains this."

He signalled for her to follow him round the jutting edge of the slope, from which they had descended. A stone relief was carved into the rock face. Stunned, she jumped back. A woman rider on a sleek black horse, no saddle or reins. Hair blowing in the wind. Her face.

"Oh my God!"

Amy toppled backwards as she saw a rudimentary version of her own features in the finely constructed carving, that seemed as ancient as it was beautiful.

"You did that!" She accused.

"Look at the stalactite falling from the roof," he answered calmly. "It's hanging over the horse's head like a shining sword. See where the rock slab has fallen away to reveal the tail," he pointed to a pile of disintegrating stone on the floor. "There's no way I could have done this. I had a night, not hundreds of years."

"What does it mean?" She was distressed now.

"Come and sit," he coaxed, finding a slab of rock that was broadly seat shaped. "I'll explain as best as I can."

Amy, still stunned, did as he asked.

"I said this place was a scoured land. What I meant is that for hundreds of years mankind has quarried and dug in this area. It's filled with disused mines. Up here the land can become desolate very quickly, with hard winters, harsh winds, snow. Its people are survivors, deeply rooted in the land. A few also became keepers of its secrets. One such person carved that relief."

"But it's so old! I don't understand! You said Choriscuro was my arinokra. What did you mean? I looked it up on Google but couldn't find anything."

"An arinokra is a linked guide who resides in Tanamaarin but will cross the dimensions to be with you. According to the energy we need, we decide the form."

"I don't know what you mean." She rubbed a hand across her brow in frustration. Disappointment overwhelmed her. "I thought you were really going to help me. Come on, let's head back."

Amy started up the slope but was halted by the sound of the strangest singing she had ever heard. The rhythm seemed to beat in her blood. And then Os began to dance, transfixing her with the way he reached out and let his limbs extend in time with the music. So fantastically strange and yet deeply familiar. Scree fell from the rock face above her as an animal leapt over her head and settled beside Os. It gave an ominous growl, bearing razor sharp canines. Shocked, Amy's mind flew to what she had once seen in a zoo. Upturned pointed ears, patterned sandy fur and the short tail of a lynx. Clear and dangerous green eyes. For only the second time in her life she could not leave the present to find safety with Choriscuro. Instead she found herself crying uncontrollably in the arms of the man who was somehow profoundly different from the Os she knew. The wild cat had disappeared.

"How did you do that? Was it an illusion?" She jerked away from his hold, panic setting in. " Did you spike my coffee? I have to get out of here! What are you?"

She scrambled upwards but slid back towards him, kicking out so that he had to swerve away.

"It's since I met you! Nothing's been the same! I shouldn't have told you about Choriscuro!"

He looked at her calmly without changing his position, leaving her complete access to the opening and the way back. Her panic subsided.

"That was what I saw last night outside the window."

"It was." He gently moved a little nearer, " I asked him to give you protection."

"You and I have become so entangled, or maybe we are just discovering how entangled we actually are." He took a minute to absorb his own words. "I'm not someone else Amy, just more of who I truly am. Last night you saw Nesu, who is my guide from Tanamaarin, who takes the form of a lynx. Once I located the cave and the carving I sent him to guard the cottage while you slept. Since Nesu came to me I have clear night vision and a physical strength beyond anything I knew previously. I can run all night if needed."

"I can't find Choriscuro."

This was the true source of her grief, a sense of abandonment from the one creature who had guarded and protected her all her life. Amy could feel that the relationship that Os had with Nesu was akin to what she shared with the esoteric stallion. Slowly, and for the first time, Os recounted what had happened to him in Lindisfarne. Amy listened, her eyes glazing with sadness, that this wonderful soul had been in such despair. As he finished recounting his story he looked across to a part of the cave she had yet to explore. "There's another carving."

Directly opposite to where her own image had been imprinted, Os gently swept away some surface crumbs of limestone. Clearly there he was. The same face, in clothes that would not have been out of place in a King Arthur novel. A sword in his left hand. By his right side sat the feline shape she had just witnessed him conjure up.

"I don't understand."

"Choriscuro has not left you."

The statement produced a wild hope inside her. Os reached for her hand and gently guided her back down the slope. She was in a daze.

"Choriscuro is your arinokra and by making the right movements you can bring him right here beside you."

She felt for the ground beneath her feet, listening for the sound of water. Anything to tell her she was still alive and living an ordinary life. But truly she had never done that. Who else did she know could vanish and end up somewhere completely different? And communicate with a horse?

"Let go Amy. Stop thinking of what you have been told is normal. Are you going to let yourself be relentlessly impaled by the version of normality that you have been given by a world that does not understand? The reason that you can't vanish and find him is that he has crossed from Tanamaarin, because it is time for him to do so. There is nothing I am saying that, somewhere inside you, you do not already know."

The trouble was she knew exactly what he was saying to her. Choriscuro had whispered to her something of the same. Not spoken exactly, more that the idea had just slotted into her mind.

"Close your eyes," he instructed.

She was standing in front of the waterfall. The cold air of the cavern, the weight of the earth above. A beat. It seemed to come from beneath. A hum. She caught the sound and began to find her voice echoing the rhythm that surrounded her. Something primitive, so ancient, calling, energising. The cry for rain from dry, parched land, the scream of wind tearing across the sea, the wash of the ocean as it reaches the shore. A hoofbeat on stone. Her limbs began to fall in with the beat, neck rolling forwards, reaching outwards, faster the hoofbeat, longer the stride as her body swayed. When the song and the dance had completed, Choriscuro was once again before her, moving freely in the joy of recognition as she stroked his head. Her conscious mind and all its irrelevant chatter, stopped to breathe in the energy of the sleek and graceful stallion, that bent to the rhythms of the earth, in a way that human beings did not.

Time had passed, but Amy had no real idea of how much time. Even though Choriscuro had left, she felt his strength in her own limbs. She could see the luminescent lines of some mineral in the roof of the cave. The soft, eerie light of glow-worms. Os was sitting above her by the ledge. He made his way downwards. The memory came unbidden, not from this life, but nevertheless her memory. Like a scene from an old movie, except she remembered the smell of the forest and the taste of the river.

The old forest, for it was old, even then, was her refuge in exile. The statuesque oaks, pines and yews gave her shelter. In the day she spent most of her time high in the leafy canopy, finding pathways between the crowded branches that allowed her to step lightly from tree to tree. She was Ellan, named for bright magic, barely a woman when they had turned against her. A new religion swept from the West, reviling her power that was steeped in the old ways. Quickly forgotten were the times that her earth lore had healed the sick, predicted the storms, prevented disaster.

She had found a hidden escarpment. A gently sloping approach that led to a sheer drop on the other side. At the top was a tarn, formed from meltwater, refreshed by rain. Here she swam every day amidst the rustle of the forest and the creatures of the air that came to rest by the edge of the water. Fear of the forest and its mystery kept the villagers away. At the foot of the escarpment was a cave that let in shafts of natural light where the rocks had cracked. Here, in the summer, she laid down bedding and made a fire for warmth. One night she awoke to find the dark shape of a mare, restlessly neighing. Ellan saw the foal in her belly ready to be born. She sat with the mare as the moon brightened. Ellan could see the sweat on the mare's coat and stroked her matted forelock as she gave birth to a beautiful foal. Black as pitch, with a fork of white lighting on its brow, he gave her his name as Choriscuro. She often shared the language of the wild creatures, not in conversation but understanding. This was the first occasion one had shared their name.

As the seasons changed water shook the trees around, poured in through the gaps, flooded the cave. She was forced to crawl high upon the slope that formed the back wall of her makeshift home. When the rain abated she turned to the sound of trickling water. Pushing away the shale she felt the empty dark space of another cavern hidden behind the first. She called to the earth, and soon the roof was aglow with small creatures who gave up their light to shine in the dark. A mighty hall of columns that reached down from the ceiling and up from the floor, meeting in the middle, wedding-dressed partners. It was here, finally, that she made a solid home away from sight and safe from danger. Often Choriscuro visited, playing, his mother watching from the hills above.

One by one, the villagers came to the old forest to find her, to ask for healing or magical ways to change their lives. She could not refuse them her gift, it never felt that it was hers to choose where it was bestowed. As her mother had taught her, she met the service that greeted her. There was a small cave by the river that she used to inhabit on most days, just by the edge of the old forest. Here, the villagers started leaving gifts of food and wine. She had learned not to trust their goodwill, knowing betrayal was always waiting the next summons by a man of power. In the winter of her second year despair had reached out to clasp her in its stranglehold. She remained a woman, cut off in general from her own kind, and desperately lonely. She lay in the snow, alone and rejected, at the edge of the frozen tarn. She felt the energy of this high place, as it gave up its name to her. Even the Romans had missed this remote hilltop from their itinerary of likely fortress points. Off the beaten track of military paths, of no likely political or commercial value ,was the Circle of the Unwoven. And it was here that Avide the monk came to her, his harp on his back.

Ellan was too far gone in her own sorrow, hovering between life and death, to fear this man of the church, or to wonder how he had found her. Wearing only his cloak to keep out the cold he pulled a blanket from his pack and covered her. He knew her name, pronouncing it El-lan. Picking up the small instrument he sat beside her and began to play. The chill wind dropped as he plucked exquisite sounds from the harp. He explained that each string denoted an emotion, that bound her in despair. As he played, the tangled anger and sorrow of rejection bowed out of her life. Shame and disappointment, the deep scars of loneliness and self-pity. One by one they were taken up by the sky, the earth, the air. All that was left was all that she needed to go on. Unencumbered by what she was not, Avide left her with all that she was and the possibility of all that she could be. He lifted her near frozen body, like that of a child and carried her down the slope. He laid her gently in the blanket, building a fire in the outer cave, drawing the rocks around to make her shelter more complete. He cooked a simple stew from what she had stored and fed her gently. Her belly had become unused to food or drink, but slowly, over a number of days, he nursed her back to life.

"Amy."

Os was shaking her gently, his face concerned. He took her

trembling hand. Amy's words tumbled over themselves.

"Avide," she whispered, tears falling freely. "I must find him again."

Os nodded speculatively. "We will find him, together."

They sat and held each other until Os guided her back to the opening. Somehow her body seemed more pliant and aware of itself, she easily jumped down to find the path that would take them back to the cottage. It seemed only minutes until they reached open air, where Amy turned back to him puzzled. "It's still light, I feel as if we've been there all day."

" Look," Os pointed at the moon. "It's the influence of the arinokra. Night vision. You'll also find you feel lighter and stronger."

"Cool," she said striding lightly beside him without difficulty. "Really cool."

Chapter Eleven

I cooked pasta and filled the cottage with the smell of garlic, basil and tomato. I needed to bring Amy's senses back to the present, even as my own lurched dangerously into the past. The night chill bit hard and we had lit the log burner. It glowed against the dusky, high hills beyond our refuge. Amy was curled in the armchair. Like me, she had found the connection with Tanamaarin. A permanent shift had occurred in her reality.

"Tell me about Avide, Os," she asked quietly.

I chose to ignore her request for a moment, making some adjustments to the herbs and spices, giving myself time to frame the answer. I left the pot simmering as I took the other armchair beside the fire.

"He was a seventh century monk in a monastery around a day's walk south of Lindisfarne."

She furrowed her eyebrows. "Real then? He actually existed? "

"Yep, though there's no written history of him that I know of. He was a friend of the Sainted Cuthbert who often visited the lesser-known monastery, the two would spend long hours together enclosed in the Carapace."

"The Carapace?"

" Avide's private quarters. A mystical place at the heart of the building, where very few entered."

"You sound as if you knew the monastery well?"

"I remember it as a monk. It was destroyed by raiders long before Lindisfarne was attacked in the following century. The memories of that time began the night Nesu came to me in Lindisfarne, in brief snatches, but clearly not dreams or imagination."

"Clearly not dreams or imagination," she repeated. "How can you be so sure?"

"The same doubts plagued me at first. Nesu scaring a bunch of my fellow Mancunians kind of confirmed I wasn't completely insane. The last two years have been partly spent learning how Nesu and I can practically operate in the modern world, without attracting online attention. He is a lynx and a natural predator, though he wouldn't normally attack a human unless cornered. Choriscuro will have all the needs and attributes of a stallion when present. They are both, however, an extension of spiritual consciousness. Our spiritual consciousness."

Amy wrestled with discomfort, turning her face towards the open landscape beyond the cottage.

"I know Amy. It's hard. At some point, however, we have to understand that's where all the magic lies. Our concrete existence is made from the spaces within."

Amy stood up, heading for the sink and a glass of water. I reined it in. "I've also been following the trail that eventually led me to Avide's Mark in Croston."

"But the church wasn't built then?"

"It was the stone block I followed. Avide used a turtle imprint that bore a blessing from Tanamaarin, visible to those connected positively to him. Not only did it ensure the stone was protected but also that Nesu could eventually find it. We worked together at night, there was much Nesu wanted to teach me before he finally brought me to the church. And then to you. When I touched the turtle imprint on its surface, the stone block opened to reveal its secret. It disappeared afterwards, so I couldn't close it."

"I saw it too! Just for a few seconds. So I could have closed it?"

"Perhaps it was more an acknowledgement of you. The contents were ready to be found."

"Why didn't you take the cross?" Amy asked.

"I'm not sure if it was pure intuition or just wanting to create a distraction from what had been removed." Os explained. "Well it certainly provided that!"

She looked thoughtful, turning sincere brown eyes towards me.

" I have felt a freak my whole life. Not truly belonging anywhere. Is that what we are Os, freaks?"

I looked at my beautiful companion and willed her to see the admiration in my eyes.

"Amy, unlike you, I have not crossed to Tanamaarin in this life. Tell me, how did you feel at the moment of recognition, when you found your arinokra dance, when you called Choriscuro to life beside you?"

"Is that what I did?"

I smiled and nodded.

"The most at peace and whole that I have felt since I was born."

"And do you think your human family or friends would understand?"

"I'd be sectioned," she told him. "Committed for my own safety in a mental health ward."

"Three years ago, I would have disavowed anyone who sees the world as we do now. The voices of Joseph Ryland, and many wonderful humans are still there in my old-world view and would despair if they could hear what I am saying. Yet, in all my time with them I never felt such love as I felt when Nesu arrived bearing the touch of Tanamaarin, the memory of my time with Avide. Your arrival brought another thunderclap of remembrance. All I can say is that I am truly at home with myself in a way I have never been before."

"What are we really, Os? Not Solars, but something of Tanamaarin?"

" I'm not sure Amy. It seems like a past we have shared has thrust us forward to this moment in time. The how and the why I don't know."

I leaned over to add another log to the burner, searching for knowledge that was revealing itself frustrating slowly. "I just can't fathom it all."

I moved to the kitchen and tasted the pasta dish, my appetite reminding me we had eaten little that day. Amy followed, arranging plates and cutlery on the table. We ate hungrily and in silence, lost in our thoughts, settling back into the armchairs once the meal was complete. It was well into the night but neither of us felt sleepy.

"You said you knew Avide as a monk in the seventh century?" Amy began.

The sparks flickered in the log burner igniting my memory. I spoke it to Amy, as I lapsed into the young man I had been in another place and time.

"Tonight, the land is clear to me. The uncluttered sky, untamed rivers, vast forests. Southern Northumbria crossed great swathes of land above the Humber and reached towards the west. I came from the house of a Giseth, favoured and blood borne relative of those who rule. My Father was lord of a great house, kin to the Northumbrian king. The times were unstable but I was Osweald, brave and skilful in battle, loved by the men I led, known for my generosity and courage. I never questioned my gift of persuading men to follow my lead, of dealing with bubbling feuds and threats rife in the northern lands. My Father, Roderick, was a learned man for the times and lately had been close in piety with the nearby monasteries. I barely noticed the quiet, watchful Avide, as his visits to our homestead increased. I really knew little of the world, fed on a diet of my own importance. I was still a young man when Bierscath and his wife Sereka entered our lives. It was a winter's day and the fire was bright at the centre of the great hall. And yet the flame of her beauty burned brighter, bringing a beacon of change into our raw existence. There were idle hour lost in dreaming of her, lusting for her, the beautiful magnificence that enveloped my thoughts.

There was a place in a quiet dell, a lake surrounded by earthy oaks where, in the spring after her arrival, Sereka and I swam naked under the sun. We made love on the soft embankment, our bed of oblivion. The touch of her skin, soft and pliant, the green eyes that carried the sadness, as it seemed to me, of a loveless marriage. Men feared Bierscath, who had great power in the southern kingdoms. He was known as cruel and merciless. Sereka had remained in our house at his command as he attended the King's court.

'I have to leave you,' she told me that day.

'No!' The boy in me screamed, though I was a grown man with a wife and children of my own.

Tears welled as she bowed her head, reluctant to tell me. Eventually I coaxed it from her.

'Your father knows that we are lovers.'

Distress raised her voice to hysteria. I pulled her closer but she pushed me away.

'What dreadful names he gave to me and to you! He fears my husband and has forbidden me to stay on pain of death!'

'But how could he know?'

'How can I tell?' She was desperate now. 'Oh Osweald, I cannot bear it!'

Tears flowed freely as she allowed herself to be enfolded in my arms. And so it began. The seed of darkness watered and growing in a heart of lust. That night, as the storm surged outside, I made my approach to the room where my father studied his parchments. The stiff lean back of a warrior bent over the table, though he was now long in years. He turned his face enquiringly as I came towards him, my hand reaching behind for the dagger I carried. Blinding light coursed through the small window, illuminating lines of weariness framed by grey-tinged temples. I remembered the younger man, gentler than the custom of the times, as he made swordplay with his son. Shame bowed my head and dropped the knife from my hand. We faced each other in terrible silence, as the metal rang out on the stone floor.

The huge oak door banged open and Avide, the monk, stood before us, his head and cloak soaked in rain. Dread and sorrow filled my father's face, as his eyes focussed on the dagger that lay between us. I stepped back in a torment of horror.

'My son,' he said, tears clouding his vision, 'what would you do? To betray and murder your own father?'

'No, my Lord,' I lied, 'you are mistaken! I could not hurt you.' The unsheathed dagger gleamed its deadly tale in the candlelight. The penalty for betrayal was death. In fear, and my own rising anger I went on. 'Tis your own doing! Who are you to say I cannot bed a woman as I wish!'

'What woman?' He replied, incredulous. 'Flavia?' He spoke my wife's name, invoking momentarily the sting of my disloyalty towards her.

'Sereka!' I shrieked. ' The woman you have banished on pain of

death!'

And then I saw, in my father's dazed and puzzled eyes, that he knew nothing of my liaison with her.

I turned towards the monk who did not speak, an expression of deep sadness written on his face, but also a steady strength that helped to shift my world back to its moorings. My lips pinched with the bitter taste of knowing I had been used like some manikin, to dance Sereka's tune. It was as if the room swivelled and the huge stones locked into place, banishing my delusion. Shame crushed my soul, that I had entered my father's room with murder in my heart. The old man reflected my own expression, as the veil of delusion fell from my eyes. All horror and regret.

'Take him Avide. I cannot see him. He is no longer my son.'

My father's words stripped away my spoilt youth. To live at all was more than I deserved. In a flash of insight I wondered if her husband Bierscath had played a part in Sereka's manipulations. Did he whisper to the king about my father's house? A cold anger stilled my fear.

'Father, I am sorry. Do not trust Sereka or her husband. They are unworthy.'

My father looked for a lie but I held his gaze. There was a slight nod before he turned his back on me forever.

Avide spoke gently. 'You are not so lost in darkness as you believe,' said he quietly. 'Come with me, and I will find you a way back home.'

And he did, though it was not the house of my birthplace. Avide showed me a different home in the quiet of the monastery, where I found more contentment than I deserved.

Later, dying, my father sent for Avide.

'Is he really changed my friend? Does he live a good life?' Christianity had swept Northumbria and the holy monks of Lindisfarne were revered in these times. Like the king, my father had embraced this faith.

'You judge, my dear friend,' Avide told him, standing aside and beckoning me forward in my monk's habit.

'Osweald,' he whispered, reaching for my hand. I held the dry, cold fingers, my tears moistening his palm.

'I am sorry Father, that I dishonoured you and myself. But know that I love you and that I found a way through the darkness of my soul to the light of life. Be at peace.'

I knew my words were the last he would hear. He died later, in my mother's arms, who did not know me. To those at my old home I had died in an accident and my body swept away in the river. Avide anointed my father, as he wheezed out his last breath. I stood aside in shadow, my habit shrouding my face, watching those I had abandoned take their places. My own son and daughter and their children, that I never came to know. It was the price I paid. The cost of it lay heavy upon my heart."

I looked at Amy, holding my breath, waiting for an exclamation of horror, perhaps rejection.

My companion looked up, compassionate eyes held mine and I knew that somehow she did not judge, somehow she completely understood. I was reminded, even as it pained me to speak this memory, of the hard-won peace I had found in the monastery. The recall of this event had no power to vanquish me in this life. "We are all traumatised by fear of darkness within us. You moved beyond it long ago."

I exhaled and placed my hand over her small fingers and, to my embarrassment, a tear fell upon them. It was a little while before either of us could speak.

"There is something more I remember," Amy began. "If I don't tell you now, it will stand between us."

My attention fixed on her elfish face, the large brown eyes that were watching me carefully as she told her story.

"A few years after I was exiled to the forest I became settled into my life. The villagers invited me back to their village but I could never *trust them again. Avide came, we sat and talked for long hours. Later, I often travelled to the monastery by the secret ways he and I had engineered. A couple came often to a quiet dell, they were lovers."* She raised her hand as I began to speak, signalling me to wait.

"The woman was truly beautiful, older, more lovely in her maturity,

and he was besotted. I acknowledged their presence and spoke with the wild creatures to leave them in peace. However, one day, the force of his agitation pulled me towards their idyll and I saw murder filled his mind. She spoke about leaving at his father's direction. I gasped and pulled back into the leaves, seeing the lie in her eyes that he did not, for his were hooded with passion and heavy with murderous intent. I left for the abbey on secret paths and told my beloved monk what I had seen. The rest is as you know."

I looked up in surprise at Amy, processing this further connection of our past lives.

" I think a part of me recognised you in the church in Croston. I have no memory, at least not yet, of knowing you in the old life, but there was something special about you when we met."

"I felt it too," she agreed. "We were both saved by Avide. We were both shaped for this life by him in Tanamaarin. I think we have been brought to this time to help him fight the darkness of this age, or even the same darkness grown again. Why isn't he making himself known to us Os? Where is he?"

I sighed, shaking my head. No creatures stalked outside the window that night. Reflected in the glass was the log burner's warm glow and our puzzled faces. Plucked from time. I looked at Amy and thought of the night before, how frightened she had been. I would not leave her tonight, but even on her own I knew that she would be unafraid. Perhaps it was the shadow and the log burner, but her face seemed to glow with a fearless strength and peace that I had only ever seen in one other.

Marcus Waterman studied the outside of the house in Urmston that Amy Rowan had inherited from her aunt Maria. It wasn't the first time he had covertly watched the comings and goings in this street. He had discovered the girl earlier that year, before the insipid Paul had mentioned her name in Croston. Waterman had also managed to build a list of the others, who were working with him at the time the cross was discovered. The name of Os Ryland interested him, particularly as his address was given as Lindisfarne. New paint on the door, flowers on the windowsill, but the small terrace building was really little changed. He swallowed, remembering the smell of neroli oil that pervaded Maria's small flat in London. The chatter of the Thames, Cinzano. A cynical smile crossed his narrow features. Yes, there was still something left of himself after all. His hand felt for the small baton that always accompanied him, lodged in a sheath on the side of his belt. A type of napoten, Euair had called it, a talisman for his protege. A leash would have been a more accurate description. The terraced house was obviously empty and had been for some days. He itched to get inside and search the place. Not even the powerful napoten could unlock the seals Maria had set. He knew to his cost any attempt to enter the property without invitation would end in violent illness. After her death it had taken him a month to recover from his first attempt to break in. And even with an invitation, Maria's place would not tolerate his kind for very long.

Chapter Twelve

On the south side of Manchester, a glass-paned room gave a view on three sides of rows of computer desks. On the remaining wall was a collage of lifeless flat screens. Cathy found the tight-fitting new suit uncomfortable and alien. Had it not been for covid, she would have joined her sister in Australia three years ago; instead she had stayed in Manchester and studied. Still, the company she worked for, Inimica, was a global enterprise, a corporate development that had been applauded the world over for their work with local communities and sustainable vision. Since covid every employee had been given the choice to work remotely. Having landed, what she considered, her dream job three months previously, she had elected for a mix of home and office. Somehow, she had managed to impress the panel of charming, intelligent and politically correct men and women who had quizzed her regarding sustainable energy and community development. It helped that she was local to Manchester and had completed a master's degree in social change, environment and sustainability.

It was Cathy's intention, at some point, to live in a CO-OP housing scheme, where the occupants were effectively their own landlord. In the interim she now rented a flat in one of the new city centre initiatives, from which she could walk to work. Her parents had given her a bed, utensils and an armchair from home. She had saved much of her first three salaries to go rummaging in the charity shops, once her initial project report was complete. As of midnight last night in fact! The first three months of her new employment had been demanding. She had thrived on the challenge of bringing people together online and face to face; of identifying key stakeholders and feeding information to her manager. Her desire to empower those who felt powerless had led her to look at the various Inimica housing schemes and their implications. She stood at the door, nervously ready to explain her first report to the man himself. This was only the second time she had seen the company owner use his personal office, situated in a corner on the third floor. More often he was absent, understood to be involved in international initiatives. She loved the idea that she too, would be able to operate on the world stage someday, but first, she needed to secure her position in the company.

Today Cathy was one of only a handful of employees who inhabited the sleek office space. Most of her colleagues chose to work from home on a Friday.

A voice that was made for the stage or at the very least, a podium.

" Come in Catherine. Ada tells me you've been working on the community plans for the new Lattice development."

He indicated a chair on the other side of his desk. Karl Venmorin looked cool and comfortable in an open shirt and light, linen pants. His hair was a honey brown, natural and full. The face of a man who knew his own power, aquiline and direct. These features were softened by disarmingly smiling blue eyes. She hadn't yet been able to determine his age but he looked around forty. Cathy was careful not to let her eyes roam towards the edges of the room where, she knew, hidden cameras were installed. She had seen Venmorin briefly at the induction, and once before when he had given a lecture at Manchester Met. He had been impressive and assured. Here, one to one, it was impossible not to be aware of the magnetic attraction causing him to be one of the most sought-after connections in the city.

"You seem to have established some really good links with our local community." He smiled his approval.

Cathy adjusted her suit, pulled her dark fringe to one side.

"Their main concern is that so much of the planned development is for two-bedroom properties, too small for families. They're worried about green space for their children to play and the amount of overseas investment." The eyebrows above the still smiling Venmorin were raised. She took a breath

and continued. "There was also a good deal of questions around the sustainability and safety of the new builds."
He nodded thoughtfully and then replied.
"In a nutshell, they'll be far more sustainable and safer than anything they have now. I know Ada is planning a meeting with the local community leads. All of these issues had to be agreed with the council before we were allowed to take the contract. It's interesting that it hasn't filtered down to grass roots level though. Perhaps you can work with Ada on making sure the local community is well represented?"
Cathy felt herself positively glowing. Here, at last, she was making a difference. To have a man like Karl Venmorin listen to her, was an amazing thing. She decided not to highlight her other concerns, leaving him to elicit them from her report. Here was a big, respected corporation working for good in a deprived urban area. And she was part of it. The blue eyes twinkled with appreciation.
"Thank you Catherine," he nodded, in a way that was somehow akin to handshaking. Cathy felt a fierce sense of loyalty ignited within her towards her new employer.
Karl Venmorin's phone pinged as she left the office. "So cool," she whispered to herself, as the clear glass melded into opaque silver. When the chief exec. was not there, what her father described as 'electro-chromic glass', was switched to icy grey and the door was always locked. He had explained, in an unexpected lapse from his strict code of confidentiality, that it was one of the most sophisticated glass systems he had seen used. It had also been infused with security features making it bullet and tamper proof. The controls were linked to the Company Director's phone and to an internal office switch that her father had connected personally.
Employees were encouraged to use the lift and central stairwell but as the building was mostly empty, she couldn't see the harm in using the nearby fire exit. Still in a heady daze from her meeting, she rounded a corner and banged straight into a well-built, suited man who dropped the envelope file he was

carrying. She bent to pick it up from the stairs but he quickly intervened to retrieve the folder himself. He glanced at her, concerned for a moment, hostile eyes above the black material face covering. Cathy understood that many still felt the need to wear masks, but most of her colleagues had abandoned the practice. She instantly reset her expression as she lifted her eyes to his, glad her earlier aspirations to be an actress had meant several years of studying drama. Quickly he moved around her and resumed his half-run up the stairs.

Cathy ignored the door to her left, leading to a large, open plan space where her own desk was lodged. Instead she carried on heading towards the ground floor and out into the main street. She kept walking until she reached the spacious precinct of St Anne's Square and lowered herself onto a stone bench. Across her knees lay the folder containing her report for Karl Venmorin, the same type and colour as that carried by the man on the stairs. On his, however, had been the even letters that spelled out her father's name. Damp blotches of rain splattered across the cardboard. She became aware that her new suit was increasingly wet and she had begun to attract some interested stares as the square had quickly emptied. Cathy strolled over to stand underneath an expensive looking doorway, smiling distractedly at the others huddled there. A break in the downpour saw her walk thoughtfully to a local sandwich cart. Ada would wonder where she had been, it was almost lunch hour. Walking back to the office she played out in her mind what she knew of her father's involvement in Inimica.

Both her parents had continued to work throughout the pandemic, though mainly from home. Her mother taught at the local sixth form college and was glad to get back face to face with her students. Her father had his own IT and security business. Even before covid, he had arranged his firm so he acted mainly in a consultancy capacity. Over the last few years, and increasingly during covid, he had spent more and more time in his study. Her mother joked about how secretive he had become. Lately, in particular, her father seemed to be increasingly affected by the lockdowns, reluctant to leave home at all.

Cathy had not told her parents about applying for the Inimica job. Richard Greig was always discreet about his work, as it often involved highly confidential material. It was only after she announced her successful employment, he told her of his connection with the firm. The Inimica installation had been the only job to demand his personal attention consistently on site, where he had worked specifically on the Company Director's office. Earlier in the year he had been brought in to handle new security and IT developments specifically for Venmorin himself. After the work had been completed, he had been instructed to submit all of his plans and company provided laptop to the director. It had given her pause for thought that her father had let slip so much detail about the office, including the fact he had installed tiny, hidden cameras in each corner. She was quietly aware that her father kept a separate PC, as many in security do, with no internet link, plus an old pay as you go emergency phone. His study was a quiet room at the back of their home, overlooking the garden. Only once had she seen the computer unlocked, when he had been called out to help a neighbour. She had entered his study to find him and saw that a flash drive labelled 'Inimica' was placed within the hard drive, in the off-grid PC port.

At work, she decided not to mention the link between them, following her father's unspoken lead. Her connection to Richard Greig, the discreet and diligent engineer, had therefore gone unmarked; her parents had never married and so she had taken her mother's surname of Austen. Why, she puzzled, would that man have a file labelled with her father's name? Presumably on his way to Venmorin's office? Was it a coincidence she had just left? It took her a few minutes to rationalise that it was very likely the Company Director intended to offer her father, who had already proved himself worthy, some further work.

"All okay," quizzed the kindly Ava Bello.

Cathy handed her a sandwich.

"Really good," replied the talented ex-drama student.

Chapter Thirteen

Richard Grieg examined his modest study. He shared a minimalistic tendency with Karl Venmorin. Anything that was significant to him personally was out of sight, the room uncluttered or Spartan, as Julia liked to say. He was dressed in running gear. It would be the first time on an outdoor route for some months, but it was necessary to take the risk. Post-covid trepidation had provided a palatable reason for his reluctance to go out, but in truth he had not wanted to risk a visit to the Order since his involvement with Venmorin. It had been with great difficulty he had hidden his shock when his daughter announced her employment at Inimica. A complication he had never expected. Richard was satisfied that, until now, their relationship had gone unnoticed by Venmorin. Julia knew nothing of his secreted life with the Order and Alison, their eldest daughter, was away in Australia. It was his intention to protect Cathy at all costs and it was for this reason that he would seek advice from the hidden collective that night.

Since covid Richard had mainly used the treadmill for exercise, creating his own home gym in the garage. Staying strong and fit had been part of his routine since his teenage years, when he had been a promising rugby player. He kept his dark hair short, now greying at the temples, though Julia reckoned he could give many younger men a run (literally) for their money. A difficult shoulder injury had ended his sporting aspirations, but he had no regrets. It meant he had met Julia at university and then the girls had arrived. They lived in a good sized semi-detached on a tree lined grove in Didsbury. The area was now considered one of the most sought-after places to live in Manchester. It appalled him that house prices had risen to ridiculous amounts since he and Julia first moved there twenty-five years ago. In those days a young couple could buy a house and easily get a mortgage. Not so now. Cathy was looking at shared housing and Alison had no chance of buying with the crazy house prices in Sydney, even with her high-powered job in marketing. It seemed so long since they had seen their eldest daughter, having been unable to travel during the pandemic. Her work had taken her travelling to North America and Indonesia last year, but she was hoping to come home at Christmas. Julia fretted that they may never get to see her again. Richard talked positively, as he always did, but the last three years had been difficult on many levels.

Julia was on a zoom call as he left the house and headed towards the River Mersey, reaching the embankment at speed. The water level was low for this time of year, though it had rained earlier that day. In January the storms had prompted more safety measures, but it seemed fair to think that the new floodgates would remain untested this month. Relaxing into his stride, he breathed in the subtle fragrances of the developing autumn and marvelled at how domestic his thoughts had become. There had been many happy years and he had eased his vigilance. Yet it was time for him to acknowledge that the finding of the Croston artefact was like a beacon to those who recognised the lost cross of the monastery whose existence had been known to only a few. And there were fewer still who knew it had been hidden with Avide's Mark. Anyone who knew how to look, could read the signs that the past had caught up with its future. He had almost come to forget the secrets he protected, the very reason he was here in Manchester.

One week previously he had received an invitation, in reality a summons, to attend a meeting with the Inimica Chief Executive. On this occasion he attended the house in Bramhall, where Ava Bello organised lunch and would have offered more, if he had been so inclined. He had, using his own technology, avoided the sensors he knew would be used. Mobile phones and fitness watches had been excluded from the meeting, on the pretence of politeness. However, Richard had created an untraceable recording device worn underneath his shirt collar.

"We've been totally satisfied with your installations at our main office," Venmorin began.

Richard looked appropriately pleased and grateful.

"There is another project on which we would like your personal involvement."

He passed across a number of building plans.

"These are properties we own and rent to our more elite clients."

Richard studied the documents closely. He knew the buildings, all in prime property locations in the city.

"We require the installation of discreet recording devices in each room from a number of angles. The recordings will need to be connected to Ava's computer for interpretation."

Richard kept his expression neutral. "What kind of recordings are we looking at here?"

Venmorin tightened his lips, aggression creeping into his tone. "The nature of the recordings does not concern you."

Richard backtracked enough to break the tension that had developed.

"I understand your need for discretion but it's really a technical issue. For example, with or without sound? Will I leave it running or use motion detectors?"

There was a slight easing of the chill that had descended on the room.

"Ava will provide you with the details. When can you start?"

Richard's hesitation produced a raising of his host's eyebrows. Richard quickly responded, but it took all of his experience to maintain a neutral expression hiding the disdain he felt for the other man.

"Can I ask about the financial package?"

Clearly, this was something Venmorin understood. In Richard's world the sum being offered was staggering and confirmed his appraisal of what the work would entail.

"I need to look through a few things first, then I'll let you have a date." He held his expression of gratitude and compliance. He had no doubt that it would have been suicide to refuse at that moment.

"48 hours," was Venmorrin's punched reply

It had been his own idea to try to take a more detailed look at Inimica. The USB, where he had stored his recording of the meeting, added to his previous collected information, would give the Order a grounding for further investigation and subsequent involvement by authorities he could trust. Unfortunately he had underestimated the resources that the company had access to and the extent of their operations. He felt the increasing risk of his failure to take up their offer in the allotted time frame. It had been impossible to speak to Gerald and Mena, which is why he had decided to take the risk of contact tonight.

The place was deserted as dusk fell, the path darker than he remembered, the trees closing in above. He had deliberately left his head torch behind but began to feel that had been a mistake. The frequent showers of the day had begun to ease off, but the sky was still heavy with cloud. He looked up to find the track back towards the road and caught a glimpse of another runner on a connecting trail behind. The stranger was quickly lost within the trees. Richard checked his tracker- 5k. Not too far now. He had a moment of self-congratulation for he felt good for another ten.

The attack was totally unanticipated, a pummelling tackle from a young and muscular male. Fractions of seconds were filled with images of shaved brown skin, baseball cap, determined dark eyes. He felt himself plummet downwards, fingers slipping through clumps of grass on the rain-soaked earth. Cold froze his heart as he splashed into the river. His breath came in ragged gasps as he found the surface seconds before the current snaked around his legs and pulled him within its dark embrace.

Chapter Fourteen

"Mum, what time did he go?" Cathy stood in her parents' living room, the framed pictures of the four of them smiling in happy times. She hadn't yet removed her coat. Julia was dressed in an anorak and ready to leave.

"It's nearly two hours. He wouldn't have stayed out that long. It's his first run for ages and what if he's lying somewhere with a heart attack?"

Cathy was unsettled as she saw her mum, usually so composed, desperately trying to stop the rising panic.

"Come on, we'll find him," she told her daughter, heading for the front door.

Cathy held on to her arm. "Which way did he go? We need some direction."

"I don't know. I was on a zoom call when he came in to wave goodbye." Tears pricked her eyes.

"It's going to be all right mum. You've tried his phone?"

Julia nodded towards the hall table where Richard's phone had been left.

"Damn!" Cathy started to feel fear rising, it was Julia's turn to reassure.

"Let's head for the river. It's his favourite spot. I have to move."

"It'll be really dark down there, do you have a torch?" Cathy was trying not to think of the lonely path that skirted the river.

Julia nodded and found a torch in the hall drawer. Cathy put her hand on her phone safely tucked away in her raincoat pocket.

Richard gasped with effort, holding the branch a foot above his head. The Mersey, fuelled by wind and rain, had forced him quickly to where it changed direction and funnelled him towards the opposite side. He had grabbed the sturdy branch reaching out over the water, knowing it was probably his only chance of survival. Deep shadow made it impossible to see the bank clearly as he tried to lever himself towards it. Richard fervently hoped that his attacker had left him for dead. Even as the thought crossed his mind, he saw lights in the distance, heading towards him. The hum of a motorboat amid the rain, voices on the water, indistinguishable snatches of sound. There was a brief moment of hope, he had been attacked by only one person. Perhaps this boat was not seeking him at all?

Exhausted, Richard summoned every ounce of strength he still possessed to swing himself towards the tree and the embankment. A release of breath as his knees struck the ground, silently thanking the tough, oak branch that had finally snapped as he swung to safety. He quickly seized the branch, wanting no sign of his escape to be visible. Cold fingers made it difficult to prise the fitness tracker from his arm, He flung it into the whirling current minutes before a shout came from the boat. Richard crawled on his belly deeper into the foliage, grateful he had not worn his hi-vis jacket. Face down, he held his body rigid as the vessel came level with him. To his dismay, the noise of the engine changed and slowed as it crawled along the river. He knew he could not raise himself to escape in time if they found him. Another shout, the boat gained momentum and noise, leaving him in complete darkness. Blindly, he continued to crawl along the grass until his skin made contact with the tarmacked path. It was only while painfully bringing himself upright that he realised that his trainers had come off in the water. Icy cold crept upwards towards his heart, the threat of hypothermia becoming very real. Richard bent to rub his legs with as much vigour as he could muster, finally persuading muscles to take him back to the tree where he could check the grass nearby. His white coloured trainers would be visible, even in the cloud covered dusk. Thankfully there was no sign. He felt a little hope at the thought that finding them further downriver would cause the men seeking him to believe he had drowned.

As desperate as Richard now felt, he knew he could not head home and his original destination was too far from that side of the river. He was certain that someone would be watching the house and fear took hold, not for himself, but for Julia. It gave him the energy he needed to reach the road. Cathy used to nag him to bring his phone on runs, but he hadn't of course. Visibly trembling, he turned off the main road into a small cul-de-sac. Tom, and Katie were away. They had left a spare key round the back, in the greenhouse. Thanking whatever deity was watching over him, he quietly made his way into their back garden. There were security cameras at the doors but Tom never charged them. There was no alarm. Gratefully he found himself indoors, stripped off his wet clothes and ran himself a bath.

Tom was around the same size. He found a hoody and duffle coat, one he had once taken great pleasure in mocking. There was a pair of jeans, a little on the long side, that he needed to roll up. Trainers that weren't too bad a fit! Ravenous, he then ransacked the cupboards and fridge. The fridge was empty apart from a block of cheese. Blessing his friends he made a quick meal of cheese and crackers. Julia would be starting to panic now. Likely she would ring Cathy and the two of them would go out looking for him. He caught sight of the clock in the kitchen. It had seemed like hours since he had left but it was less than two. She would have started worrying around the ninety-minute mark when, he guessed, she would call Cathy. Had he said which way he was heading?

Richard, in Katie's dark Micra, had pulled quietly into a drive, a few houses away on the opposite edge of the cul-de-sac. He wore a beanie hat and Tom's duffel coat. The house was owned by John, a nurse, who worked night shifts at the hospital. He kept a sequence of house lights on for security, but the front garden remained in darkness. Richard was familiar with his set nights, as they had a tacit agreement with John to keep an eye on things for him, take in deliveries etc. He got out of the car and feigned entry by the back door. Silently he apologised to his wife and daughter for the anxiety he was causing, as he sneaked back to watch from behind the hedge in the front garden. It proved a perfect vantage point. The hedge was low enough to give a view of his house and entry to the cul-de-sac. also the rear of the first few terraced houses on the main road. Julia and Cathy came out of the house, he could see the strain on both as they linked arms together and hustled towards the main road. Richard guessed they would head down to the river.

It was a good five minutes before they finally showed themselves. Professionals by the way they moved, two dark figures filed out of the back of a terraced house that fronted on to the main road and, due to the curve of the cul-de-sac, was also perfectly positioned to overlook his home. Once he heard the noise of a gate opening Richard knew they were in the narrow ginnel between his own garden and the house from which they had emerged. Like a lot of the homes, the terraced house had gone up for rent six months ago. He worked in his study most nights at the back of the house, but how long had they been watching him? It sent a shiver of fear down his spine and justified his decision to temporarily cut his most important and hidden connections.

'Focus,' he told himself. Two males, young, lean, fit. They must have climbed the fence at the back. The families to either side had young children and would be busy with bath and bedtime. He stopped his mind from dwelling on his girls, remembering their infant excitement as they played in the bath. Focus, he had to focus. He was in good shape but not a fighter and no match for the men who, even now, would be plundering his private study, having disabled his camera and entered through the back. Richard used pen drives and a PC unconnected to the internet. The PC was easy to get into, all the files on the hard drive were simple, household information. The pen drives were with him or, at least right now, were underneath the tea bags in Tom and Katie's kitchen. He hadn't tried them, hoping that the soft plastic pouch inside his shorts pocket had saved the memory sticks he had intended to deliver to Gerald and Mena. There should be no trace on the main computer. Richard dismissed the idea that Venmorin had discovered his deceptions, he had been too careful. Having had more time to think about the events, he believed his attempted murder was a product of the causal throw-away attitude they had to other people's lives. It would have stung Venmorin to have felt he had misjudged Richard, to the extent that an immediate positive response to his offer was not forthcoming. The sum he had offered was mouthwatering. On his pen drive Richard had contributing evidence to Venmorin's intention to entrap influential public figures, installing sophisticated means of surveillance and recording what they would prefer never to be seen. None of it would stick in court but together with what he had managed to copy during the installation, it was all building a case. However, even he was shocked at their ruthlessness. Richard quietly got back in the Micra and drove towards the primary school.

A path ran parallel to the pavement, hidden from the main road by a tall hedge. It meant a safer route for parents and children walking to school and shielded the houses from noise pollution.

He parked in a side road and made his way along the path, gambling that Julia had opted to look for him down by the Mersey. It was fully dark now and cold. The rain had kept most people off the streets. Julia's voice was harsh with strain. "We'll have to phone the police."

Richard tried to keep the choke out of his voice as he came close enough on the other side of the hedge, for them to hear.

"Julia, Cathy, don't stop. Pretend I'm not here." He frowned as his words came out tense and sharp.

There was a quick intake of breath and a scuffle, one of them pulling the other along.

"Thank God," Julia was near to tears.

They listened, increasingly fearful, as Richard recounted as briefly as he could, what had happened to him that evening.

"There's no time for questions," he told them, as they began to speak. "We're all in danger. I think the house is bugged and being watched. Act as if you haven't seen me. I'm okay. Go round to Tom's to water the plants tomorrow. I'll be there. I love you both."

"But," Julia began.

"Dad," Cathy called at the same time.

" We're coming to the end of the path. Don't look round. I'll see you tomorrow."

He watched them walk up the street, without turning back. 'Well done,' he told them silently, as he made his way to the Micra. After arriving back at their friends' house, it was with a sense of great gratitude that he climbed into Tom and Katie's spare bed, finally giving in to utter exhaustion.

Chapter Fifteen

Richard had been sat just out of sight of the window since five am. The dark morning was damp with the residue of overnight rain. Cold pressed against the windowpane as autumn began to settle in. A ghostly, stone pair of hands, cupped to hold water for the birds, were outlined in Tom and Katie's sleepy, moonlit garden. He was still processing the events of the previous evening, that here he was, holed up in their house, reluctant to risk going out in the light of day. He hoped neither Cathy nor Julia would draw attention by coming over too early. He had swept the house, as best he could, without equipment and found nothing in the way of listening devices or cameras. There was no reason that those who were seeking him should have noticed how close they were to the young couple. Covid prevented regular contact with everyone so there had been little coming and going between them. Tom did some work for Richard but it was on a consultation basis only and had not happened for some time. There had been a conversation between Julia and Katie about keeping the indoor plants watered and checking on the house, which had been agreed when both couples had met at the supermarket. For the hundredth time he went over in his mind how secure they were in the borrowed abode. He could not think there was any other choice but to take the risk, hoping his attackers believed him dead. It was important they also believed that no incriminating evidence had been kept. In summary that he and his family were now irrelevant to their scrutiny.

It was after nine when the back door rattled as Julia entered. He kissed his wife briefly and then motioned her beside him. He pointed upstairs and then quietly went up to check, from the side of the bedroom window, she had not been followed. He couldn't see anyone. Downstairs Julia reassured him regarding the conversations he knew would have been monitored. She had said out loud that she couldn't work and had cancelled tutorials, that she needed to go for a walk to clear her head. He explained to her his actions to reassure the attackers he had been swept down river.

"They would have checked my smartwatch."

Julia gasped, her hand raised to her heart. She seemed to have aged overnight, or had he just never noticed the deepening lines around her soft blue eyes? She hadn't bothered washing her hair, which had lost its usual spring and curl. It covered her head like discoloured straw. Julia, seeing him notice, self-consciously passed a hand over her head.

"I look like Wurzel Gummidge," she laughed, chokingly.

He reached for his partner and held her while she sobbed into his shoulder.

"Richard," she began. Unable to speak, she fumbled in her coat pocket and brought out a letter.

> Julia ,it's over. I can no longer continue to deceive us both. I am in love with someone else and have been for some time. You will not be able to contact me. My life no longer belongs with this family. Richard.

Richard was furious, almost ripping up the letter, Then, thinking better of it, slid the sheet into his pocket. After all it was no less than he had expected. A confession of an affair, an explanation of his disappearance. The forgery was first class, but a totally ridiculous assumption of what he would write, written by somebody who had no concept of their real relationship.

" They took most of your clothes while we were out looking for you. Also your phone, and iPad. They left the computer."

The phone was all business, the iPad mostly internet shopping.

"They'll have easily by-passed the security on the computer. There's nothing hidden on the hard drive, just the household accounts. That should keep Cathy safe."

"Cathy," her voice reached alarm pitch and he instantly regretted his words.

" It's okay." He took her hand. "Come into the utility room, there's a flask and a couple of chairs, no window."

She followed him into the converted garage where they sat opposite each other.

"What do you mean Cathy safe? Jesus Rick, what's happening here?"

"Did she go to work this morning?"

"Not willingly, but in the end we thought it best for her to go."

He poured coffee from a flask, as he tried frantically to figure out where she and Cathy would be safest. He wasn't sure if the one place he could go would accept Julia, and in particular accept Cathy. Alison he hoped, was unreachable and uninteresting to them.

"You need to tell me what this is all about!" Julia was becoming increasingly alarmed.

" I will as soon as I can. I don't want to put you in more danger. They have to think they killed me."

"What?" She was standing again.

He wished he wasn't putting her through this.

"What do you want me to do? You don't want me to use a phone? " She had seen the regret in his eyes, the fear he was trying not to show. He stood and turned, unable to face her. "How could I ever think I could have a normal life?"

It was barely a whisper. He turned and placed his hands on her shoulders, she was frightened by the wildness in his eyes. Richard's voice croaked, he could not manage the words of final separation, they just wouldn't come. "I don't know how to explain this to you."

Julia, who never ceased to amaze him, guided him to an armchair in the sitting room and sat on a stool opposite. carefully avoiding the window. "Richard, you have done nothing wrong. You are the best father, husband and human I could have wanted to be with. I believe in you. Tell me."

And he did.

◆ ◆ ◆

"Cathy, you're not yourself, is something the matter?"

Ava walked across from her own desk, as Cathy tried to bring her concentration back to work. The other woman's beauty, the compassion in her eyes, tore at her need to discuss all that had happened the previous evening. But she had the script.

"My parents are splitting up. My dad ran off with someone last night and my mum is devastated."

Ava nodded sympathetically.

" I'm really sorry to hear that. Look, leave the project for today. Would it help if you worked from home for the rest of the week? That way you can put your hours in but have more flexibility for your mum."

Cathy, her eyes filling with genuine tears, nodded her appreciation.

"Thanks Ava, that would be great. I'd like to be with my mum right now."

She gathered her things, unaware of how closely she was being watched. Karl Venmorin switched his screen from the office camera to type an email to the man she had seen climbing the stairs two days previously. Her employer was still furious he had not known of the connection between Richard Grieg and Catherine Austen until last night. All his resources and she had slipped right in alongside him. He followed the camera positioned on the main staircase, watching Catherine leave the building.

" A complication," he said to the face on the screen.

Ava, in her private office, nodded agreement.

"A shame," she said, her eyes prodding his.

"All of it," he replied. Greig would have been perfect for the other side of their operation.

" You've spoken to Caleb?"

He nodded gravely. " Greig is almost certainly dead. How much does she know?"

Ava shook her head. "On the face of it, nothing. At least we have eyes and ears on both her and the mother, if she works from home."

Venmorin nodded, it wasn't his way to praise or thank his chief assistant.

" If Caleb only made the connection last night it's unlikely she knows anything."

"Agreed," Ava said solemnly, "but can we take the chance?"

Venmorin stood up. " No, I doubt very much that we can. She's gone to her mother in Didsbury?"

Ava nodded. "No doubt she'll head to her own place first to pick up her things."

"Put Caleb on surveillance at the flat, just in case. Get him to do a search once she's gone."

Ava scribbled a note and watched as Venmorin ran his fingers thoughtfully over the chair where Cathy had been sitting two days ago. Even now, knowing that she was Richard Greig's daughter, he was reluctant to give up his intentions for the unusually alluring young woman.

"Caleb found items belonging to Greig on the embankment, miles downriver. The body will have been swept out to sea. It might look suspicious if the daughter disappeared as well at this point."

"The team are still in Didsbury," Ava told him "We can watch the mother and daughter for a few days more. As for the long term...."

"I'll decide after I've given the matter more thought."

 He picked up a file effectively dismissing her. Ava pressed the 'leave' button, which meant Karl Venmorin faced the screen version of himself. He smoothed out the lines of aggravation in his expression. Both father and daughter had seriously disappointed his expectations.

Chapter Sixteen

We returned to the Greenhow cottage in late November. The wind was fierce as I pulled our bags from the car. Amy, after many long days on the moors, had gone to lie down. The days were short, the evenings dark and cold. I lit the log burner and used the pay-as-you-go phone I had bought for keeping contact with our families. Amy made brief calls, her people were used to her travelling and being unavailable for long periods. I had seen my parents only briefly in the last two years, meeting in various towns for a meal and an innocuous chat. Their patient kindness did not hide their hope that I would return to Lindisfarne with them. I sighed, hearing the disappointed resignation that I had no plans to go home for Christmas. I put down the phone and saw movement outside the window, not unlike that which Amy had seen that first night in the cottage. I opened the patio doors and returned to my chair by the log burner as Nesu curled around my feet. He had come to me uncalled, bringing another memory of the long past.

Avide woke with instructions to put on my most serviceable brown cowl, as he himself was dressed. It was early morning in spring, the wind whistled through my ears as we galloped a treacherous path through the forest and east towards the sea. Another hour saw the skies blacken with cloud.
The wind snatched my breath as it swirled, pushing us from the path. Only Avide's gentle coaxing persuaded the horses to carry us through the building storm. The weather lifted trees and hurled them across the path behind us as we left the top road and headed down the valley towards a small village. The river had flooded, the waters still rising. Already the storm had destroyed life and swept in its wake the small homes that had dotted both sides of the river. Together, we gathered a pitiful group and guided them to shelter above the valley

with what belongings they could retrieve. Avide knew of a noble house on the far side of the valley where the thane allowed our small, beleaguered group to find food and shelter in the Great Hall.

Avide and I gratefully broke our fast with the lord and his household. It was late afternoon when we set out to meet the others of the Order, whom our Lord had instructed to follow and clear paths in the forest, should they find them blocked. As we went through the hall and out towards the stables a heavy set soldier, sodden with ale, held a blade to a young woman, already distraught with the loss of her child of less than three years. As Avide moved nearer, the soldier turned his blade towards him. I stepped in front to protect my lord, searching for a weapon nearby. Avide slid beyond me and to my horror the soldier struck. The blade clattered on stone as its owner, wide-eyed, leapt backwards. Avide simply ignored the man and carried on as if uninjured to attend to the girl. The blade disintegrated as it lay bloodstained in front of the soldier, who howled with fear, bringing spectators from inside. Gently Avide and I lifted the girl and gave her care over to the villagers.

Overlain with this record of what had happened, I saw another. It was as if I could see what was happening in two different ways at the same time. Something akin to possessing, in addition to my physical sight, an internal set of eyes. Like the strings of the lyre, they attuned to the sweet peace of spirit I had come to know in the monastery. It was the first time that the misshapen rawdin, covered with symbols of its own distorted dimension, was visible to me. The creature whispered in the ear of the soldier and I could see lust define his intention. The poor girl fell to the floor and her aggressor closed in further.

"They are the Rawdin and have no power," Avide told me, "apart from what we give them. Know that their purpose is to occlude the light. They often pursue targets where those with great potential for powerful good are subject to self-destruction, through one manner or another. It leaves entry for the Rawdin's black goading to do some ill and then to become lost in their own darkness."

Awe-stricken , I saw a golden glow encircling Avide, as he moved around me towards the soldier. It seemed his body was made more *of light than flesh. As the soldier lunged, the sword pierced its target between the ribs, but immediately particles of light in my master's body shifted to surround the blade. The cruel metal combusted to nought as it made contact with the intense brightness of my lord and friend. I gasped and would have bowed before Avide but his look warned me not to make issue of this occasion. The ghostly rawdin had vanished. Once we had tended to the girl, Avide went to speak quietly to the soldier who, in his fear, backed himself further against the wall. Speechless and dazed, he went without struggle when the Household Guard came to take him.*

I knew now how I had recognised and been able to name the rawdin seen in Lindisfarne. Even before then, there had been many times when my work as chaplain took me to places of despair and self-destruction. I had not seen but felt the rawdin's noxious presence in the many hells we have created. Nesu, in his own particular way, helped me understand that his dispatch of the rawdin in Lindisfarne had not gone unnoticed. That Jarinbissar's grim shadow network had relayed his action through invisible spider lines of consciousness that were, even at this moment, searching for me. I understood that our time in the Dales had played an important part in keeping us both safe. Equally I knew that it was now time to return to Manchester to find the next part of our jigsaw.

The phrase 'New Normal' had become popular towards the end of the pandemic. These words often came to Amy throughout the first few months of profound transformation, following the events in the cave at Greenhow. Like her companion, Amy felt as if she had entered another phase of life, another aspect of herself that had previously been unreachable. She and Os had stayed together, travelling to remote landscapes where Nesu and Choriscuro could be manifested to form. During this time they came to understand their deep link to Tanamaarin. Choriscuro became a physical manifestation of that link and even when he was not there to touch, she could feel his potential physicality within her heart. She had no idea where it all fitted in with current spiritual or religious thinking but also little cared. She was certain, beyond doubt, that the light from that dimension reflected a love that was so far beyond her human experience that she wanted to bathe in its presence every hour of every day.

Their needs were simple, both had enough savings to see them through. The arinokra dance came naturally, calling her spirit horse into form. Os and Amy were very close, but what Amy originally saw as possible romance had taken a different direction. Os slept on a pull out bed in the living space. Entwined by their past, driven by the same purpose, there was an unspoken acknowledgement that they had both found true family. Equally entangled in a previous age, they remained at the mercy of unbidden memories to reveal an ancient history that rebounded forcibly to the present day. It was of deep concern to both that no further memories had presented to either as they rebuilt the powerful bonds that had simply lain waiting for them both to revive.

Os drove back to Manchester as winter approached, going ahead to sort out the flat while Amy shopped for lunch. She sat outside a coffee shop, underneath an outside heater, relishing the buzz of the city as it celebrated its growing identity as somewhere to visit for its own sake and not merely for the football for which it is famous. Strangers smiled at one another in the freshness of a fine cold day Overlooking Piccadilly Gardens she sipped a flat white, watching the ever diverse crowd weave in and out of each other's lives.

It was autumn, the forest aglow with rusts, golds, yellows and browns. And the evergreens that never undressed. It was from the top of one of these that I watched, secure in my invisibility, my sage linen, brown skin, auburn waves of hair plaited over my shoulder. A ripple ran from leaf to leaf to alert me to his presence. He looked up and saw me, his view travelling like an arrow to my exact position. I did not move, pinned like a dove by the sheer beauty of him. Taller than most, a body that was gifted with the grace of movement. Dark hair, sleek in the afternoon sun and his eyes a clear, iridescent blue.

"At last, I have found you."

What sort of man was this? A power that both repelled and compelled me. A rush in the river that yet could direct the river itself.

"You are Ellan."

He spoke quietly but his words came clearly to me, their tones carrying the force of his will.

"And you?" I asked.

" I am Bierscath." His eyes examined me in the way that mine had lingered upon him. I read his surprise.

"So you are the witch of the forest?" He was laughing now. "A rare jewel indeed."

"And now that you have found me, what is it that you want?"

He affected humility as he climbed down from his horse, but there was no humility in this man. Bierscath limped towards the tree.

"I need a balm for my foot. My horse trod upon it as I was heading north and I remembered hearing that there was a woman in this forest reputed to offer healing to those that asked. I have coin."

"Most do not venture this far into the forest to find me."

"You well know that I am not most," he asserted, laughing.

I sprang to the ground. Choriscuro nudged through the undergrowth. The foal was now a handsome stallion and he had come to me ever since his mother had been taken. Neighing restlessly he placed himself between me and my visitor. I soothed my horse and stepped around him to find that Bierscath had seated himself on a nearby rock and removed his leather boot. There was indeed a swelling and the appearance of recent injury.

"You have a long journey ahead?"

"I do."

I let my fingers touch his skin and felt my own tingle in response. Still, I would not take him to my dwelling for herbs and leaves to wrap his foot. Nor was I willing to leave him to fetch what I was wont to use. Instead, perhaps because I felt the need to assert my *own power, I called silently to the energies of restoration that I knew so well, placing his injured foot within both hands. When I removed them, the foot had returned to normal size and was as if the injury had never occurred. Later, when I looked back, I could see the triumph in his face that seemed, to my delight, to offer only admiration at that time. I tell myself how lonely I had been, but the truth is I had never desired a man before. I desired Bierscath.*

This was the beginning. The next day and the next and many following, he returned to that place. I persuaded the trees nearby to scatter a bed for us beneath an arch of branches; the horse chestnuts to discard their fruit outside our forest chamber. Bierscath drew in my whole being, only later did I find I had been swallowed into darkness.

The coffee was a cold splash across her sandals as the metal table toppled to the pavement. Amy jolted upright, alarming a middle-aged couple walking nearby. They stopped, clearly worried by what they saw on her face. She accepted their help to pick up the table, and a young waitress hurried over to retrieve the cup, offering to replace her drink. Amy gave her thanks, shaking her head, anxious to leave. Having tried so often in the past weeks to force the memories of those times, she began to understand the mercy of their infrequent bursts into her consciousness. They superimposed themselves on the present with such a disabling sense of reality that she felt more in her previous life than the one in which she now existed. Of all she had recalled to date, this had been the most profoundly disturbing. Even now, as Amy Rowan, she had been bitten by a remnant of the passion that Ellan had shared with Bierscath. Amy, thankful that the waitress had placed her shopping bags in her hands, wandered aimlessly in the Northern Quarter, trying to process the implications of this new knowledge. It was clear that Ellan knew nothing of Bierscath's marriage to Sereka at that time. It was the first of the memories she would not share with Os.

Chapter Seventeen

Angel Meadow was around her before she realised. The visions of history were still present here but less painful. Amy acknowledged that since that day in the cave at Greenhow, her relationship with the planet had changed. Her brain had begun to process things in terms of pattern and her perspective had outgrown her current existence. She was acutely aware of links to the natural world in a way beyond language. Bringing Choriscuro to presence in the world she inhabited meant that his consciousness was partly imprinted upon her own. Amy found she had less need to analyse with her brain, trusting her intuition and instincts in a more pronounced way. A young woman, perhaps in her early twenties and strikingly pretty, sat on one of the benches. Amy readily recognised the forlorn look of desperation mixed with fear. She settled beside the stranger who jumped nervously.

"It's good to see some dry weather," Amy commented conversationally.

The younger woman smiled weakly and nodded.

"It poured rain last time I sat in this spot."

Instead of answering the stranger stood, distracted. "I'm sorry but I'm late. Nice to meet you." The accent was Mancunian, local. There was a touch of regret in her expression as she turned, heading along the path and towards the old Tobacco building.

Amy sat a little longer, not wanting to directly follow her reluctant companion, who obviously preferred to be alone. She thought of the many times she had sought refuge on a park bench, an empty church, walking until her legs told her it was time to stop. Seeking peace in a chaotic existence.

On entering the flat, Amy was quickly alerted to the sound of intense discussion in the living room. Crossing the kitchen quietly, she heard Os' soft and reassuring tones. The same voice she had heard on the bench spoke tearfully. "I didn't know who else to speak to Joseph. And you being a chaplain, I feel I can trust you."

Amy recognised the female attraction the young woman had for Os. After all, until recently, she had felt it herself. Her friend turned as she entered the room. The stranger was shocked to recognise the woman she had rebuffed on the park bench.

"This is my close friend, Amy," Os smoothly introduced her. "And this is Cathy, who lives on the next corridor."

"I can make myself scarce," Amy offered, smiling. "It seems like you need some privacy."

Cathy shook her head. "No, it's alright, really, I'd better get back." She stood up to move.

Amy reached for the coat she had left in the kitchen on that first day. She held it up. "Please stay. I was just fetching my coat."

Os looked thoughtfully at them both.

"Look, Amy's a nurse, who worked with me in a charity group. I promise you can trust her. Something tells me that we both need to hear your story."

Amy looked at Cathy, who nodded and sat back down. Amy replaced the coat and moved quietly to sit on a stool at the side of the room.

Cathy hesitantly glanced a couple of times at Amy as Os explained that he was no longer a hospital chaplain. She seemed to ignore this fact completely in the relief of being able to pour out the details of what had happened to her family. Os listened without comment as she went through the events of the previous evening. The forced charade of believing her father's infidelity after the aggressors had ransacked his study and taken his belongings. Amy's heart went out to the exhausted young woman, her words tumbling together as she told of her father being attacked and knocked into the river. She started to pull at her fingers, her body trembling as she finished her tale.

Os brought her attention back to the room. "Prior to this happening, had your father behaved any differently lately?"

" We thought he was just like loads of people, nervous about going out after the pandemic, though it seemed out of character for him. We tried to persuade him that he could still go running but he was adamant that it was too much of a risk."

She looked up at them both.

"Running is my dad's thing. He loves it. The treadmill is okay, but he would run for miles along the river. It was as much about getting out in nature as the run itself."

"Okay, has this has been the case since the restrictions ended?"

Cathy looked thoughtful.

"Mmm," she rubbed her chin. "Actually no. It was after he did the work for the Inimica firm earlier this year."

"Inimica?"

"A big development corporation, who try to build communities and restore run down areas of the city. They're part of a worldwide network of similar businesses. I work for them."

"Did your dad get you the job?" Os was trying to gauge any connections but Cathy looked offended.

"No. In fact I didn't tell either of my parents I'd applied until afterwards. We have different names," she told him defensively, "so they couldn't have known who my father was."

"How did he react?"

" They were both over the moon for me!" She stopped, rethinking the moment when she had given them her news. A bright light after the shadow of the pandemic, as her mother had described it.

"Actually, it was more my mum. Dad smiled and said he was thrilled for me though. But then I don't think he hung around for long. I discussed it mainly with mum."

Cathy grew more thoughtful. " Something that did bother me."

Os nodded that he was listening. Amy continued to observe silently, nodding reassurance.

"He's like Mr Confidential. Never ever, especially with security work, gives any detail of what he's installed or arranged."

"This wasn't the case with Inimica?" Os encouraged her to go on.

"He told me that he trusted my confidentiality. That there were hidden cameras all over the place, barely legal, and where they were. Also some of the secret arrangements that he'd made for Karl Venmorin, the boss," she explained, "and how sophisticated it all was. And expensive too."

"How do you like working there?"

"It's great," she returned immediately, then hesitated. "I just thought dad had misunderstood."

"But," Os encouraged.

"But just before my dad was attacked, I crashed into a seriously built man on the stairs, who was carrying a file with Dad's name on it. We aren't supposed to use those stairs."

"Your father's name?"

She nodded her confirmation.

" Is he a dark-haired guy, about my height?" He stood up.

Cathy looked puzzled.

"Take a look from the window, standing here."

Os placed himself at an angle that hid his body but meant he could see out of the glass pane, and then waited for Cathy to slide into his place.

"Oh my God!" She shot back towards the chair. "That's him! At least I think so. He was wearing a face covering but I'm pretty sure it's the same person."

"I spotted him arriving when I got up to make you a drink. Your window fronts the other side?"

She nodded, her face paling, jaw tightening with agitation. " Just where he's standing, it gives him a clear view of my window. I sit and have my meals at a table right by it."

Amy came alongside Cathy, who seemed to respond to the other woman's calm manner. The suited and booted figure down below could have been any number of young corporate executives that used to lunch in the more expensive parts of the city. He was positioned so that he could easily slide behind the hedge, it would have made him invisible to the main part of the building. Os' view from the corner meant he could see down the lane towards the bridge and the river.

"I'm guessing," said Os, with a grim look on his face, "that they've made the connection between you and your dad. He may be waiting for confirmation that you're not in there before he makes his move," he added.

Cathy jumped with fright at Os' comment. "But why do you think he'll come inside? How would he get a key?"

"I doubt," he told her seriously, "that it would be a major problem for him. But from what you've told us, I'm guessing he isn't expecting you to be home for long today. He's probably fishing for something to give him a clue as to whether you know anything they think you shouldn't. Once he's sure no one's home I think he'll just try to tailgate entry. On the other hand, if he does know you're here, he may have other intentions."

Seeing the panic rise in the young woman, he added, "Or maybe he's just here to observe."

"How about all three of us going to mine?" Amy said quietly.

Os nodded thoughtfully, raising his eyes towards Cathy whose face was a mass of confusion. It was her desire to escape the man who had looked at her with such aggression on the stairs that brought a weak 'okay' from her lips. Amy turned towards the other woman.

"Can you get to your room and pick up your things without going to the window?"

Os moved to the sofa again and waited for each of them to resume their places.

" Why don't you let me go?" He put out his hands for the keys. He looked thoughtful and Amy guessed, that like her, he was hoping the man was working alone and there was no one already waiting in Cathy's flat. The young woman nodded, handing over the key to Os.

"I have a small case packed on the bed. I was going to stay with Mum," she told him. "My purse, phone and iPad are in a red cloth bag in the main room."

Amy tried to hide her anxiety from her companion, collecting her own things together. Neither she, nor Os, had unpacked the bags that were still in the back of the car. To the relief of both women, he returned in ten minutes with Cathy's bag and purse, handing her back the keys.

"Cathy, I hope you don't mind, but I switched off your phone and took out the battery."

For the first time the young woman seemed to hesitate in her trust, sending a horrified look towards Os.

"If they're that high tech, with corporate resources, I'm guessing they're gonna track your phone."

Cathy let out a sigh and nodded, placing the disabled phone in her bag.

"I need to get in touch with my mum, she'll be frantic."

"Won't she think you're still at work?" Amy commented. "We can ring her later on, from town."

Reluctantly, Cathy agreed.

Fifteen minutes later they had loaded the Nissan and covered Cathy with a blanket in the back seat. The chosen observation point of their visitor meant that he was able to see cars exiting from the underground parking area. Os noted the careful examination their visitor gave the car as it turned out of the building and headed for the city centre.

Chapter Eighteen

Amy hadn't been home since her time away with Os. As they pulled up outside the old terrace in the centre of Urmston, she hoped fervently that the heating would work. Over the pandemic period she had installed new windows, a solid front door and a new boiler. She wondered what Aunt Maria would have made of her two visitors, Os in particular. Her shrewd eyes would have missed nothing, yet she didn't judge either; just holding the space, as she always said. She felt a familiar surge of grief shoot through her belly. It had been eight years since Maria had passed away, beginning Amy's travels. During and since the pandemic, she had made the most of her time in the house, but there was much that she would not change. The attic, filled with Maria's books and personal effects, had not been touched. Downstairs she had felt more able to decorate and arrange things in her own style. The comfort of her aunt's energy remained integral to the building however, and she was grateful to find it welcoming her back home.

Amy found herself checking the street for watchful eyes, as she opened the door and helped Os to usher in the troubled girl. A high-ceilinged hall led to a welcoming and spacious sitting room, where an old sofa was covered in a brightly patterned throw. There were two bookcases, a cosy old-fashioned fireplace with a modern gas fire, her aunt's old rocking chair and a telly.

"Fingers crossed," she told them, switching the fire on, encouraging the pilot light with a gentle blow. Once it was established she found the switch for the boiler and turned on the central heating. To her great relief, it seemed to be working fine. She had painted the walls a soft, lilac white, choosing to keep some of Maria's cherished pictures, including one of the old priory at Lindisfarne.

Os went over to look more closely. "Have you been?" he asked.

"Never," she replied, though she wondered if Ellan would disagree.

"It's somewhere I've always wanted to visit," added Cathy.

"I know it well," Os told them, turning quickly away.

Amy showed them around the house which contained two spare bedrooms. Os and Cathy took a room each. He pointed to the stairs leading to the third floor.

"Just a lot of old things left by my aunt," Amy told him easily, leading the way downstairs again to the small dining room with a table, through to a good-sized modern kitchen.

"I think," she said, opening cupboard doors, "that before we do anything else, we need to find something to eat."

Os looked grateful as she pulled various ready meals from the freezer, adding the shopping she had brought from town.

"I'll nip down to the Spar for some milk," she told them, checking the fridge. "Stick the kettle on."

It was great that there was still an alternative to the supermarkets, even if the old corner shop with Mrs C, (nobody ever knew what the C stood for) a motherly woman, shrewd and kind, was now a modern mini market. It was a hundred metres from Amy's house and she popped in regularly. At the back of the shop, there was a view out toward her street. Picking up the milk she caught sight of a woman in a green jacket, who appeared to be showing particular interest in Os' car. On her street, many commuters were in the habit of leaving their vehicles during the day and heading to the nearby metro station. Os hadn't parked directly outside her house, where her own mini stood, but a few doors further down the street.

The woman took out her phone and ran her fingers quickly over its surface. Was she typing some message? Amy moved out of sight as the stranger lifted her face towards the shop. She was tall and very lean. A pronounced chin added a sternness to features that might be described as handsome rather than pretty. The dark blue eyes, hard as steel spikes, surveyed the whole street before they returned to her phone, where she continued her message. Amy watched the woman take long strides across the road, as she stepped towards the back corner of the shop. She was able to see the green jacket slide cross the opening and on towards the town. Amy hurried back home, taking Os aside in the small kitchen. "There was someone looking at your car with a lot of interest." She gave him details of the episode outside the house. "Do you think it's to do with Cathy?"

Os nodded.

"Too much of a coincidence otherwise." He poured the milk into the coffees.

"I don't think I gave our waiting friend outside the flats enough credit." He looked thoughtful. "That's very fast work."

"Come on, we need to speak to her."

Settled on the couch with their drinks, they told Cathy about the incident.

"Might not have been anything," she responded. " The woman may have wanted to buy a similar car." She did not recognise Amy's description.

Amy's eyebrows raised. "Really?"

"Well, a newer version maybe." Cathy smiled, for the first time, she realised, since her father had gone missing.

"I am still in the room." Os grinned. There was something about Amy's comfortable house that seemed to lift them all.

" How long have you lived here?" he asked.

" I inherited it from my aunt about eight years ago. She was very special."

Both Os and Cathy seemed to want her to continue, perhaps enjoying the fact that they could share a different subject matter than the problems they currently faced.

"I always felt that my Aunt Maria, rejected by her family as weird, blasphemous and gullible, was able to see and feel things that the rest of us could not."

Cathy nodded with encouraging interest.

" She had a totally different way of looking at the world. She believed in the magic of the planet and that as we walk upon its surface we interact in so many different ways that are beyond our conscious mind. She spoke about the different interplays of so many energies. She told me that she had cast a layer of protection around the house, sensitive to darkness, refusing to tolerate its presence within the walls. Every day she went to her private space in the converted attic above us. I haven't been able to bring myself to change any of it. It's still full of wonderful old books about crystals, herbs, alternative medicines and healing. We had a very special bond."

Amy felt herself getting choked with emotion. It was very rare that she could talk about her aunt like this, with people she felt she could trust. The freedom with which her aunt breathed in this world, the openness of mind and acceptance of every living being, had been so wrongly labelled as witch like and dangerous. There was nothing sinister in someone who could accept others as they were and offer them an alternative way to heal themselves. Amy's own experience of traditional healthcare made her extremely aware of the complexity of chronic disease. She was always open to anything that might offer support to those whose lives were dominated by pain and illness.

" I would have loved to have met her." Cathy reached over to squeeze Amy's hand. "My mother sometimes calls me a little 'fay'."

Os looked quizzical.

"It just means I seem to pick up strange vibes around things at times." She looked a little embarrassed. "I wonder what your aunt would have made of our lady visitor?"

"You could be right Cathy, that it's nothing at all," Amy pondered, " but I think we need to take care."

"And if you were right Amy, and I already trust your instincts, it could be I've put you both in danger."

Cathy looked infinitely sad, as if her whole world was crashing down around her. The brief moment of light-heartedness had been so quickly swallowed by the reality of their situation. It took a little while for Os and Amy to reassure her and clearly exhausted, she allowed Amy to lead her back upstairs, where she could sleep undisturbed. Downstairs Amy and Os shared a meal and moved into the small dining room where they were less likely to disturb Cathy. This contained a table, four chairs and little else. Amy refreshed their coffees and gently closed the adjoining door.

"Worse scenario?" she asked Os.

"They took pictures of the cars that left the Tobacco building today or maybe had access to the CCTV in the car park. If so their tracking resources and equipment are very scary and Cathy and her family are in a lot of trouble."

"It sounds like her dad's mixed up in something pretty serious." Amy agreed.

"There's more to it than that. I don't believe in co-incidences. There's something about her."

"I know just what you mean." Amy nodded. "I feel as if I've known her before."

"I think I need to check out this Venmorin guy."

Amy reached for her bag. "Let's at least do the Google thing first." The internet search painted a perfect picture of a man heading up a company that was part of a new wave of industry, purporting to bring new life and prosperity to previously neglected and run down communities. Inimica had won a host of awards. The smiling faces of Karl Venmorin and his assistant Ava Bello appeared in various countries across Europe, fronting several laudable projects. "They certainly don't look like bad guys." Amy closed the computer.

"Nope," Os agreed, " they don't. But then they never do."

Chapter Nineteen

Amy is a rare creature who feels like family in a way that my actual family have never done. Cathy, in the short time I had known her, more than in passing each other on the stairs, scared me. Or at least, she had made me scare myself. There was something visceral, primal, in how I had begun to feel around her. I was finding it harder and harder to be objective. I was glad to have a reason to leave them both, sneaking out of the back gate into another street where Amy had left me her mini.

The security at Inimica was, as expected, comprehensive and discreet. Apart from the staff who were alert with regular inspections of the building, there was also a raft of cameras and alarms. It was indeed, a very professional outfit. There were enough pictures on the internet for me to recognise Venmorin and his assistant, a graceful black woman known as Ava Bello. They emerged from the building in the same car, a black Mercedes, and headed south towards Stockport and the Cheshire border. That is where Cathy knew Ava lived; she was unsure of Venmorin. I followed. It seemed they lived, if not together, then in the same house. Or mansion? It was in an out of the way part of leafy Bramhall, traditionally inhabited by footballers and a long way from Amy's beloved street in Urmston. As they pulled in and I drove past, I could see there was a winding drive with a computerised gate security system. There were lights on, in what looked more like a stately home than a house, so I presumed some staff were on the premises. As night closed in I found a quiet area to pull off the road and park up, sliding the mini behind some bushes. I found myself easily able to climb the trees adjacent to the eight-foot fence, dropping down into the grounds on the far right of the property. Stealthily I made my way across the lawn towards the back of the house. My enhanced senses detected the presence of dog kennels, so I opted for the other side of the building, finding an enclosed and carefully constructed courtyard. I stepped behind white trellising covered in winter foliage. Venmorin and Ava sat with drinks in an immaculately designed living room, log fire blazing. I melted into the shadows, heading for where a small side window had been opened and placed myself directly underneath. I knew that my hearing was now acute enough to pick up the conversation inside.

" She seems to have completely disappeared. What about the mother?" Karl Venmorin's voice was self-assured and firm.

"She received a text message from Cathy saying that she had to work late and would see her tomorrow."

"Did we trace the mobile?"

"Hers. Outside the fish market in the city. No trace when we got there."

" You said she was heading home to her mother this afternoon?" I heard her put her drink down and step restlessly towards the window. I ducked down as she made her way to the glass doors. It was a clear night and the moon was almost full. I caught the suppressed anger in her expression as she looked out towards the garden. "That's what she told me," she was moving back towards Venmorin, " so I was surprised when Caleb reported that she hadn't arrived."

"And he found no trace that she'd been in her flat?"

"Nothing. Looks like she hasn't been there since yesterday."

"Routine checks?"

"We're keeping surveillance on any cars that left her building from 2pm, just in case. There were only a few."

"We may have made a huge mistake in letting her go." He sounded tense.

"Maybe we shouldn't have killed her father."

He snapped his drink on a wooden table.

"Maybe you should have known she was Richard Grieg's daughter! Close the window," he ordered, before leaving the room.

Ava Bello waited a little while, slowly finished her drink, and then did as she had been instructed.

I crept towards the deepest shadow until she too had left the room. I had heard all I needed to hear.

Chapter Twenty

Amy ran, exhilarated by the freshness of a clear wintry day. She headed up to Flixton where there was an old Victorian walled garden, tended by the community. Squirrels scampered up an oak tree and out onto the top of the red brick wall as she ran alongside, stopping at the end of the wall to take on water in what was really a lovely space. Rain was heading towards them once again, her vastly more acute sense of the weather told her it was already in the air. The area had lost many businesses during and shortly after the pandemic. Things were still pretty grim. She felt the usual guilt about not being at work and then wondered if she would ever return to her life as a nurse. It was gratifying how much more speed and stamina she seemed to have. She flicked her thoughts away from acknowledging the strange life she was living. In truth it had always been strange. Perhaps this was the reason why her aunt and her had got on so well. Os had so quickly become her anchor. And Avide. The memory of him so strong. The need to find him was like an urgent programme written into her DNA from the beginning, but to which she had just awakened.

Arriving back in the street Amy slowed to a walk. There was a large black van parked outside Tim's house. It didn't belong to her friend and neighbour on the opposite side of the street, who had been working in London all year. The windows on the side of the van were blacked out, but her peripheral vision, as she crossed the road, had become far sharper in recent weeks. Undoubtedly there was the same man at the wheel who had been in the park outside the Tobacco Factory. And the woman in the green jacket was now sitting beside him. Amy picked up into a jog again and ran past the house to the end of the street, doubling back into the narrow alleyway at the back of the row of terraced housing. The gate she had recently replaced, was lodged tightly into the wall and was locked with a bolt on the inside. She hoisted herself up enough to slide the bolt, and once in her little yard, made sure it was firmly closed behind her. A soft knock on the kitchen door brought Os to let her in.

Amy opened her mouth to tell him about the van but he was already talking in rapid sentences, brows furrowed and eyes reflecting an unusual anxiety.

"Slow down Os, what did you say about Cathy?"

"She looks awful, something is seriously wrong."

"Hang on." Amy had a medical kit in a plastic box, that she had used for home visits during covid. She grabbed it from a kitchen cupboard and headed to where she had left Cathy comfortably sleeping the previous night. Rapid and noisy breathing sounded as soon as she climbed the stairs. Once in the room Amy noted the pale, clammy skin.

"Do you have any pain, Cathy?" she asked, gently taking her hand and checking the pulse.

Cathy shook her head, clearly frightened as she submitted to Amy's painstaking examination.

" All pretty normal," she stated, replacing her blood pressure cuff and thermometer. Summoning Os to help, she sat Cathy up so she could auscultate her chest.

"It seems okay apart from the number of resps, which have calmed down a little."

Cathy gave a little cry and her breathing sounds became noisy again. "I feel as if the walls are closing in," the words were snatched between gasps.

"She's in panic," Amy told him, trying to get the girl to slow down her breathing, with a little success.

"I need to get to my mother," Cathy croaked.

Amy nodded. Let's take her out the back into the fresh air. You get her downstairs and I'll set off and pull round to the street that runs at a right angle to mine. Let her sit for a few minutes in the garden and then head left out of the gate. I'll get our things."

Amy had a quick wash and changed, figuring that Cathy would calm down once out in the open. She did not even glance towards the van opposite as she opened the mini, deliberately unhurried, her heart fluttering. In a shorter time than she could have imagined, they were sitting with Cathy in the back seat, windows opened. The young woman looked like a ghost as they set off through the narrow streets and out towards Stretford.

As Amy had predicted, Cathy had responded well to the fresh air and seemed more herself. Her colour started to improve and she was able to talk in full sentences. Amy watched in the mirror as Os, who had been supporting her, relaxed his arm, reluctantly she thought, from around the girl's shoulders.

"I don't know what happened. I just woke up and couldn't breathe!" Cathy pulled at her throat. Trying to head off another episode of distress, Amy directed Os to a small cool box with water and snacks, in the pocket behind her seat.

"Have a drink, Cathy," she told her. "It's not surprising that the events of the last two days have started to take their toll. I'm not sure taking you to your mother's house is the best thing. Look, let's have breakfast somewhere and talk things through."

"No," Cathy was determined now. "I need to get back to her. We'll have to take a chance. I need to know what she's found out from dad. If you drop me off by the bus stop, maybe they'll think I've come from that direction."

Amy caught Os' nod in the mirror.

"Okay Cathy, I'm heading there now. Give me the post code." She tapped the keys of the sat nav and covered the distance in thirty minutes.

"Here," Cathy instructed. "There's a housing estate towards the river."

Amy turned the mini into the quiet cul-de-sac as Cathy explained. "If I get out here, I can walk down to the bus stop without anyone seeing you drop me off. There's a cut through from the estate. Pull into the drive behind the hedge, I know the couple, there's no one home at this time of day."

The hedge was pretty high on either side of the drive.

"Cameras." Os nodded towards the front door.

"They're not working," Cathy reassured him. She slipped out, taking her overnight bag and started towards a path on the other side of the cul-de-sac. Once Amy and Os had joined the main road she turned back towards the house. Minutes later she was knocking quietly on the back door of Tom and Katie's place. Her dad, his face ashen, opened it and quickly ushered her inside.

◆ ◆ ◆

Richard gently untangled himself from Cathy's sobbing embrace. He led her into the kitchen and listened to her account of what had happened the previous day.

"If it hadn't been for Os and Amy, I'm not sure what would have happened. I don't understand what's going on dad?"

Richard steered his daughter away from the windows into the utility, where he had spoken to his wife.

"Cathy, I discovered some things about the Inimica company and Karl Venmorin when I installed some of their security systems. They operate in every part of the world and most of what they do is legit. In Manchester it's not entirely the case."

She sat down beside him, her face still very pale. "I don't understand."

" I am almost certain that Venmorin ordered me killed."

"Oh my God!" Deathly pale now, she told him about the file with his name on it and the watcher outside the flat.

"Tell me about this Os, is that his name?" Cathy nodded in affirmation.

"Well, that's what he calls himself now. He was just Joseph, a hospital chaplain, when I first knew him. He had a fiancé."

Richard looked thoughtful. "And did he explain the change of name? Is anything else different about him?"

He noticed that Cathy had become quite animated talking about her neighbour, colour coming back into her cheeks.

" He's not engaged anymore." She shrugged. "He's with a girl, they're close, but I'm not seeing romantic close."

"What's her name?"

"Amy. Oh, and he's not a chaplain anymore."

"Really? What does he do now?"

She shook her head. " He didn't really say."

"And this Amy?"

"She's a nurse. Not sure where though."

Richard stood up. "I'll make you something to eat, your mum has brought some food."

Cathy stood up, shaking her head. She still had no appetite. "I should go to her."

"No Cathy," he replied thoughtfully, "you can't go to her."

Richard put his finger to his lips to stop her reacting. He moved back into the kitchen, checking the windows. A moment later Julia appeared, sliding into the utility area, breaking down in tears when she saw Cathy.

Richard took both their hands.

"I need to explain something to you Cathy."

He repeated the information he had given to Julia, while she carefully watered the plants in the bay window. His wife crossed back to them, to give them both a brief embrace, before Richard and Cathy sneaked out of the back door, using the cut-through that led out onto a neighbouring road. Julia checked the house for any signs of Richard's presence and then, satisfied they had done all they could, returned to her own home.

Chapter Twenty-One

To her relief, Amy saw that the van had gone, as she manoeuvred the mini into the gap in front of her house. There was no sign of the watcher from Angel Meadow, or the woman in the green jacket. Hopefully they had decided there was nothing of interest here for them, or even better, that Os had left his car and gone into the city. She quickly let her friend in through the back door, having dropped him off a few streets away, explaining that the surveillance seemed to have ended.

"Do you think they followed us?" She looked worried.

"No. There was no sign of anyone following us," he replied, his face rueful. "Let's not take any chances though. Keep our heads down."

He went to sit at the table, waited for her to join him before continuing. "I want to know more about this Venmorin guy and this company Cathy is working for."

" I have a friend who might be able to help," Amy told him.

"Will he come here?"

"I'll ask," she replied.

She chatted on her phone for a few minutes in the kitchen and returned to the dining room.

"No problem."

James arrived later that evening. There was still no sign of the van or its occupants. Amy had worked with James in a GP surgery, where he had been asked by the doctors to investigate an alleged fraud. The Practice Manager who had, in fact, been syphoning funds, lost his job shortly afterwards. Amy suspected her friend's talents strayed from the strictly acceptable standards of the NHS. Currently he was part of a team that worked to prevent cyber fraud and terrorism. It gave him access to some areas of cyber space where others could not venture. On the occasions when James was not glued to his computer screen, he spent his time in outdoor sports and hiking in remote areas. He and Amy had struck up a friendship that grew closer during some brief trips away in small groups in between lockdowns. On one such trip to Snowdonia the relationship had deepened. A few months later however, and without any rancour, they tacitly agreed that they were more suited to friendship than romance. His Liverpudlian accent greeted her cheerfully, as she opened the back door of the house. James held out his hand as she introduced Os, his slim figure looking small against the other man's taller and more robust build.

"Where should I set up?" He shuffled his laptop off his shoulder as he followed Amy into the dining room.

"Here okay?" she checked. Even before Os could pull up his own chair to the table, her friend was seated, his fingers running across the keyboard.

Amy returned from the kitchen with coffee, sliding in beside Os. James leaned back, swinging the screen around so the other two could see. His baby blue eyes and blonde hair gave him an ingenuous look that belied the forensic ruthlessness with which he carried out his job. On the screen was a photo of Karl Venmorin with a 'summary report'.

"It's copied from a trusted source," he told them.

It gave an account of activity similar to the material they had found available on the general web. There were no criminal activities recorded against him, but a number of investigations had taken place as to his possible involvement in an array of schemes including money laundering.

"Never enough evidence to pursue," James told them, "but he and the woman he works with, Ava Bello, have been right there on the cusp of some very dodgy deals. There are some who think it might go further, people seem to disappear very easily around these two."

Os whistled.

"That's not all."

James tapped the keyboard. "It's highly likely that he actually works for this man."

A picture appeared on the screen, showing a group of men and woman at a social gathering. James enlarged the screen to highlight a hazy image of a figure in an expensive-looking tuxedo, his face side on.

"Poor as it is, this is possibly the only image available of this person. It took me a long time to hunt it down and to identify that this is indeed Elijah Tregothan."

He looked up to see if there was any reaction from his companions. None. Amy continued to examine the photo but said nothing.

"Despite the biblical inference," James continued, "he's suspected of being the real power behind a multitude of worldwide operations. To those in the know, this elusive person is a billionaire and apparently a camera-shy philanthropist. You won't' find him listed in Forbes, as his money trails are like a spider's web. My belief is that he is the purveyor of quiet but intensely effective evil. The usual suspects in these cases are into human trafficking, drugs, slavery, arms and political unrest. The retention of power through the influence of money and resource or the withholding of it. The disruption of progress by the creation of a fear-driven populace."

"Sounds like something of a crusade for you," Os said softly, watching Amy's friend become more agitated.

James took a breath. "He came to my notice during a particularly cruel episode of human trafficking involving children. The financial walls were good, the money trail had more twists and turns than a giant maze and it took me months to track down his name. I found a connection through a receipt in Vienna, that I suspect someone should have destroyed. I'm learning to recognise the pattern he creates. I've come to understand that his penchant for invisibility is at war with a need to control."

He ran his fingers through spiky hair. "But trying to get anyone who might have dealings with him to talk, has proved impossible."

"Can I take a screenshot of that image?"

Os stood, ready to find his phone which he had, like Cathy's, disabled.

Amy felt as if someone had stolen her breath. She turned towards the window and tried to relax her breathing.

"I'm gonna say no."

Os sat down again, frowning at James' firm statement.

"My advice is to stay away from this man. Don't even carry his image on your phone."

" We're trying to help someone," Os told James, who held up his hand.

"Trust me on this. I have my reasons." He wiped the screen and hunted in his case for a package, which he laid on the table.

Os looked speculatively at Amy, whose face was now very pale.

"I've brought you two burner phones. They're set not to show their numbers on ringing. My advice is keep them just for talking to each other. There's a good amount of credit on them."

Amy reached for her purse.

"Not necessary." His eyes softened as he looked directly at Amy. "Just promise me you'll be careful."

Amy nodded, still feeling shaky. "We can't thank you enough, James."

Once they were alone, Os made a note of the name James had given them.

"You okay," he asked her.

"Just need to catch up on a bit of sleep," she said, heading upstairs, avoiding further questions. On her bed she let her eyes close. Another long-hidden memory began to play out in her consciousness.

I was invisible to the highly dressed troop of men that hunted below; they rarely looked up from the trails of deer or wild boar. Even had they done so, the white rock I sat upon was hidden by the forest around this time of Bealtane. Roderick and a few men from his House were on horseback, hounds tripping behind. Scouts rode back and forth to the main group, urging the band forward. By now Osweald was ensconced in the monastery with Avide. I watched as Bierscath inveigled himself into a position where he was next to

Roderick. Gradually, under whatever pretence he had invented, I saw Bierscath drop back, as if losing control of his mount. He let the horse drift towards a thicker, enclosed part of the wood. Roderick sent his men onwards towards the hunt and I, who knew the dangers of that place, saw the black hearted intention of his companion. Behind a large huath bush, inches from where Roderick now stood, was a cliff edge, a hidden gorge. Bierscath had steered him to this point beyond the known paths. It would be a simple matter to knock him from his mount into the gully below and serve it to his House as a hunting accident. I signalled to Choriscuro, waiting in a cave below. We were as one in those times, and as he came out of the shadow I pointed to where the two men stood. Bierscath, in the act of raising his left arm, paused, recognising the flurry of whistles I used with my horse. In moments my mighty stallion broke into the grove, sending the two horses fleeing away from danger. As both mounts escaped towards their companions, Bierscath turned back. He looked up, blue eyes turned to ice. And though I knew he could not see me, I saw that there would be no more passion between us. My heart wanted to cry out, to reach him, but his black soul was revealed fully to me that day. Ever after I named him Euair, for the poisoned tree. I remembered Osweald, my brother, though he did not know it. And I thought of our father, how he had been saved from death a second time.

Chapter Twenty-Two

Sleep was not an option. Thought was a cyclone of unwanted knowledge and memory. And fear. Flashes of light caught her attention as they crossed her window, was someone using a torch below? Amy pulled on a sweatshirt and made her way across the room to look out upon a ghostly illumination of the small garden, as moonlight filtered through wispy cloud. The solar lights between her pots showed that the back gate, though closed, was unbolted. Os' door was shut tight, she knocked gently but there was no response. Was he in the garden? She made her way softly downstairs. The open curtains in the living room allowed the lamplight outside to confirm that there was no sign of the van or any further surveillance. Amy stepped silently towards the dining room, where she was halted by a sound from the kitchen. Barely audible, she could nevertheless distinguish knocking at the back door. Os was locked out! She smiled as she entered the kitchen and opened the back door.

Adrenalin coursed through her body as she was confronted, not by Os, but a total stranger. He was very lean, but her experienced eye also noted the wiry muscularity of a regular runner or maybe cyclist. He appeared in his fifties, closely cropped black hair turning grey at the temples. She was aware of some sense of familiarity. He held a small torch in his hand.

"Amy?" A mellow, musical voice. "I'm sorry," he looked around, uncomfortable, lowering his voice even further. "Look, I need to speak with you. My name is Richard. I'm Cathy's dad. It's how I found you."

Relieved, she opened the door. "Come in," she stepped aside as he entered the kitchen.

"Is Os here too?"

Amy nodded and indicated he take a seat in the dining room.

"Where's Cathy? Is she okay?"

"She's being watched," he whispered.

"This will sound ridiculous," he took out what looked like one of the machines the delivery men used, a small electronic device, "and I know I sound paranoid, but for the safety of us all can I sweep your place for listening devices?"

She hid her discomfort and allowed him to check the ground floor. When he headed for the stairs she was more troubled.

"Sometimes they're placed in the floor above but can still pick up our conversation," he explained. She nodded but went ahead to warn Os. Quickly, she flew back to the landing, noiselessly opening the door to Os' room. It was empty, the bed undisturbed. On the bedside table was a heavy book she recognised from her aunt's attic study. She picked it up. 'Geometric Patterns of the Spirit' by Livia Raumsnal. There was a colourful assortment of interlocking shapes on the cover. The pages were encyclopaedic in number. Inside it was filled with many geometrical sketches, odd looking text, and pencilled notes made by Maria over a long period of time. Amongst all her books it was the one her aunt had seemed to treasure the most. Where the hell was Os?

Footsteps by-passed the room she was in and headed towards her own bedroom. She made out the sounds of drawers being quietly opened and closed, the wardrobe door being carefully shut. A few minutes later and Richard was knocking gently at Os' door. She let him in and watched carefully as he checked the room.

"All clear." He sank wearily onto the bed. "Where's the man Cathy calls Os?"

It was Amy who noticed the sounds from the attic stairs, hardly audible. It took a few seconds before the door burst open and Os, moving more swiftly than she thought possible, had pinned the visitor across the bed. The implacable animal power of her friend seemed to swallow the room. Amy stood back in shock at the revelation of his lethal potential. Quickly, she reached forward to place her hand on his back, feeling the hard knot of muscle that corded his neck. He turned, eyes a wild grey, one hand still pressed on the neck of the older man.

"It's okay," she told him. "You can let him go."

The stranger looked pale and terrified, breathing hard as he adjusted himself to a sitting position. Os looked into the steady eyes of the other man.

"Who are you?"

"I'm Richard, Cathy's father."

The voice was a little shaky but firm. He stood up and held out his hand.

"You must be Os? She told me you had helped her."

Os took his hand. "I'm sorry, we're feeling a little spooked at the moment and not expecting visitors in the middle of the night."

Richard, Amy noticed, did not take his eyes from Os as he backed away. Suddenly weary of all the tension, she sank into the armchair at the bottom of the bed, her arms curling around the 'Geometric Patterns of the Spirit'. Richard's eyes opened wide.

"May I borrow that?" He took a step towards the armchair, but Os moved his body across the small space.

"I think you need to tell us a little more before we start lending you anything," he said quietly.

Amy's tone was softer. " Maybe we could do this back downstairs over a cup of tea?"

She took the book and placed it carefully in her bedroom, noting that everything seemed undisturbed before following the two men downstairs.

Os had grabbed a sweatshirt and was in the process of putting it on when she entered the small dining room. Her friend helped her with the drinks, remaining strangely quiet, leaving her to lead the conversation with their unexpected visitor. She saw no point in being subtle. "Why are you here?"

Richard glanced at Os, whose face remained quietly composed as he took a sip from his mug and placed both hands in his lap, leaning back into the chair. They waited until the man, who called himself Richard, took a deep breath and continued.

"I guessed," he shifted his earnest gaze to Os, "and hoped you were here."

Os remained silent, waiting, focusing his gaze on the other man. "Why?" Amy questioned, frowning.

"I don't know how much you know about yourselves yet. I recognise you both, though you do not know me."

Os' expression did not change, but Amy was becoming increasingly uncomfortable.

"I'm quite certain we haven't met before," she told him confidently. And yet, there was something.

Richard waited for Os to comment and another heartbeat for Amy to say something else. Silence. He nodded towards Os. "You were once Osweald, a monk brought to the monastery one stormy evening in Northumbria."

Os sat straighter, focusing on the other man's words, but still silent.

Richard turned to Amy. "You were Ellan, forest dweller and friend to Avide."

Amy looked at Os who leaned forward and almost whispered his response. "Avery?"

Richard exhaled deeply. Amy thought she could see the glimmer of tears in his eyes.

"Once, many lives ago, I was Avery." He held out his hands to Os who took them, holding the other man's gaze with his own grateful eyes. Os turned to Amy. "Avery was a young monk, the youngest at Lindisfarne. He was close to Cuthbert and often frequented our smaller monastery that was hidden in the crook of the River Tyne."

Richard continued. "In those times of veneration and the making of saints and miracles, the truly miraculous went unknown and unseen within the 'Mainisstir Na Gaoithe Fillte'."

The words acted like a magical charm for Amy. "The Monastery of the Folded Wind," she responded.

Richard's use of the old Gaelic had opened a chink in her mind, into which flowed a vision of shimmering halls, where sunlight filtered through high arched windows and music ran like a system of streams beneath their feet.

"You remember?" Richard smiled, the first time she had seen

him do so.

"No, not really," she explained. " I just get snatches." She tugged at her hair in frustration. "Nothing I have done to unlock the memories has worked. I feel as if it's all there, the knowledge, those other times in another life. Yet they will only come when, and if, it suits them."

"It's the same for me," agreed Os, "only I've just had a little longer of knowing who I am."

Richard had visibly relaxed.

"And you," Amy asked, "have you held this knowledge all this life?"

The older man shook his head. " It was earlier this year," he explained, sipping his wine. "I was contracted for a job by a very prestigious company."

"Inimica?"

He nodded. "Most of it was straightforward installation of tech, writing a bespoke software system that would link to what they already had."

"And then?" asked Os. Richard looked weary beyond words. "And then," he continued with an effort, "I was asked to meet Karl Venmorin, having dealt only with Ava Bello, his assistant, until that time. He was charm itself. The job went well, but lately I refused an offer to work on his more," he lifted his hands and made inverted comma marks with his fingers, 'delicate' projects."

It all connected with what Cathy had told them. Os raised an eyebrow in encouragement, as Amy leaned in closer.

"He sent out some pointers that I could earn a great deal of money becoming involved in the other side of his operations. I didn't take up the offer but I haven't felt safe since. The night I met Venmorin everything changed. One moment I had only the knowledge of myself in this life, and then it was as if someone had opened the wall of the world. I could clearly see my life as Avery, and the shapes of the lives I have lived in between. I knew, with perfect clarity, that my purpose was to find the two souls I had known in the days when I was Avery, in the service of Avide. Cathy got a job there, hiding her connection to me, so that we could continue monitoring the company. A few nights ago I decided to go for a run. I had to get out and think, desperate for fresh air and the sound of the river. The rest you know from Cathy."

"Tell us about Avide," Os requested. " It's obvious the monastery did not survive."

Amy looked expectantly at Richard. "It's the one thing of which we are both so certain. We have to find him," she exclaimed.

Richard paused and his eyes examined each of them very carefully, before letting them roam beyond them both to another world.

"Not long after the destruction of the smaller monastery by raiders, Cuthbert made his way to the Farne Isles to live out his days reclusively. I remained in Lindisfarne until the end of my time."

"Avide?" encouraged Os.

"No one knows. Some say he was killed by raiders, others that he left before that time."

Richard suddenly slumped forward.

"You look as if you haven't eaten or slept for days," Amy told him, acknowledging the dark shadows under his eyes and the delineated cheek bones. "I'm going to make us all a meal." The older man nodded, looking grateful.

Amy busied herself in the kitchen, picking out the ingredients to make a homity pie, one of her aunt's staple meals and easy to make with cheese, potatoes and vegetables. She needed the time to absorb the memories that Richard, or Avery, had invoked. Amy tried to remember him from that other life, so shrouded by the distance in time. Not just time, she realised, there was something else, a resistance from her to think back to days where life had been so ungentle.

"Oh Maria," she whispered, desperately missing her aunt, "you would have known how to help me."

Once the meal was in the oven Amy stood at the window fixing upon the way the small pebbles in her pots became luminescent in the moonlight. She pulled a coat from a hook and went out into the autumn night, trying not to scrape the painted metal chair as she took a seat by the small iron table. It was barely seconds later, breathing in the scented air, that memory enveloped   her.

It did not matter that the conversation had taken place fourteen hundred years ago. The words and his presence were with Amy now, as if the earth had held it safe in her own private locker of time.

"Avide, did you want to speak with me?"

"Always El-lan."

She felt wrapped in the warmth of his energy, making herself comfortable sitting cross-legged on the soft rug. As always, he wore his monks' robe, the simple white linen cloth. He sat on the edge of a deep stone well that was at the centre of his private indoor space. Ellan had traded the rough woollen robes that kept her warm in the forest for a brown, nun's habit. She had washed in the river before entering the cloister through the women's gate. She had been aware for some time that not all who were part of the monastery could enter this space, it simply did not exist for them. The first time she had come here she had followed Avide through a tree-lined arch to a standing stone that gave way at his touch. Later, when she came to it alone, it gave way to hers. At other times however, she noticed that the entrance changed appearance, though always recognisable to her. Sometimes it was a solid, rough-hewn door, at others silken soft fabric. At times there was an arch set in a garden wall, at others an open gate. Avide had told her that it changed according to the individual who entered and that she would be able to recognise the many imprints that had been left by each. In the Carapace, for that was how he named this space, the air was charged with a peculiar essence. As if he had captured the secrets of a freshly travelled breeze from a mountain top and sealed it within.

Avide dropped his hood and handed her a stone cup of water from the well. It never failed to touch her, how these simple actions were part of his rich language of love. The water was sweet and cool and made her skin tingle. His face never aged, or, she wondered, was that merely her perception? The long brown hair, the colour of oak bark. The facial bones, irregular in their lines, the mouth full lipped, the jaw long and set, a nose off centre. His eyes were the colour of falling autumn leaves, flickering in firelight. There was, she had often acknowledged, a liquidity about him, the grace of a meandering river and the mystery of the sea.

"You are very precious to me," he told her, smiling lightly.

She, who had been cast away by the world, had found it hard to accept that this man, who was so much more than man, could truly care for her. And yet he had found her as she lay dying and brought her back to life. She had witnessed his compassion and kindness, often unknown by those that benefitted from it. Unlike most of the monks, he understood her primal beliefs, the earth magic she carried within. Her love for him was the centre of her being and was beyond any other obligation or attachment. And yet it was neither possessive, nor flesh-entwined, nor familial. He was the lake and she the lily, he was the mountain and she the orchid, that bloomed beneath its looming strength.

Avide reached into the well and lifted from it a small object. He signalled for her to open her hand before placing upon it a triangular stone. It was smooth and cool to touch. She held it up and saw that, although essentially blue in colour, it was filled with flecks of diamond white. "There will be a time," he brought her gaze back to his own, "when you will need this Mark to return to me. When your mind will watch this moment from afar and remember these words. Go now and hide it where only you may find it again. And El-lan, when the time comes to retrieve it, be alone and tell no one that you do so."

There had been joy in this discovery that she could step back into that pocket of time once more, feeling the deep and infinite presence that abided there. It also left her with a restless doubt. She was no longer Ellan and her connection to the monastery of long ago had yet to be reforged. This was a different time, there were other considerations. Amy wanted to share her memory with Os and Avery, to discuss what she would do.

Ellan had been skilled in lybcraft, the magic of the times, in what was now called the Dark Ages. The meagre history of that period was written by men, most of them clergy. Her people did not read or write in the way of later scribes. They used complex symbols, storytelling and the house of memory to pass on their lore and to communicate what was necessary to be known. The power she exerted as Ellan was mostly a matter of intuition and knowledge, learned from her mother. Added to this, her years alone in the forest, though often imprisoning her in utter hopelessness, had also honed her abilities. They had brought a comprehensive understanding of natural forces, a practical and skilled connection to the plant world, and an ability to be open to things beyond her cultural and personal experience. It came to her then, what she needed to do. She would not dishonour Ellan's devotion to Avide.

The more Amy acknowledged what she had to do, the more she felt uncomfortable. There was much that she never wanted to know again. Years of sadness sang their mournful song down the ages, reaching her even now, safe in a Western World, free from want, accepted and liked by many of her peers. Obviously, she was already plunged past a point of no return. Even if she never again performed her arinokra dance, Choriscuro inside her could not be denied. Avide's words had been uncompromising. She made her decision quickly and left doubt behind as she raised herself from the garden to a kitchen full of the rich smells of home cooking.

In the dining room Richard and Os spoke in soft whispers of another time and place, when they had been Avery and Osweald. Amy placed the meal before them, having collected plates and cutlery, adding another bottle of wine and glasses. They were so deep in conversation that they barely responded when she told them she needed to catch up on some sleep. She closed the doors of the dining room and living room. Quietly, Amy made her way upstairs to her aunt's quirky attic and picked out the notebook that Maria had always carried with her. The attic had a Velux window through which the moonlight gently shimmered, illuminating a picture of Amy and her aunt which she added to her pack. An overwhelming instinct to leave the house seized her. She had decided to tell Os not to worry, that she had some private task to do. That thought was squashed with the need to leave at once.

In her bedroom was an embroidered purse she had bought in Istanbul, and in which she held her most precious objects. In a hidden corner behind the bed, was a storage space where she kept her 'run fast' rucksack, for the many times she had needed to get to the airport with little notice. It contained her passport, cards for her savings account, some cash and clothes, all packed tightly. Although it was bulky, she squashed into her bag the book that had so interested Avery. She knew every creak in the stairs and avoided each of them, as she descended back to the hall. There was hardly a sound as she closed the front door and made her way to the mini that was parked a good few doors down the street. The dawn had just begun to show over Barton Bridge as she headed north. With any luck, she would be back tomorrow before they realised she had gone.

Chapter Twenty-Three

I sat listening to Richard, seeing his pain and disappointment that we did not know him. Both Amy and I had retained the basic facial features that we had worn so long ago. This was not the case with Avery, who had obviously lived many different lives since that time. It was not until he mentioned Ellan, speaking of her being a friend to the monks, that I began to see a vague outline forming and then finally, I knew him.

Young Avery stood at the edge of the river, looking across to the other side. Behind him loomed the great stone walls of the monastery, its arches and mullioned windows peering out at the sunlight of a new morning. The building, gifted by the King of Northumbria, sat in the crook of the river and was surrounded by great trees and many contemplative pathways. Cuthbert, as was often the case, would be enclosed with Avide, leaving Avery and the others free to roam about our home. He was a particular favourite of mine, being near in age to what my own son must have been. I hailed him from lower down the river and steered my coracle towards the bank. He had clearly been waiting for my return and came to meet me. Together we unloaded baskets of foraged roots and fish, the sum of a two nights journey.

Richard bowed his head in relief as I spoke the name by which I had once known him. He smiled as Amy too, had acknowledged him as Avery. His existence had never been chronicled in the histories of that time, but to my knowledge, he had lived out his life quietly in Lindisfarne. Amy, in her usual thoughtful way had left us alone to discuss the long years since we had last met, offering to make a meal for Richard who looked half starved.

"It is the way of things," Richard sighed, "that humans in general do not remember their past lives. Often, only the truths that were found in those previous times, travel with them into the next. I speak mainly for myself, for since you knew me in those precious days, I have walked this earth many times, yet only the essence of them remains with me."

It occurred to me, that as he looked at my features he saw the intermingling of two lives, in the same way that I could clearly see Avery and Richard.

"And yet," he went on, "I believe you both still wear something of the same countenances that were Osweald and Ellan."

Amy had laid out the table for food. We gratefully ate the pie she had left us, being so engrossed that we barely acknowledged her saying she was heading to bed.

"If there had been lives before I became Osweald, I cannot determine. Only that something of relevance to the strange times we live in, prevailed in Northumberland in the seventh century. As a result of this both Amy, as Ellan, and myself as Osweald, were plucked from the cycles of rebirth. In Tanamaarin we were prepared for a time to return to new lives, centuries after we had last lived out a human existence but retaining a closeness, even in our DNA, to those we had lived in that particular period."

"Tanamaarin is real?" Avery asked wistfully. "There were words spoken amongst us, but no concrete knowledge of its existence."

"I don't think my human brain can find a form to fit it into." I tapped my head. "It's why the knowledge remains locked in here." I placed my hand over my heart. " I have no memories I can share, just deep certainties that arrive like paving stones before me, leading the way." I told him of my revelations in Lindisfarne and of finding Amy in Croston.

"But what exactly brought you to Croston?" he asked. I could see that he was refreshed now, his mood uplifted.

"Nesu," I replied, watching his response closely.

"The lynx! Is he with you here? I remember he was your shadow. You made a formidable pair." His eyes were sparkling now.

Avery looked around the tiny dining room, as if Nesu might appear beside him. This was the final hurdle. I relaxed, fully confident that he was indeed Avery of the Lindisfarne monastery and friend to Osweald.

"He is here," I tapped my chest. "Nesu is an arinokra, coming specifically at my call and only if he is willing. A physical manifestation linked to our existence together in Tanamaarin."

"Fascinating." I could see he was excited by the concept, wanting to know more. "Of course, back then, we had no knowledge of the other dimensions entangled with our own," Avery commented. "I always suspected that Avide moved in circles beyond us. But you said it was Nesu who brought you to find Amy?"

"Not just Amy."

Avery was astonished. "Avide's Mark! I thought it lost with Avide himself!"

"There had been talk amongst all the monks about a particular power linked to a stone that Avide sometimes carried. Rumour said that Cuthbert had witnessed his dear friend walking through a door into another world. Once it was reported that it transformed Avide into a mighty sea monster." I nodded and grinned, sharing his wonder.

"Go on, please," he encouraged.

"One evening in April, I noticed the moon being particularly bright, shining into my bedroom. I got up to look out and there in Angel Meadow, was Nesu. I hadn't called him to me and knew instinctively that he wanted to show me something. I went out to find him but he was no longer there when I arrived. When I made my way to the spot where he had been standing, I found a discarded leaflet. It was for a homeless charity working from the old church in Croston. When I looked at the place in more detail, I found links with Aiden from the early monastic years in the North. I signed up to help. I felt the tug of Avide's Mark almost as soon as I entered the oldest part of the church. Amy arrived two days later. I didn't recall her as Ellan then, but there was something about her. It took me a little while but by intuition, and perhaps having handled it previously, I found the hiding place."

Avery was wide-eyed. "You have it then? Avide's mark?"

" I have it," I told him.

"Is it safe?" He seemed deeply concerned.

"It's right here," I reassured him.

Avery seemed uncertain, as humble as I remembered him.

"Would it be too much for me to see it?"

I shook my head. "Of course not. It's in my room. The library of Maria, Amy's aunt, is fascinating. To my astonishment, I found what I think is a reference to the Mark in one of the books."

"The Geometric Patterns of Spirit?"

"Yes. And Maria had made notes, a remarkable woman."

I led the way, excited to share my discovery with my trusted old friend. As I turned to bring out the Mark from its hidden nook behind the bed, a terrible gnawing fear assailed me. Syllables I had not heard in this lifetime crawled into my ears in rasping shards of harsh evil. The language of Jarinbissar. They held me in shock for vital moments, as a silicon like material encircled my waist. Even as I started to twist with all the strength, endowed by my arinokra, pain stabbed me to immobility. Avery's voice had changed from its pleasant humility to a dark arrogance, as he intoned the foul rituals .

When I looked into his face it was unrecognisable from both the Avery of long ago and the gentle character with whom I had shared my meal. I had seen his expression before, eyes livid with enduring hate, mouth pinched with cruelty. The rabid obsession of those lost and locked in Jarinbissar. He pulled the scroll roughly from my grasp. I had led him straight to Avide's Mark. I saw the murderous intent, choking on vocal cords that were useless, paralysed, as the dark figure of Avery crept towards Amy's bedroom door. How I had failed her! A howl, haunting and grotesque, rang out as he marched back to my bedroom alone.

"Where is she?" The voice was barely human.

He pulled on the cord, whispering further dark words. "Where is she?" he repeated dangerously.

I felt speech return and hope lift me out of my sense of doom. I answered with a smile and he knew, in an instant, that I had no more knowledge than he. As I began to goad him he pulled hard on the cord, intoning syllables that returned me to silence.

There was noise from the accompanying houses that had been disturbed by the dreadful howl. In moments he pulled me down the stairs and into the kitchen. He pressed a speed dial number on his phone, as he shoved me into the garden. Opening the gate, Avery turned to push me forwards into a black transit van, sinister in the early morning stillness. He pulled a rod-like instrument from his jacket and let it touch the cord around my waist. It was all I was to remember for some time.

Chapter Twenty- Four

Amy grew drowsy as she passed the turn-off for Lancaster. It had been her intention to make her way to Northumbria that morning but she had not slept, nor eaten, since early the previous day. In her haste to retrieve the object hidden so long ago, she neglected to factor in time to do either. Slowly, she was coming to terms with the long-ago existence that intruded so forcibly into the life she lived now. Ellan's power, she realised, was not hers. It was part of the forest dweller's life back then, grown from all that she had experienced and a deep connection with elemental forces. As Amy, in this time, her world was sanitised and vastly different. Even with Choriscuro, she still lived in this modernity, requiring a far different set of skills.

A sign for Carnforth, somewhere she had avoided since Maria's death. Some years previously her aunt had invested in a holiday lodge, that was only an hour's drive from Manchester. An exhausted quarry had become the basis of a lakeside resort, near to the small market town at the top of Lancashire. It had been a personal haven for Amy as a teenager. Almost every weekend of the summer in her fifteenth year, had been spent with Maria. They had used the location to travel to the Lake District and the Yorkshire Dales, climbing mountains, swimming, visiting caves and generally avoiding the inevitable conflicts that were a daily occurrence at home. She had made local friends and even had her first date whilst staying there.

Amy's mother had inherited the lodge on her sister's death. Characteristically her mum complained that it was a costly misuse of funds during the pandemic, bringing in no revenue but requiring her to maintain the ground rent payments to the holiday resort. Amy knew that her mother planned to sell the lodge but had still not got round to emptying it of Maria's contents. The many hints she had dropped to encourage Amy to do so had been deftly ignored. She sat up straight and held the steering wheel more firmly as she felt her eyelids begin to droop. It seemed that it was time, after all, to revisit the place on her own.

It was still early morning when she pulled into the site. Amy swallowed as moonlight skimmed the water of the lake. Mahogany-stained wooden lodges were dotted amidst large pine trees and carefully cultivated flower beds. The sounds of wildfowl echoed in the sleepy resort, reminding her of the hours she had spent listening, as they proclaimed their presence on the lake. She smiled, little had really changed. Maria had picked a lodge that was out of the way of the main site, set back and largely hidden by a hawthorn hedge At the very edge of the resort, it backed on to the River Keer where, in the past, Amy had delightedly spotted kingfishers. Today the river was more a stream, gurgling quietly amongst long reeds. It took her only a few minutes to retrieve the spare key from its hiding place under a solar powered water feature, still in the cool, calm night. She breathed in the smell of pine, the moist air, happily accepting the illusion that she was somewhere more exotic than North Lancashire. Maria had pottered about in the small garden for hours, endlessly sweeping leaves in the autumn with an expression of pure joy on her face. As if that thankless task were the most worthwhile work in the world. Amy wiped her now wet cheek impatiently, only to find that her tears began again as she opened the door.

It was as if her aunt had never left. Spotless, the lodge had been cleaned regularly as part of the contract she had with the resort. The same cosy furniture, a modern kitchen and two bedrooms. The patio doors led out onto a terrace with a direct view of the lake. The sense of excitement that she always felt as she arrived came flooding back. It seemed to have banished her immediate need for sleep. Even after she had unpacked and refreshed the lodge, it was still too early to call Os using the burner phone provided by James. She shrugged off the discomfort she had felt when James made her promise to put her own phone, without its battery, somewhere no one else would find it. He had advised that they commit to memory each other's new number. If possible, he told her, she was to use a public place to phone from. Amy was still restless with her decision not to give Os at least some idea she had left but reassured herself they would not notice her absence until later in the morning; very likely he and Richard would have been in conversation for some time after she left. There was a motorway services within walking distance. It made sense to get some breakfast there, and it would be a good place from which to phone her friend.

A grey dawn finally arrived. Amy had barely entered the cafe area of the services when the rain began hammering against the windows. She made her way to a corner seat at the back of the building and found she was really hungry. The poached eggs on toast were quickly disposed of but she took her time with what was a really good cup of coffee. The shower subsided as she emerged back into the main car park. Taking out the phone she called Os, a little unsettled that there was no answer. Probably still asleep, she decided. Between the food and her own exhaustion, it was clear, as she made her way back to the lodge, that she would have to get some sleep herself.

The smell of wood and the feel of fresh white sheets folded around her, brought sleep in minutes. Later, she would be grateful for the persistent 'beep' of a reversing laundry vehicle at a nearby lodge. Waking disorientated and way too soon, she did not feel so charitable. Amy gradually registered her surroundings, the neat bedroom and the sounds of the lake. She sighed her grief, catching sight of her watch on the bedside table. Almost 1pm! She picked up the new phone, but no missed calls. James told her the number could not be traced, but he had still insisted that she be cautious where she used it. She had a brief panic that she had remembered Os' number incorrectly but finally assured herself this was not the case. She had a quick wash and pulled on her pants and shoes, a change of T-shirt, and headed back to the services. This time she didn't go right into the cafe and parking area but positioned herself near the petrol station at the entrance. Her gut began to wrench when Os didn't pick up within the first three rings. Almost giving up, she sighed with relief hearing the voice at the other end, only to find herself greeted not by Os, but by Richard.

"Hello," he answered tentatively.

" Richard?"

He sounded relaxed and relieved. "Amy, we were getting worried, where are you?"

She ignored the question. "Where's Os? I need to talk to him."

"He's just gone out to look for you."

"Oh, Damm," she should have told him where she was going, he might be putting himself at risk. "Tell him I'm ok, Richard."

"But where are you Amy?"

Her eyes caught a flash of light over the green fields in the distance. As she looked more closely, she saw a different set of hills, more rugged. A path appeared on the left where Avide emerged in his white robe. To the right, Avery arrived from the river. The arched walkway of the monastery ran between the two. Avide came on to the path below when Avery turned to collect his foraging. Her beloved monk then moved back, behind the side wall, watching through an open arch, as the other man hurried towards the main entrance. There was such a sadness in Avide's expression that Amy wanted to rush towards him. She understood the sadness, it was the look of one who had been betrayed by someone they loved.

"Amy? Amy? Where are you?"

The Lancashire hills were now heavy with rain. The memory had lasted seconds but would stay with her indelibly.

"I have to go Richard, tell Os I'm okay." She had kept her voice firm and even, as she had needed to do in so many difficult conversations. Inside, she was deeply shaken. During the fifteen-minute walk back to the lodge, her plans were changed entirely.

Chapter Twenty-Five

Marcus Waterman set down the phone he had taken from Os. Through large windows he looked out upon far reaching and carefully cultivated grounds. He had lived most of his youth in the city of London, where his father had worked in another arm of the Inimica group. He preferred much less open space than was provided in Ava Bello's home. In his infancy, he had been handed over to be groomed as a member of Euair's close personal staff. His mouth twisted in remembrance of the cruel games that the adults had played around him and with him. There could only be guesswork as to the real age of his self-styled guardian, who still looked little older than when Marcus had first joined him. Of course, this was never seen beyond those outside his close circle. If there were any circulating images, they were quickly traced and destroyed. After puberty, a confused and terrified teenager, he had been taken to the house in Vienna and became more exposed to the dark machinations behind a luxurious lifestyle. Here, he first witnessed the billionaire's entanglement with Jarinbissar. Perhaps he was the only one still living that had done so. It went far beyond anything that he could have imagined or wanted to remember. It was enough for him to understand that resistance was futile, that the power he had witnessed would feast on the human world until it was completely consumed by the darkness that was its essential nature.

Waterman stood up and walked around the large ornate desk in a library full of priceless classical books and first editions. Bello's idea of wallpaper. It was in Vienna that he was subjected to painfully intrusive methods to reveal a history of Lindisfarne that involved him personally. Having still retained some private corner of his own consciousness, the young man had, at first, dismissed it as another manipulative bend in his guardian's winding route of coercion. Until the memories began and did not stop. He knew, felt immediately, the truth of his existence as Avery. A monk in the famous monastery of Lindisfarne, a favourite of Cuthbert, in that long ago period of time. A self-mocking twist of the mouth as he acknowledged the bitter remembrance of the point in time that had dictated the continued pattern of all his lives since.

There had been one chink of light in the person of Maria Sullivan, but he had distorted and destroyed their friendship, not knowing how to trust such a thing. It had been the reason he alone, well used to the ironies that beset his path, saw the significance of a few lines of conversation. A chance overhearing of Ava reporting to Venmorin that no trace of Catherine Austen had been found in the surveillance of Martin Street. He had questioned Ava carefully, hearing the account of Richard Greig, his assassination, and the daughter they had not known they employed. He saw their fear as they admitted failure in connecting the two. Inside the organisation Marcus was well aware that he was feared for his closeness to its leader. That he was known as The Ghost due to his silent ways and ability to fade into the background whenever it was necessary. He had performed his own surveillance of the street in Urmston, melting into the shadows of the back alleys, using his own powers. He had almost broken cover when he discovered that Cathy Austen was being assisted by Osweald and Ellan returned. Clearly, though having new lives, they had retained the same DNA patterns given centuries before.

It had been a calculated risk to assume the identity of Richard Greig. Logically, only her father could have informed the girl of her danger, sending her into hiding. He must therefore have survived the assassination attempt. He gambled that neither Os nor Amy had ever met the man, surmising that Cathy had been plunged into desperation and engaged the help of a friend in the building. To find the girl had run into the arms of the very individual he had been seeking! Such was the trust accorded to him that Marcus had been able to keep his discovery secret, until he could bring his prizes to lay at the feet of the man he despised and worshipped in equal measure. It bothered him deeply that Amy had slipped through his fingers and to recognise that Maria's niece had once been the formidable witch of the forest, who even Bierscath had feared. He enlisted Ava's assistance in the search for Amy, as she knew better than to ask who he was chasing. Her equipment had taken a fraction longer than standard to find what should have been an unfindable location. A service station. Clever girl. They would follow through anyway and no doubt she would ring again. He called Caleb.

I wanted to weep with frustration, but even tears would have been impossible in my bound state. Whatever he had used had left me unable to move. Internally I growled my furious and impotent rage. I suspected he had placed me in an underground room. The ceiling was low and thick, the walls, though covered with plasterboard, were irregular. An arched door, that appeared to be composed of a few hundred years of solid oak, was clearly original. Modern cupboards had been installed. There was a screen, not in use, but I couldn't see any cameras. In my eyeline I could also make out what was probably an ensuite, and a bed. I had been propped and tilted slightly, in a deep leather armchair, my hands resting on the sides, my neck supported by a padded wing back. I wondered if this was some kind of escape room, a hiding place, perhaps part of the original building. The irony that it was probably an old priest hole was not lost on me. It gave me a glimmer of hope, however. I was sure that these people would own many buildings to house those they had stolen, I very much doubted that this was one of them. My best guess was that I had been taken to the mansion I had found in Bramhall. A voice came through a microphone, a screen switched on, the face of a stranger that I had thought was a friend, directly in front of my eyeline.

"Good afternoon, Osweald." Avery spoke with self-congratulating arrogance. How could I have been so deceived?

"Soon, feeling will return, if a little painfully, and you will be able to have the meal that will be sent down to you, in a small galley box behind your chair."

The impersonal pronouncement stopped. The joy of finding a real connection to the Monastery of the Folded Wind sank bitterly into the misery of betrayal. At least they didn't have Amy. My mind wrangled between the puzzle of Amy's disappearance, and relief that she had left.

The man in the grey suit looked official and hard-nosed. Gilly Thompson was pretty hard-nosed herself and there was something about him she didn't like. She was almost certain that the woman he was looking for had been floating around outside the petrol station that afternoon. Gilly remembered her being very attractive, a pixie-look, with her short black hair, big eyes and a slight figure. She hadn't come in, but she had that troubled look about her that she knew so well, it had appeared in her mirror enough times.

"I need to see your cameras." He was very sure of himself.

"Sorry, I can't help. I don't have any access, it all goes to the main site." It was the simple truth, she kept her expression neutral. Chills climbed up her spine as he stood staring at her.

"Excuse me," she smiled at the old man who had ambled forward to pay for his petrol, forcing the policeman, if he was what he said he was, to move to one side. In her peripheral vision she could see that he continued to weigh her up. When he took the space in front of the counter again his charmless brown eyes screwed into a half smile. It wasn't a good look, noted Gilly as she took the photograph he handed to her. Definitely the woman she saw this afternoon. She shook her head, allowing a look of concentration to cross her face.

"I would have remembered if I'd seen her, I've been pretty busy though. She handed him back the good image of the woman. "Is she in some kind of trouble?"

He took the photo back and grunted what she thought might be a thank you. Or maybe not.

Caleb was already calling Ava Bello. "No sign, nobody remembers her at the petrol station. Someone at the services said he thought she'd had breakfast. Dead end though."

"Did you see the camera footage?"

"The assistant said it goes off site."

"Give me the name of the garage and exact location." He did.

"Five minutes."

He looked around the local area. A mini roundabout just outside the town and five minutes from the motorway junction. She could be in Scotland by now.

Bello rang at four minutes 30 seconds. "I think she walked."

"What? Why?"

"There were no cars in the garage at all when she phoned. I checked the wider CCTV of the site, although it wasn't complete. But I don't think she would have known to stay clear of the cameras."

"We don't know anything about her really, Ava."

"My gut says she walked."

Caleb shook his head, tightening his lips. "If you're wrong I'm going to use up valuable time."

"I'm not wrong." But she had been wrong before. Rarely, very rarely.

"There's nowhere for her to stay in walking distance apart from at the services." Even as the words were said he remembered the lakeside resort he had passed at the bigger roundabout. Bello had already hung up.

Chapter Twenty-Six

Amy sprinted back to the lodge, her mind running over the conversation with the man who had presented himself as Cathy's father. The fleeting glimpse of Avide's mistrust long ago as he watched the monk Avery. Her own deduction that Os would not go looking for her without the only method of communication they shared. He would have tried to ring her at the very least. He would not have forgotten the number, she was certain. Avery, she concluded, was not the friend they had imagined. The sense of loss was immense; he had been part of that long ago existence, the Monastery of the Folded Wind, and had now corrupted its memory. Rapidly her mind began to evaluate the implications - was he really Cathy's dad? How else could he know where they were? As fast as these thoughts skittered across her mind, she pushed them away in the fearful certainty that Os was in danger. If she was right, they would come looking for her. Could she trust that Inimica's technology would not find her?

As a precaution, despite the sense of urgency, she checked around the lodge for any signs of disturbance, or other cars nearby. It was the weekend but still very quiet. It was a risk to delay, but she would take the time to perform something her aunt had taught her many years previously. She unpacked a stick of hazel wood, a packet of herbs and essential oils from the holdall that contained, what she called, her aunt's 'witchy' stuff, that she had removed from the attic. Clearing a space in the bedroom she used the hazel to make a circle and placed herself within it, touching specific oils to her temples, as her aunt had done the day she had lost her grandmother's locket. Maria had told her to imagine being on top of a mountain, but instead she remembered how it felt to be on the roof of the forest when she had been Ellan. In imagination she stood again in the open space of flat rock that was level with the treetops. The finding spell had been used by her aunt to locate previous objects they had lost. She had no idea if it would work on people. "Os," she called softly, "where are you?" Only mist, a blank sea of impenetrable of fog. She placed her hand on her heart. "Help me Choriscuro," she whispered. Slowly, painfully slowly, the mist thinned. The woodland fell away and she saw in the distance the familiar terrain of Manchester city centre, the Hilton hotel and Co-op building. Beyond this the southern edges opened up, pulling her towards the airport. Some part of her mind jumped in alarm that Os had been smuggled from the country, but the scene quickly changed to views of a town with which she was familiar and a building with which she was not. A huge house in the middle of impressive grounds. A large yew tree by a high stone wall. It was undoubtedly the place Os had discovered Venmorin and Ava Bello. If only we had known she would need directions!

Amy, her heart heavy, acknowledged that there was a remote chance that the lodge may no longer be safe. It was close by to the services where she had spoken on the phone to Avery. There was a link to her through her mother's ownership. James could be right, they wouldn't be able to trace her, but she felt the reach of these people may be wider than even he had conceived. Carefully, she removed all traces of being at the lodge, moving with speed and deliberation. As she passed the entrance to the reception area a familiar figure, his back turned away from her, was deep in conversation with one of the cleaning staff. Fear stabbed as she thought of the man she had seen in Martin street and Angel Meadow. She willed herself to keep a steady, slow pace as she drove past checking closely in the mirror. Once away from the resort she pressed hard on the accelerator to join the A6. Clearly it was necessary to avoid the motorways even though it would add another hour to the three-hour journey time.

Apart from picking up a sandwich and using the facilities in a local supermarket, that did not have CCTV, she did not stop. It was getting dark when she arrived a few miles outside Bramhall and made her way to the stables, where she had learned to ride as a girl. Over the years she had occasionally visited to do the odd ride. The owners had diversified into providing luxury holiday cottages on the original farm site but had continued to run the stables. The car park was busy, but two high sided vehicles provided a screen for her mini as she positioned it between them. The stables were on the far side of the site and could be accessed by a track that ran around the edge of the farm. She was familiar enough with the place to look as if she belonged, should any visitor notice her, and had a good knowledge of the family routine. It was very likely that their evening meal would be in full progress, and that they wouldn't miss anything from the tack room until morning. Most of the visitors would keep to their family units or veer to the communal area on the other side of the farm building. The tack was kept in a locked barn next to the stables, with the key hidden on a hook in the outdoor toilet facility. It was a matter of minutes, but felt much longer, for her to pick up the equipment she needed.

The weather was changing, clouds drawing in as she made her way towards an old barn at the edge of the site. Behind this was a small field, boxed in by hedgerows, where she and her friends had hidden from prying eyes. She had forgotten how heavy the riding gear was and laid it down gratefully in the barn. Amy paced across the field struggling to still her thoughts. Os' face loomed large in her consciousness, strained and alone. Had she been wrong not to answer the phone? There had been several missed calls but after she had answered the first, to find once again that only Richard was on the other end, she made some excuse about driving and had no longer responded. She had taken out the battery and stored the phone in the car. But what if Os had been trying to ring her? Why hadn't she just driven back to Urmston! Amy stopped and made herself breathe steadily. She had been so certain of what she would do only thirty minutes previously. What do I know? Every fibre of her being said that events had already overtaken them, that she was being hunted, her friend taken. The memory of Ellan is real and strong, she told herself. I have to trust the power of who I once was and the emerging power of who I now am.

A sound amidst the rhythm of the rain. A whisper of wildness, a feral longing. She placed her hand on her chest and breathed, letting nothing else cloud her mind apart from the image of Choriscuro. Slowly her legs found the movement, beating out in time with her heart, in time with the hoof beats that drummed in her ears. Her head dipped and raised, nuzzling the damp air. Arms raised, she called on all that she had once been and all that she was now. When she lowered them again, and opened her eyes, he was there, standing before her, grazing, raising his eyes to hers. Amy went across and placed her arms around his neck, allowing her head to be pulled into his chest by the powerful head, letting tears of relief flow against equine muscle. Lightening flashed and thunder came close on its heels. Rain poured as she brought the stallion into the old barn, where he allowed her to load him with blanket and saddle. Patiently he waited until she had fitted bridle, reins and bit. She fastened her helmet and breathed deeply. "You have to help me find him. I know you can."

Amy shook her head as humour raised itself in a sense of the ridiculous that she was talking to a horse she had just brought into being. It was quickly replaced with an urgent need to find Os. The shower had abated and the evening closed in, as she rode across the countryside, lost in the memory of a woman long ago riding the untamed lands of Northumbria.

Chapter Twenty-Seven

Avery entered the room alone, from where I could not see. I had no idea of time and no evidence that I was, in fact, at the house in Bramhall. I had been released from the dreadful paralysis to eat and use the spartan toilet. As instructed by Avery on screen, I returned the plates to the small chute, examining it for any opportunity of escape. I placed my head inside to look upwards, only to find a tight three-sided metal box. I narrowly avoided decapitation, for there was barely a sliver of sound to warn me to pull away as a sliding metal slit came across to close the opening. No sooner had this locked into place than, from the opposite direction, slid a perfect square of matching wall. At first I thought Avery had come to reinstate my immobility but his leisurely stance, leaning, half-sitting on the desk, seemed to offer some reprieve. I fretted at the cord around my waist, that bit into skin even though it was not tight. It appeared silver at first glance but on close inspection was flecked with another substance. I guessed, from my own repulsive reaction, it was a product of Jarinbissar. The several raw burns on my hands were from ineffectual attempts to remove this thing that had cut my connection to Nesu, an injury which smarted far more than those to my hands. Avery held the metal rod that had previously been used to immobilise me, I guessed that it triggered some reaction when connected to the cord.

"A napoten." Another cynical upturn of his mouth. " I am never without it. A powerful gift indeed."
My eyes caught the scroll he held so arrogantly in his other hand. Avide's Mark. I felt nauseous that he should be handling what had been given into my protection. He followed my glance.
"Hardly what I expected." I did not comment. " I don't think you will be alone for much longer," he continued. I waited,

suppressing the fear that he wanted me to feel.

"I should have guessed that Maria would have been involved."

"Maria?" I wasn't expecting that.

Avery 's mouth pinched together. For a fleeting second he was the old, old friend in Amy's dining room, sharing memories with me.

"She and I were at university together in London. It was only after she had gone that I suspected her own link to Avide. Maria played a close game, far closer than I ever imagined. It was only after her death that I began to investigate certain aspects of her behaviour. We were very close but she never mentioned her niece who, I later learned, was central to her life. I never imagined that the house she had left contained such treasures. Earlier this year, additional to my official duties," his eyes turned cold, "I decided to make my own enquiries. After all," he said without emotion, " it was because of me that her aunt was murdered."

I gasped in horror despite myself.

" It would be a lot easier for you to tell me what we want to know, than have it extracted by my employer."

"Venmorin? Bello?"

The sound of his joyless laughter chilled me. "So you know about them. They are aware only that I have a prisoner and they are required to follow instructions. They should be back very soon."

At least his comment added to the likelihood that I was where I thought. I had been wrong in my assumption that he was their employee. That is, if I could believe anything he told me. His voice became the hideous whisper I had previously heard. "How do we activate the Mark?"

" I genuinely haven't a clue. I was hoping that you would tell me."

He examined my face. "Then we will have to wait for the girl."

Again, I gave no response.

" We tracked Amy. The phones you had were good, but not good enough. If she has retained anything of Ellan, and I believe she has, she will try coming for you."

My stomach lurched. "She doesn't even know you are... what you are. Or where to find me."

"I think you underestimate your friend, Osweald."

"You don't have the right to call me that."

"Maybe."

"Were you as treacherous back then?"

He laughed, a sinister laugh. " Oh yes."

"And Cuthbert? Avide?"

"I was expelled from the order not long after your death."

I had yet to recall the circumstances of my death in the monastery, but I would not ask him or believe whatever version of events he might offer. He seemed to understand this.

"If it is truly the case, that you do not know," he held the rod like a baton, ready to use, "then this little thing will do its job again." The thought of being unconscious and then paralysed once more sent jolts of fear and panic through my mind. Equally, I was determined to hide this fact from my betrayer. At that point, without warning, a surge of white light blanked out everything. There was an instant when I thought he had once more applied the rod, but a quick check of movement in my feet brought assurance he had not. A voice inside my mind. Amy. Muffled. It was as if she had somehow opened a corridor of thought between us, where we could push out information for the other to collect. She was nearby.

'Where? Where are you?' Although it was Amy, there was an accent I didn't recognise.

'The house is called Asters. In the cellar, I think,' I found myself replying, silently.

The connection was tenuous, a fragile string of shared consciousness to which I clung with all my concentration.

"I'm still here Osweald," stated Avery, coldly. "Open your eyes!"

I felt him move nearer when I didn't respond, the cold baton crossing my forehead, snaking down my shoulder. "When it reaches the cord at your waist you will be immobile again."

I opened my eyes, cutting the connection with Amy.

The screen blinked behind him and he moved backwards to see it, retaining one eye on me. A light touch to the keyboard. An image of what I recognised was Venmorin and Bello, entering the building. I sensed his irritation. "It seems our conversation is ended for now."

He placed the baton on the desk and pulled out ordinary, plastic ties from his pocket.

"Sit down," he ordered.

I grasped my opportunity, powering into him, even as he reached for the baton. It fell to the floor as the desk toppled and the computer screen crashed. If I had been right that meant the only camera in the room was now out of action. Avery was unconscious on the stone floor, and I was able to turn him over to find Avide's Mark in his pocket.

The room reverberated with the sound of pounding against solid oak. I scrambled around for a weapon and saw the baton on the floor. Splinters of wood shot across the small space as I dived into a corner. Keeping low I pulled off the jacket Avery wore and used it to pick up what he had named a napoten. He began to stir but, as I leapt to one side, the door finally smashed open and landed upon my helpless captor. Horse's hooves and a stallion neigh filled the small room, as I took Amy's hand and leapt up onto Choriscuro's back behind her and out into the night. We were already across the field and into the trees beyond the house when it erupted with noise and bright lights. Choriscuro was magnificent as he jumped hedges and fences, my burnt hands stinging with the grip on Amy's saddle. The baton, rolled up in Avery's jacket, was safely wedged across my knees.

The moon, which had lit our way in our mad dash across the countryside, slid behind clouds. We rolled off Choriscuro's back and Amy ran to stroke his head. Even as her hand touched the sweat covered, heaving body, Choriscuro disappeared. Amy fell upon the abandoned gear. I felt, rather than saw in her, the shock of his absence, for I knew how it had been with Nesu. I began to talk but she hushed me to silence. Quickly we gathered up the equipment and I followed her stealthy trek along a path that led down beside a barn and into what appeared to be a holiday complex. The moon was still shrouded as I waited at

Amy's instruction, while she returned the things she had taken. I was still stunned by her engineering my escape, as she drove the mini out of the complex onto roads I did not know, but which she clearly did.

Chapter Twenty-Eight

Amy channelled the still swirling adrenaline into steering the mini down narrow country lanes, heading back towards Manchester; avoiding the main roads as much as she could. She hated the idea of relinquishing the car but it was known to Inimica now. Somehow she needed to find another vehicle.

"Where are we going?" Os' head ached, nausea kept coming and going.

"I should have picked up on it earlier," she told him. "What Avery said about Cathy, as if she had deliberately gone to the company to ferret out information. She said that wasn't true. That her father knew nothing until after she'd got the job. What Avery said would be the point of view of someone involved with Venmorin, believing that she would have deliberately suppressed the link between her father and herself. I don't think Avery is Richard."

"I agree." Os found relief in the assumption that Cathy bore no relation to his persecutor. "We were just swept up in the fact of finding Avery again and another link to the monastery. He told me he was expelled from the order later."

Amy frowned. "He knew or guessed that Richard didn't die. We can only hope Cathy and her family are okay."

Os nodded thoughtfully. "He was after Avide's Mark."

"What?" He told her in detail what had happened in the cellar, patting his jacket where he had placed the scroll.

"I'm still not sure how he knew that we would know about Richard," Amy puzzled. " Or that Cathy had sought our help."

"He seemed to have known Maria."

"What?"

"Watch the road," Os admonished, as the car rumbled over the edge of the pavement.

"They were at university together. I don't know any more than that." His voice sounded tinny to his own ears.

Amy stopped the car. She wanted to understand more about her aunt but saw that her friend's face was covered in sweat, he looked pale and clammy.

"What did they do to you?" Amy's voice broke, upset she had not given any thought to his condition.

He signalled to the back seat. "That's Avery's jacket. Wrapped inside is a kind of baton or rod he called a napoten. He bound me with this cord. Os lifted his T-shirt to reveal the snaking material around his waist. When it connects with the baton I'm rendered unconscious and virtually paralysed."

"Shit, how do we remove it?"

Os raised his hands to reveal the raw burns. "I've tried, it just won't come off. And I can't access Nesu with it on." Answering the question he knew she was about to ask.

Amy was appalled.

"And I know where we can get another vehicle not registered to either of us."

He pressed a button by the window letting in fresh air, breathing in deeply.

"Right," she said, switching the engine back on, "tell me where."

Julia was still trying to absorb what Richard had told her. She had been plunged from comfort and a sense of wellbeing into a nightmare of survival. It had stirred something inside her, a courage she did not know she had. A determination to protect and support her family in the face of murderous enemies. Richard had kept Cathy with him, fearing that she would be in danger returning home. Julia had returned home alone, trying her best to pack a few essentials for them all. It was 4am. As instructed, she picked up her bag, leaving both her own and Cathy's phone inside the house. She had earlier turned off the cameras and phone notifications that, Richard had informed

her, were being used to track entry and exit from the house.
"With any luck," he had said, "if they're still watching, they'll be relying on them as alerts to any movement."

Dressed in black, keeping close against the hedgerows and beneath the trees, she moved as quietly as she could. Several times she stopped, hearing only the scurrying of neighbourhood cats and other night creatures. Julia looked around methodically at each change of direction. Richard had insisted on meeting her himself though she and Cathy had thought the risk too great. It was with great relief that he was exactly where he was expected to be, at the edge of the long path that was sheltered from the road by a tall beech hedge. Richard signalled her to follow, as he led onto the track which led down to the Mersey. Richard shivered with the memory of his near death, as they followed what he called his running path, this time taking the higher lane, a good distance from the river.

Richard was taking Julia to where he had left Cathy. The place he had been going to the night he had been attacked. A small farmhouse of which ownership had been dutifully transferred to named householders of many generations, all members of a hidden order established in the seventh century. Richard took a sharp left off the main track into a wooded area. The track was little used and overgrown with nettles. After another mile they crossed a road and climbed a stile. The moon was waning, hidden behind clouds, but Richard would not allow any lights. At some points they walked hand in hand on a route with which he was clearly familiar. The soft light of a cold dawn appeared as they finally reached the end of their journey. An unpretentious, small gate and a gravel track that led to a detached bungalow with fields either side. The kind of place thought Julia, where they might be visiting elderly parents, except that they had none. The woman who answered the door, quickly for this time in the morning, appeared in her seventies and wore a blue dressing gown. The smiling eyes beneath round glasses reassured Julia as she ushered them quickly inside.

◆ ◆ ◆

Waterman staggered across damp grass to the gap in the hedge made by the fleeing pair. The dogs were howling and fast on the chase. Concussed and bruised, he found a brook that edged the property, splashing water on his face. Wet and disorientated, his intense training had honed his instincts for survival. The first thought had been to reclaim his prisoner but this had dissolved in the realisation that the napoten had been taken from him. Like the worst form of addictive drug, he could never divided himself from Euair's powerful chain. That morning he had relayed the information that he had found Osweald and was holding him at the Asters. The instruction in reply had been swift. Do not move him. No one was to have contact with the captive. Euair would come.

Marcus knew that his dark rage would seek him out.

Fear drove him onwards now, following the brook to the road and then to woodland on the other side. The dogs had dashed across the hedge on the path of the horse. In some area of his brain he delighted in this proof of his assumptions. The pair had moved beyond, and faster, than even he had anticipated. On the other side of the woodland there was shelter and food in the form of an old shed for storing firewood. He would steal what he needed from the farm shop at the front of the building, which had a storage shed nearby. It wasn't the first time. It was his practice to rehearse escape routes and challenge his skills. Not far from Maria's house he had hired a garage. In it was a vehicle, new documents and money. A long walk and one he could not make without rest and food. Already, even with the adrenalin circulating in his blood stream, every step required dogged will. He was probably the most valuable tool that his guardian had forged. And just like that he had decided he would rather be dead than continue in that role. Too late of course. And no one would believe him, or at least no one that mattered.

Chapter Twenty-Nine

The hospital was busy as usual on a Saturday night but most of the coming and going was around the Accident and Emergency Department. Amy had done some agency work on the site but couldn't claim to remember the lay out. Os directed her away from the main hospital boulevard to a small car park, near to what had been his office. He had received, in a will, the donation of an old, but very serviceable, Land Rover from a grateful patient. In fact it had been left to him personally, but he had never registered it in his name, only in that of the chaplaincy. He had used it to provide outreach work to vulnerable relatives, often delivering and teaching the use of an iPad to maintain a connection with sick family members during the pandemic. All his small team had been insured to drive the vehicle but he knew it had been little used since he had left. Sarah, his previous assistant, had written to him to collect the Land Rover and suggested registering it in his own name, as they could no longer afford its keep. Os transferred to her enough money to maintain the vehicle until the end of the year, when he planned to give up the Nissan. Knowing that his own car was compromised, he had messaged Sarah earlier in the week to say he would come and collect the Land Rover as soon as he could. As it was originally often used out of hours, he had arranged for a box to be placed outside the multi-faith centre, containing the keys to the vehicle. Amy quickly retrieved them at his instruction and tapped the steering wheel approvingly as the Land Rover stuttered to life. The momentary triumph rapidly altered to fear for her friend as she helped him from the mini. His skin was slick with sweat, his breathing shallow.

"I know it's working for us tonight but this is a seriously poorly lit part of the hospital." Amy looked around the deserted area, separate from the main building.

"I know," he replied. "It's a bit of a black corner. I had to make sure we came out here in twos when we were using it. I don't think anyone will even come looking."

"Still, security might notice the mini on its own."

"We'll have to take a chance," Os grunted, as he tried to heave himself into the Land Rover.

Amy climbed up to steady him in the rear, noticing a small indent in the shape of the wall in front of them. Moving the Land Rover backwards, she then jumped back into the mini and manoeuvred it into the space. The protruding bricks on either side meant that the vehicle's registration plate would not be easily visible and the car less noticeable. It was something, she supposed. Reluctantly she locked the mini, transferring her bags from one vehicle to the other.

"I'll come back for you," she patted the mini and jumped into the driver's seat.

The engine sounded reliable and, to her relief, had over half a tank of petrol. Os winced as she made heavy work of the gears.

"We have to get you some help," she told him.

"I've been racking my brains," he replied. "I can't come up with anywhere that isn't more than an hour's drive away." He was writhing in pain now.

"We're in a hospital Os! I'll take you to A&E."

"No! Amy!" She had stopped the Land Rover in the middle of a path, not yet on the main hospital site. Os seemed oblivious to the distracted look on her face. "I can't do it Amy. I have to rest." In a few short minutes his condition had deteriorated further.

"I'm taking you to A&E," she told him firmly.

"No!"

In her heart she knew that the hospital could do nothing for him and most likely they would be further exposed to those who had engineered his capture. She needed to buy time. After swinging back round to the mini, she opened the back of the Land Rover. Os could hear shuffling, Amy's breath coming in sharp gasps as she shifted things around. The back seats had already been removed and old carpet lined the floor to make the vehicle more serviceable for carrying supplies. Gratefully, Amy saw there were some boxes of blankets, towels and coats. She appeared at the passenger door looking resolute. "I've got rid of anything we can't use and put it in my boot. There were some items that proved very useful though." She made her voice cheerful. Having cleared the back of the Land Rover she had created a makeshift bed, with the blankets and a small pillow from the mini used for taking naps in the back seat on long journeys. Amy had wedged the baton underneath the passenger seat, still wrapped in the jacket as Os had carried it. Amy had used the remaining blankets, a couple of boxes and her own holdall, to create an area where he could lie down and not be rolled from side to side by any movement of the vehicle. Very carefully Amy supported Os as he edged out of the seat, at one point scraping her own skin against the cord.

"Bloody hell!" She lifted her hand up, scrutinising it in the half light. The cord had sent a jolt of electricity up her arm.

"It didn't burn," noted Os.

"Come on."

With difficulty he edged himself into the manufactured space, gratefully stretching his long limbs to ease pressure from the cord. Amy was going through her kitbag. She treated his burns, making him take some simple analgesia to ease his discomfort. At first she thought he might vomit the tablets, but the flask of water she always carried helped to ease them down. Exhausted, he was almost asleep when she closed the door and made her way back to the driver's seat. She ducked beneath the steering wheel, having spotted a security guard heading in their direction. Once he had left she drove the Land Rover out of the hospital grounds, to a quiet street nearby. Hunched up in the darkness, hearing the gentle breathing of Os behind her, she shook away the tears that threatened to come. "Oh Maria," she whispered, "I wish you hadn't left me."

Her rucksack! Yesterday she had noticed a paper sticking out from the back of the heavy book when putting it away, unable then to give it much thought. Once the area was clear, she gently eased 'The Geometry of The Spirit' from her bag and, using a small torch, she quickly found what had been in the book's jacket.

In Maria's slanted handwriting was a note addressed to Amy. Carefully, her heart beating faster, she opened the folded page.

'Just in case I'm not around and you actually get to reading this book, (how well she knew her niece!) and you need help, go to the place where we first met, between 9am and 10am any day. Friends will find you. Stay safe my love. Maria.'

Amy searched her mind for family events but couldn't remember the first one her aunt had attended. Os stirred beside her, placing his hand on her arm. "Amy," he told her, "this is the same kind of darkness we faced before, a very long time ago."

The words seemed to be a last effort before he drifted off again, exhausted, but they brought her another memory.

Avide had been called to a land beyond Rome. I felt a terrible foreboding in his leaving. Unlike the monks of Lindisfarne he was not subject to the dictates of the church, though I had never questioned why. It was the day following his instruction to hide the Mark.

"There is a very urgent matter of balance in a faraway place," he had told me. I knew him well enough to see the decision to leave had caused him some distress.

"When do you go?"

"Now," he sighed.

"And when do you return?"

He did not reply, placing his hands on my shoulders. All the words I had framed were gone.

"You are needed here, El-lan," he said softly. "Osweald will walk with me along the river."

Stricken, I returned to the forest, feeling as alone as the first day they had banished me. The next morning I knew that Osweald would return along the same path and went to meet him, wanting news of my lord. I was never to share with him the knowledge that he was my half-brother.

I came across Osweald, still some way from the monastery, a golden rod in one hand, a sword held limply in the other. I saw his eyes were glazed and hopeless under the hypnotic power of Bierscath, whom I had long since named Euair. I called out as the dark-cloaked figure of my former lover drew his dagger. Without haste, arrogant eyes turned upon me. He cut a symbol in the air between us and I saw beneath his human shape the writhing black threads from which emanated a shadow, black as the pit. In the years between our last meeting he had learned to make a weapon of hatred, a shield of anger, a fortress of greed and power. He was utterly entangled with Jarinbissar, the dark source. My people, of which I was the last, had long ago evolved an immunity to this net of evil. The light energy of Tanamaarin wove through our DNA and left us impervious to the black arts that imprisoned Osweald. The Mark that Avide had given me was in my pocket. Clasping it tightly in my hand I moved towards the captured monk.

"You can do nothing for him," laughed Euair. "The napoten holds him at my will and should he live he will be ever entangled with Jarinbissar."

I curled my fingers around the golden rod, feeling the darkness inside. I threw it back to its owner, aware, even in that short time, that its victim could not release himself from its power. The elements of the instrument had been fashioned directly to ensnare Osweald. Euair gasped that I remained unharmed. I rubbed the Mark, unseen, on the hand of my half-brother, who had begun to come back to his senses, erasing the taint of Jarinbissar.

"Ellan."

Osweald had been a mighty soldier and still held himself strong and agile. He had taken to wearing a sword again and I had seen him train in the forest in secret. Even before I , he had understood the battles gathering near. It was one thing to come upon him in surprise and subdue with deceit. As ever, the most cruel, are often the most cowardly. Even before Osweald was fully standing, his enemy had raised to his saddle.

"The witch of the forest has saved you this day." I could see he still

wore the shock of it." Scuttle back to your master. You will soon see all Avide has built laid to waste."

Os' noisy breathing, grey light filtering through dusty windows. She needed to move. Platt Fields! She had been about four years old and wandered off unnoticed from the family gathering in the park. A woman who smelled of flowers had sat on a bench, watching her practice her tumbles on the grass. Without hesitation, Amy had taken her hand when offered and Maria had returned her to the gaggle of cousins and other family members. Much later her aunt had given her instruction about the dangers of taking a stranger's hand so willingly. The truth was Amy had never felt so secure in her young life. The note said that if she went to that place between the hours of nine and ten help would come. She checked her watch. Seven am. The trip would take about twenty minutes. Platt Fields was a local park that hosted events and generally provided a green space for locals and visitors. Latterly, when she and her friends had spent time there as student nurses, there had been some problems with drugs and alcohol. Amy made the decision to stay where they were for a while. She started to flick through the pages of her aunt's book to see if she could find more information about what she now knew was a napoten, still lodged under the passenger seat.

At eight-thirty she headed off towards her old student haunts of Fallowfield, taking a roundabout route and watching to see if anyone followed. On a weekend the roads were still quiet at that time and she felt secure there was no one in pursuit. Warily, she slid the Land Rover into the parking area, deserted on this Sunday morning. Amy found herself in desperate need of some sleep. She made sure the door locks were in place. Ten minutes, she told herself.

An hour after Amy closed her eyes, a woman in her thirties, sleek in a blue jumpsuit, passed the vehicle, seeing its driver asleep in the front seat. She took out her phone and wrote a brief text, waiting on a nearby bench. Within fifteen minutes a Ford van pulled alongside. Amy came abruptly to wakefulness at the sound of the passenger door being opened. So much for the door lock! Wriggling upright, she barely registered the youngish man, who slid into the seat before the driver's door was also opened by a woman. A prick in her thigh brought the terrifying realisation she had been injected with something. 'Oh no,' she whispered. 'Why did I come here?' She turned enough to see that Os had barely stirred and his breathing had become even more ragged. She had failed them both. It was to be her last conscious thought for some hours.

Chapter Thirty

A sick emptiness, dry mouth and a head feeling full of sand. Memory destroying the frail rest as it flooded in.

"Os!" Amy sat up straight, on top of a single old-fashioned bed in a rustic room of whitewashed stone. Clean sheets and cover, all oddly reassuring. Light sneaked in around a plain blind that told her it was day and not night. She was still clothed in her leggings and sweatshirt and had been laid on top of the covers. Recalling the fear she had felt when they had been taken, she was relieved and confused to find herself able to move freely. Clean clothes from her bag were folded neatly on a chair nearby. Gingerly she shifted to the edge of the bed and managed to stand up. A little unsteady, but she had barely eaten over the last two days. The blind was easily raised but the window was locked. Green fields, a few sheep and a glimpse of a stone wall on either side of the frame. Ground floor.

It was difficult to stay upright as dizziness threatened to overwhelm. Amy doggedly made her way to the other side of the bed where a jug of water and a glass had been placed on a table. She drank thirstily, gaining strength. There was an attached bathroom, another unexpected benevolence in her incarceration. Gratefully she splashed water on her face, noticing that her toiletries had been placed ready by the sink. An old wooden wardrobe contained her bags from the car. She reached for her trainers on the floor beneath and had to kneel down, her head in her lap until the room stopped swirling. Her mind flew back to the terror of being overwhelmed and taken against her will. Anger flared to be quickly overtaken by fear for Os. Determinedly she pulled herself upwards. Moving more freely now, she felt able to try the door. To her surprise it opened easily, the old-fashioned lock had not been secured. The corridor was plain, freshly painted in terracotta and spotlessly clean. No guards outside the door.

The last thing she expected. Singing. Voices that were both male and female. A music that reverberated around the walls. The Latin chant was beautiful, reminding her of memories left behind long ago. Hope, despite all her misgivings, made its way into her heart. Following the corridor to its wider end, looking for a chapel or a meeting place, brought her to a room much like the one she had just left, a little bigger, where a group of men and women in normal dress, were singing the chant. She could see bed covers peeping out between those that were gathered in the small space, most had their eyes closed. One person who did not was fixing his attention on the bed with an expression of grave concern. She slid in front of them, crying out when she saw the occupant of the bed. Os, grey and sickly, lay unconscious amid the group of men and women. Silence. The group parted and she stepped towards the bed, looking around for a sphyg, a pulse oximeter, instruments she could use to better gauge the status of her friend. There were none.

"Amy." The voice melodious and kind, from the man who stood nearest to Os. Fair, greying hair, round features, he radiated a calm competency. A woman from the top of the bed turned and immediately came to embrace her. Cathy!

"Oh Amy," she was in tears. "They've tried everything. Gerald," she nodded towards the older man, "has discovered that the cord around his waist is poisoning him in some way. We can't remove the cord or even touch it." She opened her hands to show the same burns she had seen on Os' fingers. "It doesn't matter if we wear gloves, it won't budge and every attempt seems to make it tighter. Os is dying."

"No," she heard herself reply, "it's not poison." She had seen it named in her aunt's book.

"It's a delnome, " she told them with authority, to startled looks from the old man and woman standing either side at the top of the bed. "This is a binding cord, to disconnect him from the power of his true self. It's made of lies, deceit and delusion collected over many lifetimes and instilled with a substance found only in the dimension of Jarinbissar." Maria's notes had added this description.

Perhaps it had come from Maria's books, the stories she had told. Choriscuro whispered quietly in her ear however, that this was the old dark magic and she had always known how to fight it.

The group made way for her as she approached Os, noting his breath irregular, skin dull and sallow, restless beneath his unconscious state. She breathed, placing her hands upon her heart and called for the wisdom of Choriscuro. In a matter of seconds she fully understood what had eluded and what Os had tried to explain. The figure of the horse was a representation of a connection to Tanamaarin. Calmly she allowed that connection, a fraction only was needed to take her out of time and space, to see the face of Ellan, that had once been her own. She thought only of the golden energy of Tanamaarin where her different lives merged into one. There was tingling and heat in the palm of her hands as she allowed that light to fill her body, returning her to the small space, eyes open and fixed on the dwindling life force of her friend. Suspending the array of thoughts that pounded at her trained nurse's brain, she removed her hand from her own chest and placed it upon Os' heart, feeling it flutter unsteadily beneath her fingers.

Amy applied a gentle pressure, willing a transference of energy, healing in the way that Ellan of the forest had done so very long ago. Very slowly she felt the vital organ gather strength and rhythm. There was a collective sigh of relief around the bed as his colour changed and breath came more easily. Each member of the group moved aside as she turned and walked around the bed to approach Os from the right. She looked around and held out her hand. "Avide's Mark."

The fair-haired man looked hard into her eyes and brought the scrap of ancient vellum from a draw in the bedside cabinet.

"We tried," Cathy intervened. "Gerald brought it towards the cord, but it's what sent Os into sudden decline. Two of the Order were afflicted by a violent headache and had to leave the room."

Amy continued to look evenly at Gerald who handed over Avide's Mark.

"Please wait outside," she told them, her eyes concentrating on Os' face, but aware of the second the last member of the group had left the room. She turned the key in the door.

"Breathe." Ellan's voice was within her own. She placed her left hand on her heart and let the right middle finger touch the centre of the X on the vellum. As she breathed in she raised her hand and the dot that had been the centre rose with her, shades of soft blue and purple. Slowly it became an apex and the X rose to form a pyramid, four sides of luminous indigo against the stark white of the room. It lifted to the centre of her palm, then moved towards the cord that entwined Os' waist. Oscillating strobes of light emitted from the almost fluid pyramid. A jolt of electrical energy passed through the Mark as it touched the cord which disintegrated, leaving nothing but a faint line around her friend's waist and a similar one on her own wrist. She knew, in some distant corner of her mind, that this fine, white scar would remain on both their bodies whilst they still lived.

Os' eyes opened. Behind her, Amy became aware of a presence she had first seen in the cave in Greenhow. Nesu. He seemed huge in the small space, a wildness of wisdom. In this wonderful feline, she recognised clearly, the essence of Tanamaarin. Nesu padded around the end of the bed and came level with Os. The rough tongue washed his face, the green eyes acknowledging Amy before the lynx vanished.

Amy looked appraisingly at Os. The grey pallor and tight-lipped tension of chronic pain had disappeared. Relief and gratitude were in his soft smile as he reached for Amy's hand. She, still holding the Mark in her right hand, reached with her left. Os' eyes fixed on the pyramid, now more blue than indigo, his gaze questioning. Carefully, she placed the Mark on the vellum. Right hand on her heart, she breathed in and placed the middle finger of her left on the apex of the pyramid and watched it return into the vellum as a flat figure X. A knock on the door. She opened it, standing aside to reveal Os smiling and very much alive. Gerald approached them, his voice and face awe-stricken. Slowly, others entered the room, surrounding the bed. Amy, exhausted, found her legs wobbling and was helped to sit down beside her friend.

"Where is this?" Os looked to Amy, who turned her head towards Gerald.

Gerald, a gleaming smile across his face, opened his arms.

"Welcome to the Ord na Farraige Eisteachta agus an tAigein Faire." The Gaelic made it sound like an ancient magic formula.

" The Order of the Listening Sea and the Watching Ocean," he translated. "Created by a secret community of monks in six hundred and eighty-five."

Amy raised her eyebrows. "Impressive."

Cathy burst forward, tears streaming down her face, kneeling by the bed and reaching for Os' hand.

"You're okay!" He gently stroked her face.

"They need food and drink." An older woman, with a soft smile had stepped forward. She looked kindly towards the trio.

"I'm Mena. If you feel up to eating, we'll arrange for something to be brought to you," she told Os. Then turning to Amy. "If you're able to walk, perhaps you can join us in the refectory."

"I'd prefer to stay with Os," Amy began.

Cathy was now placed between the two friends. "I'll bring my meal here and watch him, see if I can tempt him to eat a little."

There was a proprietary expression on her face as she encouraged Amy to leave the room, adding her thanks to those of the others.

Os looked weary, his eyes flickering closed, then open.

"I'll be fine Aims," he told her, voice croaking. You go."

Gerald coughed and gave a slight bow towards Os.

"Let me formally welcome a long-ago former inhabitant of the Mainisstir Na Gaoithe Fillte into our company." He put an arm out for Amy to link. "And also Maria Sullivan's niece and, if I am not mistaken, in another existence, the mysterious woman of the forest, befriended and much loved by our founder, Avide."

The shock felt by both Os and Amy translated into a momentary exchange of glances. Mena clucked, taking Amy's other arm. "Give them time Gerald," she admonished, leading Amy into the corridor where the smell of food was incredibly welcome in her famished state.

Chapter Thirty-One

Ava Bello sipped her cocktail but found it tasteless. She wore the soft white satin dress that clung to her curves distractingly but felt uncomfortable in its possessive grasp. The red ruby that so often took flame from the sumptuous, expensive surroundings, was as dull and lifeless as a trodden acorn around her neck. Her voice was hoarse from the screaming rage that had descended upon them both. She and Venmorin had torn through the building after finding that both Tregothan's prize and Waterman had gone, mere minutes before they went to find them. Too late, they had chased across every route of escape. Waterman had told them little, apart from the necessity of using the cellar room for a prisoner important enough for Tregothan to see personally. He had insisted that only he have contact with the mysterious captive, sending home all but Bello's personal assistant. As was their habit on a Saturday, she and Venmorin had spoiled away the afternoon in an orgy of gratification. The houses holding their enslaved victims were in the heart of the suburbs, unseen and unnoticed. Ava had little to do with that side of the business. She saw her interventions as acts of kindness, gifting those who gave her pleasure and never acknowledging her abuse of power, that had been stolen from the victims of Tregothan's trade in human life. As Waterman had once said, she delighted in doing the right things for the wrong reasons. The bitter poison of her spent rage twisted and turned in the fear that loomed over them both. Tregothan was flying to Manchester the next day and they would face him before the weekend was over.

Venmorin, stony, white-faced, sat opposite. Like Ava he had indulged the red mist of his temper. Two of the dogs lay dead, unable to fulfil their master's unreasonable commands to find the man who had escaped. There were no cameras on the hidden cellar door. Something or someone had battered the solid oak door. How anyone outside could have found the entrance? The staff knew nothing of its existence and entry to it was adjacent to the nearby woods, well disguised. Their bolt hole. Of all the buildings they owned, this should have been the safest place to keep him and there would have been no witnesses to whatever end was planned for their captive. The instructions were clear. Tregothan himself would interrogate and deal with him. He was merely to be held under Waterman's supervision until the elusive head of their organisation arrived. Instead, Venmorin and Ava had returned to find they had lost both captive and capturer. Their frantic search had proved useless. Their efforts made impossible by the fact that a rider had trampled the little used bridle path near to the hidden entrance. It was only the intervention of Janice Lamb, Ava's personal assistant, gauging that both her mistress and Venmorin had finally calmed down, that brought some relief. She ran baths for them both and provided dinner. Ava showed her gratitude and her mercurial temperament by embracing the thin figure, who Amy would have recognised as the woman in the green jacket that had monitored her home.

Venmorin was exhausted but adrenaline pumped around his body, tight with the knowledge that Tregothan would soon be here.

"Will he kill us?" Bello asked him.

"Probably," Venmorin replied. Running was not an option, there would simply be nowhere far enough. It mattered little that they had done nothing wrong in this instance. It was their patch and therefore their responsibility.

"What of Waterman? What do you think they will do to him? He is, after all, Tregothan's pet."

Venmorin shook his head. "I doubt if he is still alive," he replied. In a second he was on his feet.

"Unless we can convince Tregothan otherwise. Unless we can make him believe that we can recover him."

Bello uncrossed her legs, leaning forward. "How? He can pick a lie from the air."

Venmorin was pacing now. "It's perfectly true that we have no evidence he is not alive."

"Blood on the floor. Him disappearing?"

"Maybe the blood's not his. Or he was injured. Taken as hostage."

"Is that what you believe?"

"No. But that doesn't mean anything."

A voice crackled from the front gate. "Mr Tregothan has arrived." Price, his driver and right-hand man.

Equally horrified, they looked at their watches simultaneously. He was a day early!

Venmorin twisted his mouth into a smile, speaking into the intercom.

"Good Evening. Opening now." He flicked a switch.

Minutes. They had only minutes before they must hurry to meet him at the front door.

"Be convincing that Waterman is alive and not tortured or left for dead half a mile away, as I suspect."

Ava straightened her dress, raised her chin and followed him to the door.

The refectory was unsurprisingly as simple and uncluttered as the rest of the building. Long wooden tables and benches were laid ready for a meal. Amy thought of how popular and trendy artisan products had become. Here it was clearly a long-established way of life. Everything looked as if it had been homemade and built to last. The pottery, a simple blue and grey, had the irregularities of individual hand-made pieces. The colourful beaded runners down the centre of the tables were carefully worked with geometrical patterns. The kitchen stove at the far end of the room was an old-fashioned range, on which were bubbling huge cooking pots. Bowls of fresh fruit, plates of rustic bread and pottery jugs of water had been placed at intervals along the table. Gerald moved Amy towards two cushioned chairs at the end. She guessed he was giving up his own place for her.

Amy nibbled at her food, a tasty stew. Though hungry, she still had little appetite. She counted enough places for twenty to sit comfortably along the main table, currently occupied by fourteen. Mena introduced them one by one. The oldest was Bernadette, a comforting, grandmotherly face. The rest a fairly equal mix of men and women, mostly in their twenties or thirties. Mena was probably in her late forties, Gerald a few years older. Her keen eye caught tension in a young woman, tall with long brown hair, introduced as Joy; she seemed vaguely familiar. Apart from herself, whose food was brought by Mena, everyone else served themselves from the stove. Mena had taken the place to her left. Close up it was now actually hard to guess her age. The virtually unlined face turned towards her. Mena's scrutinising gaze was as uncompromising as her aunt's had been. In fact Amy found herself reminded so much of Maria that she needed to dab her eyes, turning her face away.

"You must be full of questions," Mena commented, when Amy had finished her meal. Even her voice had the same soft, reassuring calm. "We'll be able to talk more in the morning when you've had a proper rest."

"We owe you an apology Amy, for the way we brought you here," Gerald told her. "I'm sorry." He glanced at Joy, whose head dipped. Amy recognised her now as the woman who had injected into her thigh.

"Our location is sacrosanct," Gerald continued. "It cannot be known to anyone outside. We had to get you both back to the house as quickly as possible."

Amy looked directly at Gerald, her voice even. "I don't think you needed to chemically sedate me. You could have at least tried to explain." Mena clucked beside her, frowning at Gerald.

"I'm sorry," the older man continued, "but we felt it a necessary, if unfortunate, way to keep you and us safe."

Amy nodded but remained reluctant to trust this strange Order who had assaulted her. How did her aunt know of them and they of her? She was beginning to understand that she really knew very little of Maria's work. There had once been an understanding between them that, when she was ready, Amy would have access to the diverse interests that her aunt pursued. Unfortunately she had been killed by a hit and run driver only metres from her home, before that could happen.

The group slowly dispersed, solicitous in their concern for both she and Os.

"Did you put the Land Rover out of sight?" Gerald was talking to Joy by the patio doors that led out of the refectory into a courtyard. Amy's enhanced hearing picked up the conversation clearly.

"Take it to Martin Street tomorrow, a few doors down from Maria's house," he instructed.

Amy yawned, smiling her need to get to bed. Her hand checked the pocket where Avide's Mark was folded. Did she notice a flicker of interest in Gerald? An hour later, Amy was dressed in a hoody and sweatpants, using her heightened vision to find her way to the nearest barn, that doubled as a garage. The Land Rover had been hastily parked. To her great relief it had been left unlocked as she had hoped, in their difficulty of managing to get both unconscious passengers inside. The keys had been removed but this did not concern Amy, who reached underneath the nearby seat and brought out the jacket, inside which had been placed the napoten. Carefully she placed it in the pouch of her hoody and crept back inside.

It was the first time that Ava had met the man in person, to whom she was ultimately responsible. The grace of movement in the short walk from the main entrance to the sitting room utterly belied his age. She knew he must be well into his fifties at least, but he moved like a man in his thirties. He wore an open necked polo shirt and blue jeans, easy shoes. She was even more uncomfortable in her formal dress. There was little expression in his perfectly symmetrical face, which she had only seen once before, one of the few to do so. Price, who she knew as a trained killer, more lethal even than Caleb, shut the door behind them. Venmorin garbled an offer of a drink. Their employer did not answer, his sharp eyes sweeping the room. Ava could see her companion trying to frame the words to give some explanation of what had happened and exonerate them from responsibility. It was something in which he excelled, practiced hundreds of times with local politicians and journalists. Whatever Venmorin had been going to say however, fell silent in the dark appraisal of the tall, dangerously still figure in the centre of the room.

Bello, with Venmorin, was used to wielding power. Their talent for presenting themselves as skilled and socially responsible was the reason they had worked together at the top of Tregothan's industry in England for so long. Many good things were done by good people under their watch, enough to confuscate and misdirect those authorities that came looking. Beneath this comforting blanket of philanthropy and constructive business ran a steady and larger stream of human trafficking and slavery. They were also masters in the art of injecting lies and mischief to create a culture of prejudice and hatred. Neither were easily confounded nor intimidated. Tregothan, in one devastating glance, had done both.

Ava, shivering, drew nearer to the log fire. How was anything in the room still producing light? The sheer power of the man and the terrible darkness he carried. The voice was quiet, resonant and emanated suppressed rage. It dried her own into incapacity.

"Take me to the room."

Neither she nor her partner bothered to verify that he meant the hidden cellar, from which the prisoner had escaped. Nor did either ask how Tregothan knew that they no longer held the man they had trapped below, or that Waterman was missing and presumed dead. Above all, they dared not ask how he had come to be at their door less than three hours after they themselves had discovered what had occurred. The pair just avoided banging into each other as they hurried to lead him through the corridor and along the hidden passage to the secret room. Venmorin pressed a button. A slight swish was the only sound made by the narrow steel door as it admitted them into the cellar. Silently, Tregothan examined every inch of the old priest hole. Closing his eyes, the aquiline nose twitched like a hound on the scent.

"No cameras?"

Ava shook her head, looking at the broken screen, her brown eyes huge and fearful.

Tregothan came over and cupped her jaw, pinching her flesh, his touch like searing fire. Her attempts to pull away were met with disdain. When he eventually released her, she turned to run but was halted by his voice. "I don't think so."

Ava's feet refused to move, standing stock still she waited for the final blow.

It did not come. She watched with a mixture of horror and relief as he turned to Venmorin. A vicious whip-like strike across the face felled the other man. Ava suppressed a scream. Venmorin crawled out of reach. Dazed, his mouth and nose bleeding, he raised himself with one hand covering his face.

Tregothan moved to the door that had been stood on end to cover the arched, open space. The massive oak again boomed as it fell to the floor, covering the blood stains. Unnoticed previously, as they had both rushed over the fallen timber, Bello now clearly saw the prints of horse's hooves on the door.

Tregothan's face paled, he took a step back as if he had been struck. His voice froze her heart.

"Ellan."

To the massive relief of the two executives, he walked over the door and out into the forest, joining the bridle path. Ava found her legs. They headed back though the indoor entrance and through the secret passageway. At the top of the stairs they pushed open the door that gave entrance to the rest of the house. The imposing figure of Price blocked the light from the hall. Venmorin ordered him aside. Price looked dismissively at the two executives.

"Your room is required," he told Ava Bello. "You need to remove your things to new accommodation on the lower floor. Venmorin will also take a room there. Ava, about to protest, was stopped by Venmorin's hand on her wrist.

"Of course," he agreed.

Ava followed him upstairs. They were still alive.

Chapter Thirty-Two

"You're starting to look a lot better." Os was on his own for once. Christmas had come and gone inside the retreat house. Neither Amy nor Os wanting much involvement. Cards to their families had been posted in the city centre by the Order. Most days Amy had arrived to find Cathy gently coaxing her friend to eat or reading to him from one of the books from the farmhouse's impressive library. Occasionally she had caught them silently looking doe-eyed at each other and Amy, smiling wryly, had left before she had been discovered. She had begun to suspect that the attention he was receiving had encouraged Os to lengthen his recovery time over the last few days. He had turned up occasionally for meals in his dressing gown but spent most of the time in his room. She watched fairly unsympathetically as he slumped into an armchair after returning from the bathroom.

"It's the fatigue," he told her. "It's so frustrating. I feel all wrung out, like a dishcloth."

"Unlike you," Amy quipped. " I've been making some use of my days. Not having the dedicated nursing of a beautiful girl to encourage a bed bound state!"

He threw a cushion at her, having the grace, she thought, to look a little embarrassed.

"Hey. You didn't have that thing around your waist, squeezing the life out of you!"

"I'll give you that," she laughed.

"Cathy said you called it a delnome."

"It's all in the book Waterman wanted to take when we thought he was Richard."

Gerald had identified Avery as Marcus Waterman. Known to the Order for some years.

Amy had decided to keep much of her studying to herself. How

Os and the Order would react, knowing she had brought a napoten into the building, she could not predict. He seemed not to recall that he had wrapped the dreadful instrument in the coat, prior to his rescue. Amy, by some instinct, had placed it in the silk she had found in the stone at Croston. As she did so the symbols on the cloth, she had previously failed to understand, were clear and informative.

" Where are the parents by the way? Cathy said she had come here with them, but they've never appeared in the refectory," asked Amy.

"I didn't want to push it by asking, to be honest. I think the Order is hiding him and want to keep his whereabouts secret."

"Well, it's a big enough space. They've acres of land with a working farm, probably outbuildings that I still haven't found yet. Quite the enterprise. You'll love the chapel! I've hardly seen Mena and Gerald, I think they're waiting for you to get better."

Os raised his eyebrows. "Maybe. I've been doing a lot of thinking."

"And?"

He went to the wardrobe and, to her surprise, pulled out jeans and a sweatshirt.

"It's time for some conversations."

"I'll give you a hand," she told him easily, stepping towards him.

He looked at her for a moment, finally seeing the nurse offering practical help and not a pretty young woman offering to dress him.

"Out," he told her.

Amy thought her friend looked fresh and handsome at breakfast, his appetite now clearly restored. Even though she had teased him about getting better, she recognised he still had some way to go before feeling fully recovered.

"Do you feel up to a tour?" Mena asked him.

"Of course," Os replied.

Mena led them towards the back of the refectory where an older section, lined with heavy stone, appeared to be part of the original farmhouse building. Amy had increasingly warmed to the older woman who often spent time with her in the evening, encouraging her to take part in group singing and gatherings within the chapel. During these sessions she found her connection to Tanamaarin felt stronger, unlike many of the religious services she had attended previously. They followed down a spiral staircase, to a basement area that was mostly occupied by a chapel to their right, its double doors open. The clear beat of Bob Marley's Song of Redemption sounded from inside. Members of the Order were cleaning and arranging flowers inside what was a space that exhibited the same simple beauty of the rooms above. A brief glance showed that this was not a typical place of worship. There were areas of seating but also floor space with individual mats. There was no one religious symbol, figures of many prophets from many belief systems lined the walls.

"We are multi-faith," Mena explained. "All belief systems that enable the expansion of spiritual growth and light are welcome to worship in this place. Some follow other paths that are grounded in earth practices passed on down the years. Once a day we come together to pray. We have retained some particular traditions we believe to have been given to us by Avide and with which all individuals here are comfortable."

There was a cosy seating area to their left, lined with shelves of books. Amy expected Mena to lead them to the soft leather chairs, where she had been spending most of her days studying. Instead their guide went straight ahead, turning right into a narrow corridor area that was in the far corner, on the other side of the chapel, and not visible from the main basement area. Mena produced a swipe card that let her into what was obviously her personal office. Amy registered the neatly stacked shelves of books, as well as a picture of Maria, on a mahogany desk. Once the door was closed the older woman went to the stone wall that lined the back of the office.

"How are you feeling, Os? I have more to show you."

Fascinated, Os was examining the bookshelves that were filled with monastic histories.

"I feel great." He looked around the small space. "What did you have in mind?"

" We are about to descend to the original monastery. Most of our Order are not privy to its existence, aware only that our house is built on the original site." She sighed. "Sadly we have been forced to keep secrets within secrets to ensure the protection of Avide's legacy."

"And yet you are willing to share it with us," Os noted.

Mena became solemn as she looked frankly at the two souls standing in front of her.

"More than any other individuals in my lifetime, I feel a sense that you belong here. That Avide intended for you to find your way to the Monastery of the Listening Ocean and the Watching Sea."

Amy glanced at Os, the intensity of Mena's tone causing her to tremble a little. He seemed to understand, squeezing her hand momentarily. Mena laughed, lightening the mood. "It's a bit of a mouthful to be honest. Apparently the original name and the Gaelic gives it more resonance. Everyone here just calls it the Farmhouse or the Field. We have lots of actual fields by the way, and a working farm. We all work together. All very sustainable and all that."

Mena turned back and reached towards a small, darker stone to the right of the wall. A slight click and it opened to reveal a keypad. Maria quickly typed. Os noted the number as '685'. The wall slid across to reveal a modern lift. The older woman smiled at their surprised expressions, stepping forward. Once all three were safely inside, she selected the arrow for down. A simple up and down were the only choices on the panel. "To all intents and purposes," she explained, "we are a spiritual retreat house funded by a working farm. Our outside contacts are handled by Art and Steve. They sell our produce from an artisan stall in Altrincham. We have a few animals and mainly grow rapeseed, which needs a lot of land, helping us to remain isolated. Bernadette, who lost her husband this year, was one of our associate members until recent times. They supported us outside the community, arranging for harvest collection and trading our crops. Our members know that this is a hidden, multi-faith Order that follows the teachings of a little-known historical figure. They believe that our deviation from the norm, in terms of a having a more eclectic faith, is the reason for our secrecy. Our total number is kept to twenty-four. Bernadette is now our front of house person for any occasional visitors."

Amy felt in her pocket for Avide's Mark, which she had kept under her pillow as she slept. They were clearly well below ground level.

Amy gasped as the lift opened to reveal a maze of arches and underground walkways. She felt for Os' hand as they stepped into what was clearly a very old building. There were irregular slabs of old stone in parts of the walls, clearly dating from the time of the Roman occupation. It was something she had witnessed before in the underground crypt of Hexham Abbey, where Roman engraved stones were used in the building. Also in Istanbul, where old Roman columns had been used to create the unique and atmospheric Basilica Cistern. Perfect examples of early recycling.

"This is the original monastery, created in secret so long ago. It is modelled on the little-known Monastery of the Folded Wind in the North."

"All of it?" Amy's excitement increased, she had already felt a wonderful sense of familiarity in the old stone.

Mena, who had been leading them through the main passageway, turned towards them, shaking her head. "Perhaps you are referring to Avide's inner sanctum, the Carapace, to which very few were admitted? It is our belief that the Carapace was or is an inter-dimensional portal, inextricably linked with Avide himself. As such, when he left the monastery, so did the Carapace."

"That, I didn't know," whispered Os. Amy remained silent.

"Of course, we have had to use many techniques to maintain and make our building fit for purpose. Some very old, some very modern."

As she spoke they turned a corner where a steel panel barred their way. Mena's touch saw it slide to one side to give entry into a space the size of a village hall. There was absolutely nothing rustic here, noted Amy. The walls were covered with large screens, the floor with computer stations. Alcoves made up both sides and appeared to be areas for virtual reality and video games. Walking past one such alcove Amy stopped to cry out in surprise. "James!"

Her friend turned, removing his headphones, shaking out blonde hair.

"Hello Amy." He smiled, a little self-ashamedly.

"We deliberately placed him with you in the GP practice," Mena told her. Her mouth widened in a half apology, seeing the dumbfounded expression on her guest's face. "I promise I'll explain later."

"They're pilot simulations," James told them, indicating the large screen in front of him. "It allows me to practice a range of scenarios. I will admit that Wi-Fi connection and keeping it secure and secret, have been a bit of a challenge."

Amy looked stunned and would have stayed to talk more but Mena quickly moved her on.

"I want you both to meet our lead and expert in all of our technical activities." She shook her head. "I barely understand a fraction of it myself."

Os and Amy followed to a door at the back of the space, which opened to reveal a man in his fifties concentrating on a screen, inside a small office.

"Meet Richard Grieg."

The pair looked at each other in amazement. Amy thought he couldn't have looked any less like Avery. A physique that made her wonder if he was ex-military and a clear-eyed benevolence in his sea blue eyes.

"Will the real Richard Grieg please stand up!"

Richard looked puzzled at Os' greeting but shook his hand enthusiastically. He then turned to Amy who received a similar handshake.

"I can't thank both of you enough for everything you've done for Cathy."

"I can't believe we didn't see it," Os turned to Amy and then back to Richard. "I'm sorry. We were led dangerously astray by someone impersonating you."

"Waterman?" Richard had lowered his voice.

Os looked puzzled. "We understand that is his real name."

"A lean and hungry look," Richard quoted.

Os nodded, somehow the reference to the sly Cassius in Shakespeare's Julius Caesar perfectly captured their late night visitor.

"May have represented himself to you as Avery?" Richard spoke hesitantly.

"He did," confirmed Os. He exchanged glances with Mena.

"I'll join you all shortly," Richard told them. Cathy's dad sat back behind the desk. "I'll just finish what I'm doing and follow you down."

Mena ushered them towards what appeared to be a store room at the back of the office. "This is a part of the Monastery we don't use very often."

A keypad opened the door through which they passed to find themselves in complete contrast to the modern office they had just left. Stone steps brought them back into the original building, but on a lower level. The energy here was different, noted Amy. She could feel the history in the rough stone walls and narrow walkway. Almost hearing the quiet shuffling of feet that came to worship along the passage. There were alcoves with electric candles, where the original old ones would have been placed. They shone their light dimly in the heavy, blanketing atmosphere of enclosure.

"A crypt?" Amy was running her hands against the stone. Os too, impulsively reached to touch the old walls. Swiftly, his consciousness was back in the seventh century.

I had Ellan to thank for my escape. I should have seen Bierscath lying in wait, had I not been so preoccupied by the wondrous sight

I had been privy to, as I reached the mouth of the sea with my lord. It was the first time Avide spoke to me without voice, soothing and calming as he transformed from man to sea creature. Even as I looked for the boat that would take him across the sea he bade me accept the change that had come upon him. A sea turtle. Though I had never seen one, I had heard men speak of such a creature. The huge segmented dome of his shell shone like studded emeralds in the sunset. The sprawling limbs gathered the water towards him as he went further out to sea. I watched, bereft, as he submerged beneath the ocean and the night began its dominance. Though I was tired, I did not sleep but turned to walk my solitary path back to the monastery.

Bierscath took me unawares. At first I feared that he had followed me and seen Avide's departure, but his words of triumphant disdain told me otherwise. A weapon I had never seen and that I hoped would never see again. He simply handed it to me like some missive and I, unsuspecting took it willingly. Shafts of pain drove through my arm, and every attempt to shake off the strange smooth roll affixed it to me further. The pain struck me down but more than this some abomination fed upon my loss. I could taste despair, severance, and a want that would never be tamed or satisfied. As I sank into the pit of its presence Ellan freed me. Her gentle brown eyes bade me keep silent, as she broke the dread embrace of the object and soothed my skin with what felt like a velvet petal. He was gone when I returned fully to myself.

I thanked the woman of the forest, who was special to my lord, and marvelled at her beauty and strength. But I could not stay with her long. I had Avide's instruction and somehow must relocate our Order to another site, south and removed from Northumbria. Not so far that we could not reach it in a few days ride. I had been a leader of men before and did not hesitate to gather my brothers. We were to leave that night and I was to return alone.

Os felt his head bump against the low ceiling. Amy looked at him speculatively.

"Come and see," invited Mena, pushing open an arched wooden

door at the end of the passage. She smiled at Amy's cry of delight and Os' look of incredulity. Instantly, Amy was aware that this had been a sacred place, long before the monks had called it so. Probably the reason that they had chosen this spot to found the hidden Order. The size of a small chapel, the chamber was cave like. It had no windows and there was a sense of being deep within the earth. However, there was light in this space, a luminescence that came from the vividly covered painting on the largest wall. A portrait of their beloved monk. The colours looked as fresh as if it had just been created, and yet, she knew that this was not the case. She had no idea what materials had been used in this vibrant representation of Avide turning from his garden, as if to greet whoever had entered the space. He stood among an array of plants in bloom, his hair hung loose and long, as was his way. His face tilted attentively towards the observer, with eyes that penetrated your heart and dug deeply into your soul. Somehow the artist had captured the inner light of his presence. Both Os and Amy had tears in their eyes. Was this then, what they had been sent to find? This sacred place that held his image?

Mena switched on the lights, another series of electric candles placed in small inlets throughout the room.

"I see you recognise our founder, Avide." She gazed at the painting herself, as if it were indeed the first time. Whatever reservations Amy had regarding the older woman, fell away.

"Thank you, Mena," she said sincerely. "Thank you so much for looking after us and bringing us here."

Mena responded by reaching out and squeezing her shoulder.

"How is it so warm?" Amy asked.

"An underground, Roman style heating system that Gerald and James managed to modernise. Brilliant really. Would you believe we have hot springs here in the middle of Manchester?"

"Incredible," commented Amy.

A large stately table dominated the space. It was covered with an embroidered cloth. Around the table were the kind of finely carved wooden chairs that Amy had seen in some cathedrals and churches. The rest of the natural walls were covered in engravings and calligraphy that she suspected had been created by the original inhabitants. Some were daubed with faded colour; they looked fascinating and beautiful, but none contained the immense power of Avide's portrait.

"We decided to meet here this morning in honour of you both." Os and Amy looked at each other, stunned.

" It is quite the momentous day," continued Mena. "All of us feel it was meant more for you than anyone else who has come here in our lifetime."

She pointed to a section of the wall in the right-hand corner. Os gasped in surprise as he saw the simple engraving which had not been coloured. The figure of a woman beside a horse stood alongside a man whose hand rested on a lynx. The carving had been made with the two figures facing away, so that only their caped backs were visible. Amy reached for Os' hand and was reassured to feel he needed her touch as much as she needed his. Mena was glowing now, as if their reaction to Avide's portrait, and the wall carving, had confirmed what she needed to know.

"There is much to discuss," she told them, a little breathlessly. "Gerald and the others will be joining us shortly, I'll make a pot of coffee."

Amy smiled at the practicality within this sacred space. Mena went to an antique dresser, within which was a very modern looking coffee machine. She placed another cloth on the table and began plating biscuits. Just as the coffee was ready, the others entered, as if on cue. Mena greeted Gerald, and Richard with a wide, relieved smile,

"I think we can proceed now."

Chapter Thirty-Three

"Where to begin?" Gerald rubbed his brow and sighed deeply. Around the table also sat Mena, Richard, Amy and myself. I had only just begun to recover from my narrow escape, and although Cathy and Amy had spent much time at my bedside during this period, both had avoided discussing anything more important than my ability to function again. I was still traumatised by the deep wounds inflicted by the delnome. It sought out my darkest fears, my deepest guilts. Had it not been for Amy, and then Cathy, I might have sunk into despair, even after its removal. It all meant I was a little anaesthetised to the shock of finding this hidden monastery in the suburbs of Manchester. Until, that was, Mena had led us into the underground cellar that looked as if it might once have been a chapel. The space swallowed you whole as you entered. Avide's lifelike portrait dominated the centre of the back wall as we entered; it took my breath away. The intricate carvings, showing what appeared to be a depiction of Amy and myself hundreds of years previously. It all felt surreal, even to me, who lived with the spirit of Nesu embedded within. I wondered if Choriscuro was whispering to Amy the way that Nesu was whispering to me. Not in words but in a kind of soft music, a rejoicing. My doubts about the Order fell away. There was someone absent however, with whom I wanted to share this time, this sense of coming home.

"I thought Cathy might have been included in this meeting." I directed my query towards Richard.

I had looked for her that morning at breakfast. When she didn't arrive my eyes tried to find her as Mena brought us through the building to the hidden room in which we now sat.

"She's with her mother, my wife Julia," he replied. "Julia was working with me late last night, trying to lay a false trail of credit and debit card use, to indicate that we are now in Ireland. I think I'm right in believing that Waterman guessed that reports of my death were premature?"

I sighed. " I'm afraid if he had any doubt, it was banished by our reception of him."

Richard took an inward breath. "Marcus Waterman grew up inside a fortress of power. James has discovered that he was given over to the care of his billionaire guardian at a young age."

"Tregothan," guessed Amy.

"You know of him?" Mena looked surprised.

"James told us."

"It makes sense," I added. "I thought he was Venmorin's employee to begin with but it became obvious he was outside their control."

"Venmorin," Gerald told us, "controls huge, largely untouchable and grossly corrupt operations. About two years ago, James noticed the presence of another, more shadowy figure, operating in the UK and linked to the Inimica company. He was very careful to minimise his presence online, or by phone, but James was able to pick up the contact. He seemed to be using Inimica's resources to follow the trail of an ex-chaplain, who appeared to have left behind his normal life one day in Lindisfarne."

I felt shocked, glad I was already sitting down. Amy placed her hand on mine. " You were very careful."

" I had no idea about being careful." My mind was racing now, wondering how he had tracked me down. "The kind of explorations I needed to make were totally off grid. More internal than external if you know what I mean?"

"We know exactly what you mean," Mena reassured me.

"Waterman was someone we have been trying to locate for some time. He didn't find you until you located the cross and Avide's Mark in Croston. It was one of the original crosses from the Monastery of the Folded Wind," explained Gerald.

"I had no idea. I needed to find Avide's Mark, but I didn't recognise the cross."

"I believe it announced your presence to those who were

searching for you. We have some evidence that it was given by Cuthbert to his friend, shortly before Avide's disappearance," Gerald concluded.

"Waterman," continued Mena, "had disappeared from our radar following Maria's death."

"I don't understand." Amy looked towards Avide's portrait, as did I. No doubt she, like me, fervently wished he was there with his wisdom and powerful understanding.

"You said my aunt was part of this Order?" Amy directed the question to Mena.

"She was part of our Order for over twenty years. Your aunt and my sister," the old woman softly replied.

Amy stood, her eyes rapidly changing colour from soft brown to flickering amber as emotion overwhelmed her. "How?" she croaked.

Mena placed a tentative hand on hers and waited until Amy returned to her seat.

"I was the result of your grandfather's time in England, when he came over to teach at the university in Manchester. He brought Maria here as a girl of ten. My mother was a lecturer at the same college and, I think, influenced Maria's later desire to come back. My mother, Eloise, later married Gerald's father, both were members of the Order. After our parents died," she looked sadly at Gerald, " I told Maria of our family ties. I think she already knew. I was educated in the school that was once on the land on which Richard's house now stands."

"Oh my God." Amy sat down again. "I have been thinking ever since I met you that you remind me so much of Maria." She was crying now in Mena's embrace. The old woman's eyes had also filled. Giving the two women some space, Gerald turned towards me.

" We know that Waterman, through the dark ways of Jarinbissar, has discovered his previous identity, several hundred years ago, as a monk called Avery. We believe that he was expelled from the Lindisfarne monastery in the late seventh century. We also know, through information passed down in our own Order, that

Avide was the one who first alerted Cuthbert to his treachery."

I reached over to Amy, putting my hand over her own. "You told me that Avery spoke about Maria, when you were captured."

"Like I said, he knew her from university in London," replied Os. Amy's brows creased. "Maria read classics and history at university. She did mention someone named Marcus that she was close to." Her voice was shaky.

"Perhaps now is the time for us to hear your story," suggested Mena.

I looked at Amy, who nodded in agreement. I spoke only about the events since Cathy had entered my flat at the Tobacco Factory, wondering again why she had not been invited to join this meeting. Amy added her own story, giving minimal detail of her rescue of me. Due to some unspoken agreement, neither of us told of our arinokras.

"I still can't believe that Joy found you, sleeping in the car park in Platt Fields!" Gerald's eyes were shining. " We have been checking the park for years every morning, knowing that Maria had written instructions that if you needed help, that's where you would find it."

"And I almost didn't read it! If Os hadn't found the book and Waterman tried to take it, I probably never would. But I still don't understand how Avery or Marcus, as you call him, found us."

Mena seemed to hesitate before she spoke, keeping a keen eye on her new found niece.

" Maria was in love with Marcus Waterman at university but decided to end her relationship in her third year. She told me that his darkness had grown and she could no longer touch the heart that had initially reached out to hers. He followed her back to Manchester and effectively stalked Maria for a time. It was during this period that she became aware of his sinister connection to Venmorin, who was known to the Order and whom we originally thought could be Bierscath. At some point it's my belief that Marcus' obsession with Maria came to the notice of the Inimica group."

"You think she was murdered?" Amy's voice rose in horror.

Mena nodded sadly. "One of the reasons I did not make contact with you is because I believed he has made it his business to monitor your movements. Thankfully you were abroad most of the time, but I think he suspected you were important. During their relationship, he revealed to Maria, that he was a reincarnated monk. Maria, by that time, had eschewed her traditional beliefs and was prepared to believe him. Once she knew he was watching her in Manchester, she stopped coming to the monastery but I met her in my own house in Didsbury, under the pretext of being her client. Waterman is incredibly skilled in subterfuge. We swept her house continually for listening devices, though I am inclined to believe that Maria had taken care of that in her own fashion. Together, using what he had told her and what I could discover, we gathered a reliable history of his previous life as Avery."

Gerald continued.

"Long ago, Avery the monk, ever restless, resentful and power hungry, was recruited by Bierscath. Avery's purpose was to disrupt the energies of the Lindisfarne monks and to penetrate the Monastery of the Folded Wind. To destroy the enemy that Bierscath most feared- Avide. However, in the early transcripts he is remembered fondly, as the monk who visited with Cuthbert, and therefore would have been kindly received by Osweald. His treachery only making itself known later."

"What happened to Avide?" I asked.

" We only have what has been handed down within the Order. When this place was built in secret, it was thought that Avide would return to the monks that he relocated. The original monastery in the North was destroyed by raiders, later revealed as engineered by Bierscath. Avide's foresight meant that only he, and another, remained when the northern monastery was burnt to the ground. Months and then years went by and Avide did not return. I am now anxious to know," continued Gerald, "if, and how much memory of that time you have both retrieved."

"It's already been a very long morning," I told him. "Amy and

I have had little time to discuss or even process what has happened in the last few days. If it's okay with you guys we could do with a little time out just now."

As they reluctantly agreed, Amy added her thanks.

"Lunch is in the refectory at 1pm," Mena informed us, opening the heavy door and leaving us to find our own way through the maze of corridors. "Take my pass for the doors, the keypad for the lift is 685."

I smiled my thanks, putting her card in my pocket. I was, by now, pretty desperate to spend some time with Amy, alone.

Chapter Thirty-Four

Amy had been very quiet in the walk through the dimly lit passageways. Every step seemed to lead them further into old habits of contemplation. The ancient building tugged at long past memories and brought another to the fore.

It was long past the time of year when the sun rose early and bedded late. The leaves had left most of the trees but still patterned the soil. Avide's absence greyed the sky, even on a good day. I watched them arguing, neither listening to the other.

"Do what must be done yourself!"

"Don't tell me, you of all people, have lost your stomach for killing."

They had dismounted and walked down the path that once led to the monastery, now ash and ruin.

"Oh I see, Sereka," Bierscath turned with fire in his eyes, "just your stomach for killing him!"

"I won't do it," she spat back.

He took her face in his hands and made the act of endearment a cruel mockery, as he pressed her jaw till tears filled his wife's eyes. "Yes, you will."

He let go of her and mounted his horse, leaving the woman alone on the forest floor. I thought I might kill her then, my arrows did not stray when they left my bow. I could have prevented the tragedy they planned, for it was clearly of Osweald that they spoke. But I had never taken a life and I followed my dear Avide in his ways of thinking kindly, on even such as she.

Amy pointed to a bench in a quiet corner away from the modernised space, taking time to quietly process what had been revealed to her.

"Exactly how far underground do you think we are?" she asked.

"Pretty far, I'd say, if the length of time in the lift is anything to go by."

"It's a lot to take in," he prompted.

"More than you know." She was wearing a long sweatshirt over her leggings, from which she pulled out a plastic wallet, hidden in the pouch in the front of her top. "Cathy brought me this yesterday."

The quiver of excitement in Os, as she mentioned Richard's daughter did not escape her. Inside the plastic wallet was a copy of a beautifully inscribed, original parchment. Os recognised the runes as possibly neolithic script; geometric circles and shapes he had seen on standing stones outside, what were thought to be, ancient burial grounds. Only two lines were written, with the recognisable patterns of the Old English and Latin used in the Lindisfarne Gospels, which included three names familiar to him.

'I, Ellan of the Northern Forest….

I, Osweald of the Monastery of the Folded Wind.'

The last recognisable entry, at the very end of the document was 'Avide'.

"Have they any idea what it says?" Os asked her.

"No, they don't," she hesitated, "but I do."

"What?" Os turned excitedly towards her.

"Hush, we need to keep it between us. There are more secrets here than we know."

"But," he began.

"I know, I trust them too. But there's something Os, something holding me back."

"Have you told Cathy you can read this?"

"No." She placed her hand on his arm. "And you can't tell her either."

She waited for him to nod his agreement before beginning her translation.

> "The change comes
> Inexorable as the forest fire that fells
> A hundred years of growth.

That re-roots.
My fingertips sink down.
Through tiny spikelets to
Soiled tubers
Wet with wind-shifted rain.
Death calls
The trees release their tumbling blades,
A sparkling shower
That whispers to the ground
The leaving has arrived.
I, Ellan of the Northern Forest
And I, Osweald of the Monastery of the Folded Wind,
Profess our love.
And our returning.
In the trembling stillness of the time
And if the world allows,
We will find Avide."

Os squeezed her hand, looking awe-stricken.

"Cathy said her father told her it was found when the chamber we were in this morning was first discovered. On the ninth of March 1994 a wall collapsed spontaneously, without any apparent reason. Behind it they found another, older wall, and the door to what appeared to be an ancient chapel."

The hairs on Os' neck began to tingle. "I was born on that day."

"So was I," Amy told him, unable to keep the tremble from her voice. They had never discussed their birthdays before.

The runes were a profound relief for Amy to read. She did not question that this was her language, her history, her undying connection to what had been lost to modern human consciousness. Each symbol evoked so much more than the simple lines of English, that she had laid out in her notebook when she had translated them the previous evening. Tears welled in both their eyes, the privileged emotion of meeting an old and infinitely personal truth. Os made her laugh as he pointed to her and then back to himself.

"Were we...?" he whispered.

Amy shook her head smiling. "Half brother and sister," she laughed back, wiping her eyes.

Os looked into her face very keenly, and then to her surprise, embraced her, somehow crossing the boundaries of the past and the present.

"Completely fits," he said softly.

Even as he released her she quickly moved back towards him as the harsh ringing of a modern alarm sounded in the quiet nook. It's discordant hammering continued amidst doors banging and people moving, tense voices. Mena appeared at the end of the passageway.

"Quickly," her breath coming in short gasps, "follow me."

She led them back to the office where Richard had been working. He and James moved between screens, typing frenetically on the keyboards. Gerald, clearly horrified, concentrated on another PC in the middle of the bigger room. Mena slid behind him with Os and Amy. The old woman yelled as an outside camera showed a view of the building above, fully aflame. "Did they get out Gerald?"

Her face reflected her brother's horror at the sight of the old farmhouse, amidst clouds of black smoke, billowing upwards. Flashes of red flame, dagger points of relentless destruction that seemed impossible against the mellow afternoon and the still fields in the distance. Shouts of alarm as a huge explosion shook the earth, knocking out the camera feed from its tree top vantage point. The sound of earth moving. Yet all seemed intact in the underground expanse.

"Oh God." Mena sank into a chair, with Amy immediately going to comfort her. Gerald was stunned into silence. Cathy and Julia were across on the other side of the room with James and Richard.

"The emergency procedures I never thought we'd have to use will mean there is no trace of the monastery from above," Richard stated, his voice hoarse with emotion. He thankfully embraced Julia and Cathy who had come to join him only minutes before the explosion.

"We need to help them." Cathy's distressed voice shook, her eyes inevitably reaching for Os.

A sudden realisation seemed to hit her. "Are we trapped?" Os came to stand beside her, placing a hand on her arm. She placed her own hand over his.

Richard shook his head. "But we can't go back the way we came. The shaft is designed to close in on itself in the event that the building above is destroyed. There's an alternative exit, but we can't leave yet. The emergency services should have arrived now," he reassured her.

"There was no warning." James, shaking and pale. Rallying, he ran to the other side of the room.

"We should have recordings before the cameras were destroyed. Over here."

He went to a corner cupboard inside which was another computer screen, quickly followed by Richard. In minutes he had brought up the scene inside the upper building prior to the fire. They scanned various areas, all showing the Order members getting on with their usual activities. Joy, alone in the chapel, went over to light a candle under a Christian figurine. She turned, her face shocked and horrified, as the sweet looking grandmother, who had let Richard's family into the building, rolled a grenade into the chapel. Valiantly Joy flung her body towards it. Flames filled the screen for seconds before the smoke-filled scene reverted to black nothingness.

"Bernadette!" Mena and Gerald cried simultaneously, coming over to join the others.

"Oh my God." Gerald, pale and shaking, placed his arm around Mena.

"Does she know about the monastery? Down here?" Os asked.

"No," Gerald answered. "Despite her age, she only came to live here recently, when her husband died. She worked remotely for the Order however, for many years."

Richard glanced at James, an agreement passing between them. "I'll look into it," promised the younger man.

"Thank you son." Gerald rose to put an arm round James. Amy looked at her friend in surprise.

"Meet my dad," James said with some pride, patting his father on the back.

"I'm glad you were both down here together when it happened," Amy told him.

" It may only have been the six of us that have survived," Gerald speculated. His words moved through them bringing a crushing weight of sorrow.

"Bernadette couldn't get inside Mena's office. Targeting the chapel, nearest to the office, may have given those in the refectory and higher rooms, some chance to escape. Do we have anything else?" enquired James.

Richard had continued to tap the screen, scanning through what footage was visible. They crowded round the computer, that now showed Bernadette, moving quickly for someone her age, ascend the spiral staircase as the explosion sounded in the chapel. Richard switched screen. With horror they watched her place a device on the small cutlery table in the middle of the refectory and exit through the door that led into the vegetable garden. Members of the Order were just gathering for lunch as the alarm rang out.

"Leave, run!" Mena cried. Gradually the group became aware of smoke. Some ran towards the refectories, others towards the garden. It quickly became apparent that the door to the garden had been made impassable by Bernadette. In the seconds that the Order members bunched against the door, and others ran for the main entrance, the bomb exploded.

"Dear God, she has killed them all!" Mena sank to her chair in floods of tears, staring at Gerald who was also crying. Cathy and Julia, weeping together, tried to comfort each other. Os went across to lend his support.

"I'm so sorry." Amy remained with Mena and Gerald. "This is because we came here."

The sadness in her voice was echoed by the absence of denial. Os' head dropped.

"No. This is no one's fault, only those who engineered Bernadette's betrayal." Cathy was clear voiced, certain.

"Bierscath," muttered Gerald.

"After all these years, and all our protections," added Mena.

"Who is Bierscath?" Cathy asked her father, who in turn looked to Gerald.

"We believe that he first appeared in Northumbria in the seventh century, but he may have been active long before that. The archived records that we have from the monks of that time, document the destruction of the Monastery of the Folded Wind by raiders from the North. However, when we excavated the chamber you saw this morning, we found another account written by Osweald, a monk of the 'Mainisstir Na Gaoithe Fillte.' Os' face registered his shock.

"It recorded,"continued Gerald, "that the attack had been engineered by Bierscath."

"May I see this document?" asked Os.

"Of course," Gerald replied. "I have a copy here. I was going to present it to you this afternoon."

He reached inside his briefcase and pulled out a roughly A4 sized sheet inside a plastic pocket. Os examined the shaky Latin script on the torn parchment.

'I Osweald, feel death's embrace as I write, betrayed by Sereka. Know that it was Bierscath who charged raiders to destroy the Mainisstir Na Gaoithe Fillte. It burns, even as I lie in the cave of Ellan of the forest, who has softened my last hours with her care. Stay safe my brothers and keep Avide's memory until his return.'

Os handed the script back to Gerald, his hand shaking, his mind claimed once again by the memory of before.

The kiss of the river as I rolled in its embrace, left stupefied and for dead. Auburn hair stroked my skin, strong arms but soft skinned, lifting me onto my horse's back. Ellan, wild and strong, took me back to her cave and administered herbs to slow the poison. I called for parchment and ink so that I could write a last warning to my brothers, knowing Ellan would see it delivered to the secret place where Avide had instructed we build a new home for the Order.

The monastery had been attacked and destroyed as Avide had predicted. I was making my way south to our new home when I came upon their camp. A group of raiders, flushed with triumph over the destruction of an empty sanctuary. As they shouted their boasts, one name flamed my ears.

"Take word to Bierscath that it has been done as he told," ordered the largest and loudest of their number, dispatching one of his men. An involuntary cry of anger signalled my hiding place to the raiders. I fought hard, as I had done of old, battle skills returning as the wine-soaked raiders came upon me. My body was lean and tough from long endurance and the habits of simplicity. There were many, but brave Nesu joined the fight selling his own life dearly, taking the sword blade meant for my breast. In rage, I scattered the last of my foe and afterwards buried Nesu where he had first come to me, in the forest.

I do not know why I wandered that evening, back to the dell where the young Osweald had met secretly with Sereka. I came to the old place where the river pooled. Blown to her side like a leaf in the wind, she stood waiting, unchanged, even after so many years.

" I knew in my heart you were still alive." Her voice was husky with longing and invitation.

Wiser now, I knew enough to refuse the wine she offered but still I felt the want of her, the need for her. The years we lived apart had vanished.

"You have hardly altered," she whispered, taking a blanket from her pack. I was no longer a boy.

"Nor you," I replied, as coldly as I could muster.

"Come then, let us comfort each other as we did before. I have suffered much in your absence."

I knew she was there under the instruction of Bierscath, but none of this knowledge stemmed my love, as surely it should have done. What she could not hide from the monk, who had spent so long with Avide, was the pain. I could see clearly that her heart bled with self-inflicted wounds. I reached out to her, my compassion stilling the *rage my younger self might once have felt.*

"You need not inflict this evil upon us both, Sereka."

There was a fleeting second of truth touching truth, her lustrous eyes lifting, a raise of her wrist. And then it was gone, given up for artifice as her lips shaped to a shallow, inviting smile. Somehow I resisted the wanting in every fibre of my being.

"Leave me Sereka, while you still can," I said coldly. Feigning anger I let my hand rest upon the hilt of my sword. Her eyes examined mine for the softness of old. Whatever she found there made her turn and replace the blanket. Moving my own mount aside, she hitched herself into her saddle, the last I was ever to see of her.

I sank to the ground as the strong flank of her horse brushed past me. My face reflected in the moonlit pool, vanished in the breeze that drifted across. I reached up to my pack for the water skin and thirstily drank its contents. Even as I placed the skin in the pool, preparing to refill, the toxin had begun to work its way to a heart that remained consumed with love for my poisoner.

The sound of Cathy's quiet weeping brought his senses back to the modern room in an ancient setting.

"It's a strange sensation, to think that you yourself wrote that thirteen hundred years ago," commented Gerald. Silence. Held breath. He repeated the assumption he had voiced at their first meeting. "I take it you were once Osweald of the Monastery of the Folded Wind and son of Roderick, Lord of Northumbria?" Gerald's statement left Cathy and James looking dumbfounded.

Os nodded his agreement. "I was once Osweald, as you say. It was Osweald who found this site and directed the building of this monastery on Avide's instruction. Before then I lived with Avide in the Monastery of the Folded Wind."

"And Amy," Mena looked closely at the younger women, her eyes red rimmed, but lightening as she spoke.

"You were Ellan of the forest and special friend to Avide?"

"Yes, I was," said Amy simply.

Chapter Thirty-Five

"Time Out!" James made a T sign with his hands. "Before we go any further, A, we all need some food and drink and B, someone should bring Cathy and me up to speed with all of this."

"And me," added Julia, a quick glance at her husband. "None of this is known to me."

"Of course," Gerald replied.

"Practicalities," Julia added. " Are we buried alive, waiting to be rescued? Are there even any supplies down here?"

" All is taken care of," Mena reassured her.

"We are many metres below ground level," Gerald explained. "A lot has changed in the last several hundred years. The real entrance to the monastery is hidden in a wall on the west side. Behind it is a tunnel that leads eventually to what is now Dunham Massey."

Amy recalled that Dunham Massey was a place many of her colleagues took their children during the holidays, though she had never been there herself.

"A full day's walk. An emergency generator will have kicked in when the connection to the upper building was lost. There are supplies down here for at least six months with a fully fitted kitchen and dining room attached. It is all accessible from this office." Gerald stood up, picking a key from his desk drawer on the way. They followed in single file, as he pressed a switch by Richard's desk that slid back part of the wall, revealing a narrow opening that would require them to pass through in single file.

Once again they found themselves in a stone tunnel like passage of the original building. After a few hundred metres, at a blind corner, a slab of stone floor dropped inwards as Gerald pressed the top left-hand corner of the enclave. A light came on below which revealed a metal ladder. One by one they followed his lead, negotiating the steep ladder and making their way along a more modern, plaster-boarded passageway, to an extensive area dominated by stainless steel. Cold assailed Amy, who shivered, quickly finding Mena's arm around her shoulders. It was like entering a wholesalers, she thought, registering the freezers, massive counter tops and endless shelves of dried goods. "Six months!" she commented. "More like a couple of years."

"We have made provision for twenty on site," Gerald said softly, leaving Amy sorry she had spoken.

"The kitchen we use regularly, it's near the lift which is now defunct. There's a route straight to it from the other side of our supply area."

He and Mena picked out a number of foodstuffs, frozen loaves of bread, butter, cheeses, dried milk and some various cans. They divided the items between them to carry out towards the kitchen. Amy wondered how she would manage to carry her share up another ladder when Gerald opened, what she thought, was a fridge door but was in fact a lift to the kitchen.

"This is incredible." Os looked around at the very homely, modern kitchen that included an electric oven and hob, as well as a small fridge.

Mena peered inside. "We have enough milk for a few days," she said approvingly. "And fresh bread." She picked up a fresh loaf from the worktop, wiping away the tears that had once more begun. "Anna made them this morning."

Gerald came beside her and held her whilst she recovered. Amy and Os looked sorrowfully at each other. Finding a bread board and knife, Amy came forward and began slicing the bread. One by one the others joined her and she found them tasks, each quietly joining in the meal preparation. She never had the money to eat out much during her travels and was a fair cook. Under her lead, a tasty hot soup was made to accompany the sandwiches. There was a round table that accommodated six quite readily. She had quietly noticed several other collapsible tables and chairs, stacked in a cupboard on one side of the kitchen. "Somebody put a lot of thought and planning into this," she commented. All of them had begun to feel the benefit of hot food and knowing that they were secure.

"Maria," said Mena quietly. "She arranged most of the practicalities."

"Ah," Amy replied, lifting her glass of wine, of which she had found several cases. " To Maria."

"To Maria," raised glasses clinked together in agreement and gratitude.

 Amy and Os had quietly informed each other of their most recent memories, but there were still many questions to be answered.

"Bierscath?" Julia looked first at her husband and then at the group. "Who is he?"

To everyone's surprise it was Amy who answered, connecting subconsciously with the psyche she had inhabited so long ago.

"Even the forest could not occlude his power. Dark he was, in every way, and terrifyingly beautiful. Ellan saw the murder and hatred in his heart, heard the craving for wealth and power in his voice. Yet most of all she saw one who had lost his way and seeks home."

Her voice was slightly archaic, her speech resonating in the underground, enclosed space. Os, not now or ever before, had seen the expression that played in her eyes at that moment. A terrible and profound acceptance of loss.

"He bound himself instead to the lair of Jarinbissar," she continued. "It reaches out to humanity with gloved fingers, soft and expensive. Writes a million narratives on ash paper, insubstantial and reeking with smoke. A tainted and distorted dimension that feeds on fear, on violence, on all that divides us from each other. He clung to his power, to his life that grasped the spoils of his dreadful actions. Bierscath became so immersed in its talons that he was granted a similar relationship to the dark dimension that the Solars had created with Tanamaarin."

"Solars? Tanamaarin?" Cathy prompted.

It was Os who answered. "The Solars are beings of Tanamaarin. A dimension that entangles with our own, so that the Solars pass between their own dimension and ours. Typically they do not leave a loud imprint on history in themselves but facilitate and guide. They always inspire and give love. The love that they carry within them is like the sun to our moon. Of a grandeur that we recognise in our hearts and for which we will always yearn. Even Bierscath, in some blinded corner of his wanton mind."

"So he didn't die?" asked Cathy.

"No," Amy shook her head sorrowfully. "He didn't. He became a creature of Jarinbissar. Over these hundreds of years he, and others of his kind, have carefully created the building blocks of hatred, prejudice, greed and fear. Above all fear. He and his ilk are responsible for every major atrocity in modern human history. Hiding mostly in plain sight, they twist and distort language and use whatever mechanism is at hand to fuel the dark energies on which they feed."

"How do you know all this, Amy?" asked Os. "Your recall of the long past has clearly grown, surpassing my own I think. But Bierscath?"

"I have seen him. It was as if Ellan had whispered her power, so that it became mine for that moment. I had only to see his eyes pictured for an instant, to read all he has become."

"You know who he is?" Gerald challenged.

"I know who he is," Amy confirmed. "But I think the Order has known for some time."

Her eyes fixed on Mena, who nodded thoughtfully. "Elijah Tregothan. But we could not be certain."

"You can be certain now," Amy told them. Excusing herself, she left the kitchen.

Chapter Forty-Three

James turned from his computer. "It's done."

"Thank you," replied Os.

"I'm still not certain," began Gerald, stopping as Mena caught his eye.

"You agreed," she told him. "Everything is different now. We must be different now."

"It's very subtle," Richard commented. "Are you sure he'll make the connection?"

James nodded. "It's not just about the computer with this man. It's what Amy said about getting entangled with his consciousness. A few times I have felt compelled to just let him know about us, found myself unable to sleep with thoughts of how stupid we all are trying to keep hope alive in such a dark world."

"You kept us safe for so long James, while discovering so much about a man as elusive as Tregothan. Thank you."

Mena put her arms around the young man, receiving a heartfelt look of gratitude from Gerald.

"Will he be able to locate us in the farmhouse?" Os kept his jaw set as he saw the look of trepidation circle the room.

"Not straight away, but I suspect it won't take long," James confirmed.

"What if he just sends his assassination team to wipe us all out?" Richard posed the question.

"This is personal," replied Os. " Waterman was holding me until Tregothan arrived. He didn't use the name, but he didn't need to. I don't think he'll trust anyone else to deal with us now."

"What about Amy? Can we let her know?" Mena asked, showing her concern.

" We agreed no contact. Nesu will alert me if she comes near enough to talk in another way."

"Telepathy?" Mena was fascinated.

"Of a sort," he smiled.

The door to the office opened and Joy entered, addressing Gerald. "I believe the phone call you were expecting has just occurred. I did as you asked and answered truthfully."

"What did he want, Joy?"

"He wanted to know about our centre, what we did. The link to our Just Giving page."

"Did he give a name?"

"From a new 'Farming Retreat' magazine," nothing else. "It doesn't exist, I checked."

"Thank you, Joy. You should all leave now." Gerald smiled his encouragement.

The young woman hesitated, trying to find words but in the end she simply nodded and left.

"It's not too late, Cathy," Richard's voice caught as he looked at his daughter who did not reply. They had been arguing since the decision had been made to evacuate the rest of the Order. He sighed his resignation with the bang of the minibus door and the sound of tyres crunching gravel in the farmyard.

"You're sure it's them? "Julia asked.

"Pretty much." Mena sighed.

"What now?" Julia asked Os.

"We wait," he replied.

◆ ◆ ◆

Waterman was dying. Once the link with the napoten was broken, it was a long, slow, and painful death. Every part of his body cried out for the connection to be restored. It was scarcely less intense now than it had been that first night, when it felt like his skin would spontaneously erupt. For the first time since he returned from university, it meant that Tregothan could not locate him. Had he known the true impact of carrying the instrument, he would never have gone near Maria. He knew killing Bello and Venmorin would be a body blow to Tregothan. He had feigned more incapacity than he had felt when Caleb picked him up, though it seemed every hour he deteriorated further. It had been easy enough to sneak into the boot of Bello's car, using his own tools to ensure he could get out at the Asters. Somehow he had found the strength to remove both bodies to the hidden cellar where Osweald had been kept. They could keep Caleb company. He had waited until the company assassin had returned to his car after talking with Bello in the grounds. Concealed in the back seat Marcus had shot him before he had time to start the vehicle. It had taken him some minutes to work out the mechanism to the newly installed entrance to the cellar from the grounds, dragging Caleb's body to where he himself had once lain unconscious. Stepping over the three bodies sprawled on the floor, he disabled access to the internal door. Now there was only one way in and one way out. Time for another sip of brandy by the fire.

Cathy could not conceive how Os was managing to sleep. Probably sheer exhaustion: he had had virtually no rest since his return the previous morning. She had tossed and turned most of the night. Finally at five o'clock she put on soft shoes and quietly made her way towards the refectory. Dressed only in a T-shirt and shorts she pulled her arms around her in the cold, dark morning. They were the only two left inhabiting this side of the building, the others had rooms downstairs, to the right of the chapel. About to make a cup of coffee, she became aware of a figure at the double patio doors. Male, tall. She quickly turned to fetch Os but felt yanked away from the connecting door that would take her back to him. A whispering in her mind. 'I have missed you my dear.' That voice. She seemed to have known it all her life. 'At last you have come back to me.'

The pull towards the bright figure at the doors was irresistible. She could see his face now in the moonlight. So beautiful. A yearning seized her and repressed all other thought. She unlocked the glass doors. As she stepped towards him, he took off his coat and she pulled it around her shoulders. Soundlessly, he guided her across the grass and down the path, where Price was waiting with the car.

Chapter Thirty-Six

Ava Bello liked to think she was a woman of taste, who appreciated the finer things in life. Her house had been filled with the treasures she had collected over the years. The really expensive acquisitions had been placed in hidden nooks in her own penthouse style bedroom that took the whole of the top floor. There were a number of guest rooms on the floor below with ensuite bathrooms, which was where she now slept. Venmorin had taken the adjacent bedroom, instructed to remain in the Asters and not to return to his own penthouse apartment in Salford Quays. Tregothan, who took possession of her personal rooms, had taken each perfectly sculpted piece, each uniquely painted canvas, casually despoiled them and then thrown them over the banister. She had been able to recover just one, a Banksy she had recently acquired, that could be restored, the rest were destroyed. Tears ran down her face as she picked up the remains of her beloved art, for which she had given so much. On their behalf she had commissioned everything from embezzlement to murder.

Venmorin had also found that some of his precious and carefully laundered shares were now worthless, all but bankrupting him, was how he described it. In fact, it meant he was down to his last few million. Venmorin sat on the bed, Bello in the chair. "At least we're still alive."

"For how long?" answered Bello.

"If he wanted us dead, we'd already be dead."

A bell sounded below. The ostentatious summons that Bello used to summon her personal servant, Janice Lamb, to attend her.

"Does he intend us to answer that?"

Venmorin nodded. "Let's go."

The beautiful, carefully designed room gave her no comfort

that afternoon. The modified lighting, log burner, aromatic flowers, did not speak to her of prosperous success. He, perfectly and casually groomed, compelled them like two misguided schoolchildren. Tregothan had his hands in his pockets, looking over what Ava considered an impressive view of rolling countryside.

"You have brought me here when I am needed for important negotiations elsewhere."

It was clear that his team were responsible for stirring the potential for hate and brutality now raging in the Middle East.

"It was Waterman," began Ava. She stopped abruptly as he turned a savage look upon her.

"Marcus is gone!"

It was the nearest thing to personal emotion, on behalf of another, that they had seen him display.

Tregothan spoke, returning to his position by the window. "I am leaving today."

Bello and Venmorin dared not look at each other lest they show their palpable relief. Tregothan's sinister smile acknowledged his awareness of it, as he turned towards them.

"You live for but one reason. The escape has forced Ellan to show herself. Marcus bound his prisoner with a cord designed to slowly poison him. It's possible he is also dead by now."

"But how can we be sure?" A disdainful glance silenced Venmorin.

"Marcus gave me one name. Osweald is Joseph Ryland."

"Anything else?" Venmorin had recovered some of his natural arrogance.

Tregothan did not respond. "Find them both. Dead or alive. You have one week."

Price opened the door behind them. Tregothan swept from the room leaving behind him a wave of despair. Bello and Venmorin strode to the position that their employer had just vacated. They did not speak until Tregothan's car had exited the grounds.

" Get Caleb," Venmorin instructed.

"Get him yourself, " Bello replied, grabbing a suitcase from a storage cupboard.

"Don't be a fool, Ava," Venmorin snatched the suitcase from her hand. "There's nowhere to run."

She pushed him to one side and placed the case on the table, proceeding to the wardrobe in the bedroom. Seconds later he heard her scream. Running into the room he found her shaking, folded into a foetal position on the floor. In the wardrobe her clothes were splattered with blood. In the bottom was the severed head of Janice Lamb.

The sound of hooves on stone became more distinguishable, as Amy left the kitchen for the quiet passageways of the original monastery. Following the sound she wove her way through the narrow stone corridors, finding herself outside the chapel they had first entered that morning. That morning! She felt as though she had lived almost a lifetime in one day. As the door opened, the glow of Avide's portrait was like bioluminescence in an ocean. 'The Order of the Watching Ocean and Listening Sea' seemed to make more sense. Tears streamed down her face as she looked into the gentle eyes of the Solar, remembering the day she, as Ellan, lay dying by the tarn. The first time she had seen the wondrous being of light, who named himself Avide. She knelt on one of the cushions scattered on the stone floor and felt no surprise to feel the touch of his hand stroking her head. In the distant past, when Ellan was troubled or bereft, he often came to her, depositing the energy of his presence in invisible touches of light and comfort. The tumble of relentless thoughts stopped their motion as she sat with her beloved Solar, unaware of passing time.

A physical touch on her shoulder, Os. She had not heard him arrive. She felt him sink into place by her side. "I can feel him," he said simply. "Do you think this is what we came to do? Have we found our Avide in discovering this old monastery?"

She shook her head. "Os, we need to leave. On our own."

His face turned away from hers for a moment. He held her hand and again faced her.

"I don't know Amy, I think they need us here. And whoever engineered this will be waiting for any survivors to show themselves."

Amy looked at his earnest face. In the dim light his grey eyes told her many things. She nodded.

"Perhaps you're right. They need more protection than they know."

She took the scroll from the inside pocket of her gilet, keeping the small notebook she had found in her aunt's room.

"You'd best take this back," she told him.

He took the scroll and placed it securely in his own pocket. "Everyone's getting sorted for the night."

Amy looked at her watch. Ten pm. Os gave her a hand up and they headed back towards the large office space, where pallets had been put down for sleeping. As there were only the six of them, each one had been placed in a way that gave most privacy and comfort in the nooks and crannies, boxed in by the available furniture. Everyone else was already bedded down. Mena wished her a good night as Amy weaved her way to her own corner, near the entrance to the hidden rooms.

She slept for three hours then quietly rose, careful to make her exit as silently as possible. At one-thirty in the morning the storage area was even more clinical and cold. Amy tried hard to dispel the images of hospital mortuaries from her mind, as she picked out supplies from the various fridges to fill one of the backpacks. It was a balance between what she could usefully carry and how much would unacceptably slow her down. There wasn't much time, she needed to put distance between herself and the others. That afternoon, before her vigil in the chapel, she had made her way along to the area of the monastery to which neither Gerald nor Mena had yet introduced them. A very similar system had been used, reflecting that in Mena's office. She guessed, rightly, that the way to open the entrance would be at hand. Literally, it turned out to be a set of plastic prayer hands that didn't quite fit the archaic environment. The fingers connected against a small pad, hidden in the wall on the west side of the building. As the wall slid open it revealed a spiral, stone stair case. She had picked up a head torch, but to her surprise this wasn't needed. Instead, dim sensor lights tracked downwards as she stepped onto the stairs. At the bottom of the stairwell however, and as she moved more deeply into the passageway, she was enveloped in darkness. The stones, so tightly impacted together, embracing each other, evoked old memories. It had been built to the same pattern as the one that allowed Ellan to enter the monastery from the forest. The smell of earth, old earth. A passage wide enough to take a woman on horseback. She placed her hand on her heart and intoned the simple words that came to her, washing the present in recalling the past.

"I, Amy, of the Watching Ocean and the Listening Sea, together with Ellan of the Folded Wind, call Choriscuro to my side."

He was there even as the last syllable was ended, the great stallion neighing, his eyes glinting in the dark and his powerful body next to hers. She fumbled to put on the head torch and climbed onto his back. What would have taken a day's walk saw her reach the end of the winding passage before dawn.

Amy slid down from Choriscuro, her arms winding around his neck, which she kissed before he once more disappeared. Fervently, she hoped she could open the door and that there was still a viable exit, constructed in the same arrangement as before. Effectively the mouth of the western entrance was a stone cave, that appeared to be a solid wall to those who came across it on the other side. She inspected the left side and saw, illuminated, the same carving of herself and Os they had found in the chapel. Tears pricked her eyes as she pressed the carving inwards. There was a shudder. She pressed again. This time the wall grated open and sluggish dawn light filtered inwards. She turned off the torch and made a mental note to recharge the batteries. A startled group of fallow deer watched her suspiciously, as she emerged from what was effectively a mound of stone in the middle of the forest. Trees grew on top and around it, making it invisible to most passersby. Without even thinking she turned back and found the closing mechanism, just where it had been placed in the Monastery of the Folded Wind. A carving of a turtle, to the right of the entrance. She spoke the word, her hands touching the carving, that would close the entrance. "Testudo," the Latin name for turtle.

Dunham Massey was quiet, although there were already dog walkers out and about. Head down, hood up, she made her way steadily towards one of the exits. The big risk was going back to the house, but it was one she had decided to take. She didn't even know what day it was. Tuesday? It was Tuesday. Carefully she manoeuvred herself across Manchester by bus and tram to the house in Urmston, the busy traffic now feeling unfamiliar and uncomfortable. She was pretty certain by now that their enemies believed her dead in the explosion at the farm. Guilt rose as she thought of all those who had died because she and Os had sought refuge there. The fact that Maria's death had not been an accident had also begun to eat away at her. Maria would have told her to let it all go.

Nothing looked out of place as she entered the back gate and opened the kitchen door. To her great relief the place had not been ransacked. That surprised her. Surely Waterman would have reported back to his employer? She spent a little time, despite herself, enjoying the familiarity of home. A shower and a change of clothes. Swapping the backpack for another rucksack, its pockets and space more conducive to what she had to take with her. Maria had given her a pre-paid travel card in the name of Amy Sullivan, holding money in a number of currencies, that she could easily convert back to British pounds. Amy privately wondered how, logistically, her aunt had managed to open the account in another name and had never used the card. Then she remembered that Richard's expertise, and possibly that of James, would have been readily at her disposal. She had never checked the card. It was kept, ironically, in a copper turtle she had brought back from the Canaries as a gift that lived on a desk in the attic. She had chosen the PIN number at her aunt's insistence, using the last four numbers of an intergalactic star, registered by Maria in her niece's name: a quirky gift for her twenty-first birthday. She gave thanks now that it hadn't been in the pack that was destroyed in the explosion. The picture of them both was a great loss to her. Looking around she picked up a wooden figure of an Asian flautist, that was particularly special to her aunt and added it to her pack. The loss of the rucksack in the farm, above all the napoten within it, had played on her mind throughout the night. Her studies had led her to believe that it could have been the key to disempowering Bierscath. Maria had correctly guessed and calculated much about the instrument used to control and inflict misery. She had never seen one, however. Nor had she, unlike Amy, the ability to read the strange symbols of the past. On the silk cloth had been written 'Infinite love begets infinite possibility'. It had been held by Avide and the symbols imprinted by him. The cloth neutralised the weapon, rendering it harmless. Studying the geometric patterns in Maria's book, and using the library in the Farmhouse, together with the power of Ellan that remained in her DNA, Amy knew that she could have gone further. It was her belief that if she could antagonise Bierscath enough to reveal the threads of Jarinbissar, then she could find the shape into which she could place the altered napoten. If she was right it was possible to reverse the powers within the malign object, using the energy of this different time to bring about the destruction of Jarinbissar. What she had not been able to solve was how to do so, without allowing the physical instability produced, to cause harm to those in the vicinity.

Amy headed downstairs to check the road outside and the back garden. Nothing seemed amiss. It was time to do what she had set out to do the day Os had been captured. Turning into the living room she dropped her bag in shock and headed for the front door. "Wait, please."

There was something different. Despite herself, she turned. "I mean you no harm, Amy. In Maria's name, I promise you, I have not come here for any other purpose than to help you."

"Marcus Waterman," she said quietly, grateful for the firmness of her voice. He looked quite pitiful, as if he hadn't eaten for a while. His clothes hung loosely on his limbs and his skin was covered in dark patches, like an apple going rotten. She pushed aside the desire to help him. He may well have concocted exactly this scenario to entice her to believe his story. 'Pick up your bag and leave', she instructed herself, but the voice faded and she did not do so. He was looking around the room.

"I had never been inside this house until the other evening, and I barely had time to notice the reminders of her."

"You mean when you tricked us into believing you were Cathy's father?" She bit on the words hard, angry that he spoke about Maria with such familiarity.

He did not react apart from a slight shrug of his shoulders. "I was more imprisoned than Osweald. When you came banging down the door on Choriscuro you gave me a chance of freedom. I took it."

She stifled the shock at hearing him correctly name the stallion. "I don't believe you. We all have choice. When you say no choice, what you really mean is no courage! You chose to be part of a sickening evil."

"And now I choose not to be. Ellan had compassion."

"I'm not Ellan," she returned.

"And Ellan knew her own power. What does your heart tell you, Amy? All your experience of dealing with those forced into situations they could not avoid?"

"You know nothing of me."

He shrugged his shoulders again. "Less than I should certainly, but not nothing. I know where you spent the holidays. The dark places you rolled up your sleeves and gave what was needed regardless."

"I don't trust you," she said simply.

" Nor should you," he said, expressionless. "I am sincere now, but you are right, I lack courage. Just now I can be trusted to help you understand what you are facing."

 Amy allowed herself to acknowledge the great weariness in his eyes and the physical signs of dehydration. "Where have you been since that night when I came to find him?"

"Hiding," he told her, "in an old haunt, not far from here."

In his pitifully bedraggled state she could not ignore his needs. " I have meals in the freezer. You need to drink some water." His eyebrow raised slightly. "Then you leave," she told him.

He gave a small grunt, a half laugh, aimed at himself rather than her.

"Your aunt made sure of that. She had many skills. No one tainted with Jarinbissar can survive for long in this house without becoming physically sick. I have no intention of staying, nor any expectation of kindness."

A wistful and terribly sad expression moved across his face. The unexpected poignancy she felt made Amy remove her coat and head to the kitchen. If she had got this wrong, then it would probably cost her life. But he could have killed her already, she reasoned, taking a homemade soup to the microwave. She picked what she felt would nourish and be easy for him after his long fast.

"Go and have a shower," she instructed. " There are clean clothes in the bedroom you saw the other night, they'll hang on you but at least they're clean." Os would not be impressed she was giving away his hoody and jogging bottoms. He nodded, moving to the stairs like a much older man. She watched him for any signs of pain or internal damage. She suspected that once he had found a safe place he'd been either unconscious or semi-conscious for some time and then afterwards survived on very little. How long had he been watching for one of them to return? He was stiff and sore, but she judged his current state to be one of neglect rather than injury.

'Meet service where it greets you', her aunt would often say.

'Really?' thought Amy. 'No. I mean really?'

Chapter Thirty-Seven

I read the note again.

Os don't be mad. I have something I need to do on my own. Trust me. By the time you read this I will be too far away for anyone except you to follow and you need to be where you are. Spend time with Avide as much as you can. I'll return soon. If not in two weeks, then consider I did not achieve what I am setting out to do and don't wait for me. Aims.

The small, neat hand was, as yet, unfamiliar to me, but I had no doubt that it had been left by Amy. My first impulse was to chase after her. *'Too far away for anyone except you'.* She had ridden Choriscuro to the exit and would therefore already be far away. *'Spend time with Avide'.* I had scoured the chapel to see if she had left some further clues but found nothing. Why would she go without discussing things with me? What did she distrust? What did she know?

These questions and others had circled my mind all morning. Everyone seemed shocked and disturbed by her loss. Mena, I thought, most of all. "I thought I had gained her trust," she whispered. "May I see the note?" I let her look over Amy's words. "As impulsive as Maria ever was," she commented, handing it back.

Gerald was firm. "We cannot go after her. She risks not only her own life by this action but, if she is found and taken, then our lives could be forfeit as well."

"Amy would never..." I began angrily, but he dismissed my words with a wave of his hand.

"I speak as it is," he said sadly.

Mena intervened. "Os, we know that Amy would never willingly put us at risk. She is following another path of which we know nothing. However, Gerald is correct. All is finished if she is taken."

" We can't just sit here." James was agitated.

"No, indeed. We must ensure the entrance is sealed," Gerald replied. "She would not know the secret word and the mechanism to do so. And we need to make sure that she is not lying alone and injured in the long passage. James will come with me. It will take us about two days."

Gerald began to stride towards the other side of the room.

"Wait," I told him. " It won't take me two days. I'll go. Nesu will let me ride him."

Gerald, despite everything, could not hide his excitement.

"It's really true that you can bring the lynx?"

They all looked around, fearful that I would do so there and then.

"I can," confirmed Os. "Tell me how to open and close the exit or entrance or whatever you call it. But I think it's needless. Amy wouldn't have left the way open."

I could see the suspicion in his eyes, certain that I would go after her. Cathy was quickly by my side.

" Be careful, Os," she said gently.

"I'll be back in the night. At the latest, tomorrow morning." I gave a reassuring squeeze of her hand.

The passageway was constructed in the same manner as it had been in the Monastery of the Folded Wind.

"Hurry Osweald."

Ellan rode Choriscuro ahead of me. I had taken the leather strap I had fashioned and placed a blanket on Nesu. "He wasn't meant for riding!" I protested. The cat was large, even for a lynx. Somehow, it seemed natural that he could bear me in this way. Nesu was swift as an arrow, as we rode into the forest together, chased by Bierscath's men.

I heard from Avide that Ellan had saved my father's life the previous day. I had gone secretly to meet her at Avide's instruction, to urge her to take shelter in the monastery, knowing Bierscath would seek revenge. Two of his troop came upon us in her cave. I fought them back, using my staff and then the sword of the man I had left

unconscious. We raced across the forest to reach the road before them. "No," shouted Ellan. "This way."
Instead of retracing my route, a little-known track which would offer most safety, she turned her horse towards a cliff edge. Furious and bewildered, I could not leave her alone. I followed and to my astonishment saw her leap from the horse and open the entrance to a cave in the wall of the cliff. Once we were inside, she pressed against the wall and it quickly closed behind us. I gasped as she made a sign in the air and watched a small light appear in the darkness, remaining ever ahead, as we covered the long passage that finally gave entrance into the women's garden.

The memory faded as Nesu padded at speed along the stone passage guided by my headlight. We were as one now and I gave no thought to the fact that another leather strap had been destroyed in my pack when the house was burnt. I lay flat on his back and whispered in his ear, no thought of falling. It was as I had thought, she had safely reached the exit and closed it behind her. We drank water and ate what I had taken from the kitchen. Nesu 's physical form needed to be fed as much as my own. I was about to turn back when another thought occurred to me. I had hardly acknowledged a growing suspicion, something I had read in James' eyes on the day of the explosion.

I spoke firmly to Nesu to stop him chasing deer and other wildlife. Once he took form, these instincts were part of his existence. It was dusk in Dunham Massey. I had spent some time in the library looking at documents of the farm and its location. I was of course, playing with all our lives, just as Amy had done, by coming out into the open. I stopped thinking and set off for Didsbury, this time across country.

The nature of Nesu was concealment and speed. Silently we travelled through fields, alongside roads and rivers, gliding unseen past groups of youths. I had never realised how wild it could be just a little way from the beaten track this far out of the city. I knew the direction in which we must travel and he was able to take me there along routes I could never have found. I thought we had been seen just once, as we passed a bus stop in the distance. An old man who wiped his eyes as he looked out at the fields on a starry evening. A glimpse only, for we had retreated into the fields again as soon as I saw we were exposed. Finally, we came to the outskirts of the farm, where a narrow track led down to the quaint looking farmhouse. It was undoubtedly the one I had seen outlined by the camera before the explosion. And it was remarkably intact! I thanked Nesu, who vanished, as I walked down the track towards the front door. It was opened by Bernadette. Her eyes widened in surprise as she saw me, before she stepped aside and allowed me to enter the retreat house that I believed had been destroyed.

Amy, feeling chilled, placed her hands around her shoulders. She needed to get away as soon as possible. Once downstairs again, Avery still looked older than when she had first seen him. She served him the soup and the bread she had defrosted and he ate, seemingly grateful for her efforts. He reminded her of so many she had seen steeped in narcotic and alcohol use for so long, reeling with the departure from what they hated and loved at the same time. All the time wary that it would make another transgression into their lives. And yet here was no run of the mill substance abuser, here was a man addicted to evil.

"You're right," he said, putting his plate aside. "I'm damaged beyond repair."

"That's not what I was thinking."

He looked at her clear eyes appraisingly. "Perhaps," he allowed.

"What is it I need to know?" She had to go soon.

"You need to know that all is not running well for Tregothan." She didn't respond. "Ah, I see you already know he is Bierscath." This was accompanied by an eerie laugh. "Perhaps you don't need me after all. I remember that Ellan was the one person of whom Bierscath was truly afraid."

"Why?" Amy, shaken, kept her expression neutral.

"She had some kind of immunity to the dark instruments which he used to entrap others. And she could read him. Ellan could look at his black heart and see through to his soul. Even though she loved him, he could never manipulate her mind."

"Loved him?"

"Oh yes, she loved him. Such a woman to have loving you and he, twisted as he was, never understanding the depth of her passion."

"And yet you did?" She was intensely uncomfortable.

"Oh I knew. I was linked to Bierscath in a way that I could not, and in truth, had no desire to change."

"Did he ever love her?" One part of Amy despised herself for asking.

He looked at her with the first glimmer of compassion she had seen in him.

"I have no idea." she saw he spoke his truth. "One might ask what is love to a man like Bierscath?"

"And now?"

"Euair." She jumped at the name, seeing another twist of his mouth. "Yes, he favours the name Ellan gave him. Euair rides the darkness, extinguishes any glimmer of light. Hopelessness and despair are his winged messengers."

"And Avide?"

"I was never privy to the conversations of the monk." The bitterness swelled. " Bierscath hated him."

"Creatures such as Bierscath are incapable of really seeing a Solar. They don't inhabit the same realms of thought, even when they are physically entangled in the same sphere." Not for the first time, it seemed to Amy, the voice of Ellan of the forest echoed inside her own. She stood up, wanting to go and to encourage him to leave. The little flautist fell from her bag, and to her astonishment tears appeared in the eyes of the man before her. "Ah, she kept it after all."

He came over and gently picked it up. "Then she didn't hate me in the end."

Amy gave him a moment and then reached for its return. He gave it up easily. She turned towards the door, as he stood up, accepting their time was at an end.

" You cannot vanquish him without Avide's Mark. It must be whole and intact before you meet him. You should also know that the baton I used is of his own manufacture. When you took it from me it meant that he could no longer track my movements."

"He can track the baton?"

"No, it is far older and more sophisticated than that. The baton is attached to another individual by him. It's a very powerful weapon and its loss deeply felt by the one who has held it."

He turned his face away. "It's impossible to give it away or lose it." Avery laughed. A bitter, sour sound, and once again Amy was presented with his ragged expression. "Osweald was one of the very few who could have taken it."

Amy didn't respond, holding the living room door open for him. He turned back to her as he stepped into the hall. "You should know about Sereka."

Amy listened to him without any sign of emotion. He saw that she had already guessed much of what he had to say. Finally, she was able to open the front door but still he had not finished.

"I think Bierscath has reason to fear Amy Rowan, even more than he feared Ellan of the forest."

Avery smiled the same eerie smile and then vanished into the evening. She picked up the crockery and cutlery he had used and placed them in the bin outside her house. She then wiped everything down.

Using what she had learned from Maria's notes, she spent some time replacing the seals on the house. Waterman, she was certain, would not live long enough to test them.

Chapter Thirty-Eight

I summoned a meeting in the chapel. I had been a chaplain and this was, after all, a retreat house. They were, for the most part, totally oblivious to the level of deception that Amy and I had been subjected. Bernadette's surprise to see me was more due to the fact that she believed I had left for London with Gerald and Mena. I decided, as yet, not to reveal the presence of the monastery or that we had been misled so drastically.

"I wanted to talk about the bombing. The simulation that you did," Os began.

"Did they show it to you?" Joy, oblivious to the distress it had caused, ran on. "We haven't seen it yet. Only Bernadette was privy to the script, all our responses were completely natural."

"It's why we all ended up dead," offered a man in his fifties, producing a wry smile from most of the order.

"Apart from me," Bernadette added. " I had to reflect on the fact that some part of me had a good time deceiving you all." She was laughing easily. "Of course, it was only a simulation. Do you have some expertise in terrorism prevention? Has James asked you to feed back?"

"He has," I told them easily. I went straight into the role of group facilitator getting them to talk about what they might have done differently, how it had made them feel, what it told them about keeping safe. Their responses seemed unrehearsed and genuine. It persuaded me that they were totally unaware of the level of threat that was really out there. The idea of it being one of their own, the Order being infiltrated by someone that could cause them harm, was utterly alien to them. I was careful to summarise at the end and set each of them a task to think of systems that could help prevent such a disaster.

Only Mena, and I presumed Gerald, had access to the office which in turn led to the old monastery, but I was confident

I could break in. However, I decided that finding Amy should be my first priority, becoming increasingly fearful for her safety. I had a quick supper in the refectory, picked up both my own and Amy's backpack, and headed out into the night. Nesu seemed no less agile for the extra weight I carried, able to increase his size to accommodate my needs. I needed time to think and I wondered if Amy had discovered the same duplicity. Where would she have gone? I came to a compromise within myself. I would try Amy's house in Urmston, and if she was not there, I would then head back to the others and confront them.

The exhaustion had kicked in after Waterman had gone. Amy decided to postpone leaving, fearful that he may still be nearby. Desperately tired, she allowed herself a couple of hours sleep, At three-thirty, she was hunting through the attic, looking for another copy of the book from which she had learned so much. It was a great loss, she had intended to go through her aunt's notes in much greater detail looking for answers. She thought of Os, the others in the old monastery and Avide's portrait on the wall.

The mornings were getting lighter, though dawn was still a few hours away. She should make a start on her journey north. After showering and having a small breakfast, Amy gathered her things, checking she had left nothing behind in the kitchen. The wind chimes she had placed on the back gate sang. Damn, she should have left earlier, what was she thinking? She switched off the light and watched with her heightened vision, the long fingers reaching over the top to dislodge the bolt of the gate. It began to swing open. 'Run now', she kept telling herself. 'Get out through the front door!' Her body remained rigid, however. Unbelievably, Os appeared in the garden. She ran out to greet him, knocking over a plant pot and having someone further up the road shout down instructions to be quiet. They held each other, breathing in the fresh pre-dawn air and finding solace in each other's presence. Amy finally took his hand and ushered him inside.

Os grinned. "I seriously can't ever remember anyone being that glad to see me." She smiled, a little abashed. "But then," he added, "I'm exactly that glad to see you too! I can't believe you're actually here. It was a real long shot." He looked around. "Is it safe?"

"Not really," Amy replied casually. "Waterman has already found me."

"What?" He looked around frantically, his memories of being held captive coming to the fore.

"Don't worry, he's gone." She started to make a drink.

"No, come on Amy, let's go. I think we've ridden our luck enough now. We can talk as we go." He was really edgy. She nodded and picking up her bag, followed him, quickly heading out of the door.

Os grabbed the bags he'd left out in the back yard. "My backpack!" She was totally bemused. "How was it not destroyed in the fire?"

"I'll explain on the way," he told her.

"Where?" she asked.

"Anywhere that does breakfast!" He laughed.

"The Land Rover's only a couple of streets away."

"I don't think we can risk it, Amy. We don't know how much information Venmorin has about you."

"Ok. We'll talk it through."

The early morning buses were heading into the city centre, so they decided to hop on one. In soft voices they exchanged the events of the previous day and night. They put their hoods up and headed for Piccadilly Station, grabbing coffee and a sandwich before moving to a quiet seat that seemed not to be covered by surveillance.

Amy shook her head again in disbelief. "It's astonishing that they duped us like that. But why?"

"I'm not really sure."

"I don't believe that they are our enemies. Is that naïve?" She tipped the crumbs into her paper cup.

Os looked up from his cold coffee, it tasted bitter. "And yet, they deliberately created a whole video to deceive us. They also deceived those people in the Order, who trust them implicitly, but they do seem to know nothing of the monastery hidden underneath their building. I got the impression this morning that they know very little of anything, to be honest."

Amy threw the crumbs onto the ground. She was surrounded in seconds by hungry pigeons. Os saw the tears in her eyes, as she stood up, agitated, flinging her coffee cup into the bin by their seat.

"God, I'm sick of not having a phone, or thinking we're being watched wherever we go." She shook her head. "I really trusted them, Os."

"Come on Amy, hold it together." He put an arm around her shoulder and guided her out of the station onto the main street. "We need to think out our next step," he said quietly, hoping that Amy's distress hadn't brought them any unwanted attention. " Apart from everything else, I haven't much more cash and I daren't use my card."

Amy held up a hand for him to stop. She dug into the bag that she had taken from the house, now placed inside the larger one that Os had brought from the Order. She took a deep breath, shaking off any sadness and disappointment she felt hearing about the betrayal. "I think I may have the answer."

She headed towards a cashpoint, bringing out the card Maria had left for her. She inserted it in the machine, tapped in the PIN and pressed for a balance. She stepped back in astonishment. "Bloody hell!" She looked at the screen again and signalled for Os to do the same. He was suitably impressed.

"Where on earth did all that come from?" There was forty thousand pounds in the account.

Seeing a stranger looking her way, Amy pressed for cash and took out £200.

"At least that's one thing we don't have to worry about anymore. God bless Maria!"

"Amen to that," she agreed. "And we can use it to hire a car. She took out the false passport and driving license.

Os smiled. "Now we're talking, but exactly where are we going?"

Amy looked at the smiling face of her friend. Surely Avide's words would not apply to him? No exceptions, she decided. Plus, there was now unfinished business in the Monastery. "Back," she told him. "I refuse to believe that Mena meant us any harm."

"Nor me Cathy," he added. "But do we really need to take the risk?"

Amy looked at him, her spirits lifting. "Yes." Every instinct had drawn her to trust the Order.

"Then we go back."

Chapter Thirty-Nine

Behind the opaque glass of Venmorin's office Caleb gave a report to his employers. He had never seen them rattled like this.

"A strange co-incidence that Joseph Ryland should live in the same building as Cathy Austen. Even stranger that his car, one that is now sitting in Martin Street in Urmston, was the one we tracked following her disappearance," Caleb commented.

"When you wrongly thought you had disposed of Richard Greig!" Ava inserted bitterly.

"Until this morning," he continued calmly, "I was sure they'd left the country. We have been up all night watching CCTV from airports and railway stations. I could have done with Janice's help."

They still hadn't told him where she was.

"And?" A tense Venmorin, prompted.

"I found this." He produced an iPad from his briefcase and brought up a recording of a man and a woman at Piccadilly Station. They had been picked up when she, looking agitated, had walked towards a camera at the entrance to the station, to be quickly followed by her concerned companion.

"He fits the description of Ryland and she, I am almost certain, is the girl Waterman sent me to find a few days ago."

"He never mentioned a girl," Bello told him.

"Her mini was parked at the infirmary where Ryland used to work as a chaplain. I was able to find out that he owned an old Land Rover and was presumed to have collected it at the weekend. That vehicle is now parked a few streets away from his car."

Ava let out a sigh of relief. "Tell me you've got them!"

"Not yet, but it shouldn't be long. The girl is Amy Rowan. She lives in Martin Street and this is very likely where Cathy Austen, if not the whole family, have been hiding."

Before Bello could ask, he lifted his hand. "That building is now empty." He looked disappointed, but did not elaborate.

"You searched it of course?"

"Of course." He had no reason to think that his men had lied when they told him it had been searched. And yet, he did.

"They were obviously heading away from the station when they were captured by the CCTV. I picked them up again at a nearby cashpoint but could find no transaction under either name. It seems that they're using someone else's card."

"Do you think this girl is the one he's looking for, Karl?" Ava avoided using Tregothan's name in front of Caleb.

"Possibly," Venmorin replied. "Good work," he told Caleb, by way of a dismissal. He, at least, knew the value of loyalty.

"I could do with Janice along as well," Caleb again told them. "We need to cover a lot of footage."

"Just go!" Ava Bello was trembling. "I'll help in a bit," she said more easily.

When he had left, Ava began pacing the office. "I don't understand how they should be connected with Greig and Cathy Austen. I don't understand and I don't like it!"

"I don't like it either. But we should be able to ask them all in person very soon. And when we do.." Venmorin relished the speculation. The sting of the humiliation they had endured, the renewed grasp of cruel power, meant there would be no mercy once those they sought had been found.

Bernadette had answered the door once again, paying little attention as Os and Amy reclaimed the rooms they had used previously. The hired Jeep was parked some distance from the path to the farmhouse. Most of the Order were out on the farm, catching up on the jobs that could be done in winter. Others were busy in the kitchen. A couple were meditating in the chapel as they passed. Os pulled out Mena's swipe card.

"How did you get that?"

"She gave it to me, remember?"

"Handy!"

"Don't suppose you made a note of the number?" His hand was on the hidden keypad.

"685," she answered immediately.

"Hmm, that would have been my guess too. The year the monastery was built."

"Not a guess then."

Os keyed in the number. After a few seconds the stone wall slid open as it had done previously, revealing the 'defunct' lift.

" We should be prepared Amy, just in case."

She nodded her understanding. "I know, this could be our biggest mistake to date!"

"Ready?" He asked.

"Ready."

He pressed the arrow for down.

Neither were expecting to see anyone in the corridor as the lift opened. The area was far removed from the office and kitchen. They were quite dumbfounded therefore to meet the whole group, preparing, under James's instruction, to build a wall in front of the lift. James knelt at their feet, a trowel in one hand and a brick in the other. He had already laid the first row. If Amy had any doubt about Mena's innocence in the deception, it vanished as she saw the utter confusion and astonishment on her aunt's face. "Amy, Os!" The delight at seeing them was almost immediately replaced by a deep frown, as she realised the lift had not been rendered impassable.

"But it should have collapsed in on itself. How did you find it under all the rubble? You were right James, to think it might be a weak spot for entry."

Os bodily picked up James and threw him into the lift. Gerald immediately moved to protect his son but James yelled for him to stay back. "Please," the IT genius told them, " I can explain."

"James," Mena said firmly, "in the office, now. Everyone in the office now."

Like Maria, Mena's voice exerted authority when it was needed, noted Amy, stepping over the bricks. In silence, they all dutifully followed the older woman, as she led the way back to the office. No one spoke until they were all seated around the table. Gerald had positioned himself on one side of James, Richard on the other.

"How and why was this hoax manufactured?" Os deliberately set the question so that he could see the reaction in every face. He had his eyes fixed mostly on Cathy, who quickly assured him she knew nothing of it.

"What hoax?" Gerald's voice rang sternly through the general cacophony.

"I'm sorry dad." James was pale and sweating. "There was no bomb. The farmhouse is all still there."

"Everyone is alive. Bernadette?" Mena was a mixture of utter relief and total confusion.

"Answered the door to us as if nothing had happened. Which, of course, it hadn't. The Order is out on the farm doing everything it usually does preparing for the approach of spring." Os turned to Richard. "What part did you play in all this?"

Richard was aggrieved. "Absolutely none!"

"It was all my doing." James looked forlornly at Gerald. " You put me in charge of health and safety. I told you I'd run an emergency simulation while you were away."

"I thought you were talking about a fire drill!"

"It was a bit more than that. I said I would film them and then feedback my thoughts. When I saw how clueless they were about danger, I got a bit creative with the graphics."

"Have you any idea what pain you have caused us?" Mena's voice was shaking.

James seemed truly shamefaced. Gerald was incandescent with rage and shamed that his son had engineered such a thing. "You and I need to talk now."

He hauled James out of his seat and into the adjacent office. For ten minutes Gerald's rants rang out, as he bombarded his son with angry accusations and despondent cries.

Os entered the room when the shouting was mostly spent. "We need him back in here, Gerald."

The forlorn young man looked at his aunt.

"I'm sorry Mena, but I had to find a way to keep them here. I knew Tregothan was trying to find you Os, and you too Amy. You have no idea how deadly he is. None of you would have agreed to the deception if you had known."

Mena put a hand on James' arm to prevent any further expiation. Something that Amy had read in Maria's notebook occurred to her. "How long have you been tracking him?"

"Months. I believe he played a major role in the terrible world events we are now seeing."

James pressed his hands over his eyes, letting them slide down his cheeks. A man under stress and very near the edge, thought Amy. Why hadn't she recognised the signs before? She looked more closely at her friend.

"Two years of war." He was talking to the whole group, an outpouring of grief. " Like most, I held my head in my hands as I listened to more stories of atrocities, pictures of children dying and dead. First in Ukraine and now the Israeli-Hamas conflict. And who knows what conflicts are to come? So much hate, so much violence, so much war. Mena told me that the world had moved on, but my eyes and ears revealed everyday how much we had not. I could feel the whole planet heaving with sorrow, that the old energies of war had lashed out. Mena said it was like the writhing tail of some sea monster rolling recklessly in its death throes. Destroying as much as it could before we could finally lay it to rest. She said she was sure that the world would come to know peace and cease the blind surge of revenge and hate, hate and revenge. After all we faced together in the pandemic, nations coming together; now all I can see is the ugly nature of our darkest selves."

Tears shone in his eyes as he looked at Os and Amy. "When I saw you two together you gave me the first hope I had seen in a long time. Like candles in a dark room. I couldn't allow you to be snuffed out."

Amy gently took hold of her friend's hand.

"You became entangled with the consciousness of Bierscath, or

Euair as Ellan once named him, the poison tree. The more you tried to live in his world, to understand how he operates, the more despairing you became. You feel the safety that has always been here in this place and you wanted us to have it too."

James buried his head in his hands, as Mena stroked his head. Gerald too, laid his hand on his son's brow. The others left them together and descended into the kitchen.

Chapter Forty

"What is it you have to do?" Os helped Amy pack her bags in the boot of the Jeep.

"I'll explain when I've done it."

"But how do we know you'll be okay?"

"Os. I 'll be back in two days." She jumped into the driver's seat. "Bye."

Amy refused to look back at her friend, as she drove the Jeep towards the motorway. An hour later she pulled in to fill up at Carnforth Services. She smiled at the assistant who vaguely acknowledged her as a familiar face. Ten minutes later Caleb's operatives reported sighting the woman they had been searching for. He knew the value of habit and had figured that she might return to finish her interrupted journey north. He had set up a twenty-four-hour watch on places where he knew she had been, including the service station. He phoned Bello immediately, reporting what he had seen and giving Ava the number of the jeep.

"Stand down." Bello's voice had lost the usual acid tone that she used with him. Did she sound scared?

"But," began Caleb.

Another voice in the background. Not Venmorin.

"I said stand down," ordered the man.

He made Bello sound sweet. Her voice was distinctly shaky as she repeated the instruction.

"Will do," he answered, clicking off.

Slowly Caleb edged the car down a small side street. His survival instinct was hinting that perhaps it was time he looked for another job. A shabby figure in a sweatshirt and jogging bottoms hobbled down an adjacent alleyway. Something familiar. He took a left at the bottom to bring the car around and to make sure he passed the end of the alley. Caleb pulled up the vehicle.

The person gave virtually no fight, as he was ushered quickly into the passenger seat. Caleb started to ring Bello, but then remembered the voice in the room with her. It could wait, he would clean Waterman up first.

Now that we could, it seemed none of us wanted to leave the old monastery. That is of course, apart from Amy who had left as soon as we had established that the Order could be trusted. I couldn't let myself dwell on it, or why she had felt unable to tell me where she was going. James was still being cared for by Mena and Gerald and Richard and Julia were busy in the kitchen.

Cathy reached out her hand. "Can I talk to you?"

I took the hand she offered, finding that it fit perfectly into my own, as we headed down the corridor towards the chapel. Under Avide's Solar gaze I let myself acknowledge that I was falling in love with the beautiful woman beside me, as we sat on the cushions expressing our concern for James and the possible consequences of what he had done.

"Why did you come back? You must have thought it was dangerous?"

"It's hard to say. It was like the world tilted upside down thinking you might be the enemy," Os explained.

"Me?" She moved in closer.

"Yes, you," I replied, closer still.

When I kissed her, I simply felt whole. There were no words needed. She leaned into my shoulder and I put an arm across hers, where we stayed huddled together, until James came looking for us some time later. He looked exhausted and seemed to accept the fact that we were in each other's arms. We put an end to his apologies before they had hardly begun.

"Where's Amy?"

"No one knows. She wouldn't tell us. She said she'd be back in two days," Os outlined, although James looked unconvinced.

He left the chapel and we followed him up to the kitchen. Richard and Julia passed no comment on our holding hands. I felt as if I never wanted to let her go. That night we joined the others in the farmhouse and Cathy came to my room again. And stayed.

◆ ◆ ◆

So much of the building work in the part of the world near Corbridge in Northumbria, had been undertaken using stones from Hadrian's Wall. It had been built by the Romans at the top of England and reached from coast to coast in its day. Amy could hear Choriscuro whispering, as she drew nearer to Bywell, on the outskirts of Stocksfield and not far from the course of the Roman wall. Once, the story went, there were two monasteries and a sizeable community, that thrived in this place. One wore white robes and the other black. In the mellow autumn afternoon, all that remained was a castle, two churches and a private estate that encompassed swathes of countryside. There was no outward sign that before either, the Monastery of the Folded Wind had graced this curve of the River Tyne. Amy had parked in a quiet spot in Stocksfield and ridden Choriscuro through the narrow lanes. Centuries fell away with each beat of his hooves. She looked down on the river, lined by trees, as she crossed the stone bridge. They stood tall and naked in the winter sunshine, a carpet of frost at their feet. Although Amy had never previously visited this place, an image of the river in summer, foliage dancing on either bank, came clearly to her mind.

Choriscuro took her to a gate, where she dismounted and he departed. The church, old in this age, had been built on the still older site chosen by Avide. Rays of late afternoon sun swept across the front of the arched doorway, a film of hazy light bathed the Saxon tower. Amy entered to find herself embraced by a sacred energy. It perfused every aspect of this portal, so lovingly kept by its custodians. The altar was pristine, shrouded in a richly patterned cloth. Engraved stone slabs, perhaps from old graves, were mounted on the walls. A wrought-iron, medieval style chandelier, hung down from the wooden rafters. An orchestra of light filtered from small mullioned windows and stained glass. Tears sprung to cleanse her vision, as a tapering white light appeared in the corner of one of the mounted stones. The slab was positioned in shade, mounted to the left of a window in a small corner of the church. A silver strand of light, captured from the fading sun, moved upwards along the edge of the stone, curling its way across the top and down the other side. It continued to do this until Amy drew nearer. She peered at the faded outline of a market cross and a figure in monk's clothing. She knew this power, even if Maria had not written about it. A story hidden within a story imprinted on stone. At the right time of day, when the light fell in a certain manner and it was greeted by a kindred spirit, the stone would reveal its hidden message within. Like noticing pixels in a picture, she could see the solid slab break down into tiny grains of dust, that readjusted position amongst themselves. Colours appeared, flashes of gold and reds. And green. A woman, in a green cloak, her face hidden, auburn hair falling as she reached down and then reached out of the stone. Amy raised cupped hands and into them dropped Avide's Mark. The small white fist retreated, and the stone slab shifted back to its original markings. Inert. Amy looked down upon the blue pyramid in her palm, watching the dance of diamond light within. One half of the octahedron that was Avide's Mark, given to Ellan for safekeeping fourteen hundred years before. Amy tucked away the precious stone in her pocket. Silently she sat in the old church as the sun set on the day. Even then she was reluctant to leave such a sanctuary, a precious dimensional crossing point, where the energies of the past and present melded together in love. Eventually she left the church underneath a clear sky, stars whispering their tinkling messages, the moon opalescent and full. Amy reached the bridge, stretching for a view of the river in moonlight. Suddenly a dark figure came out of the shadows and placed himself in the middle of the lonely road. Amy, still bathed in the energy of that afternoon, took some time to make out the shape of the man, who seemed instantly to swallow any light.

"Hello, Ellan."

'Euair,' whispered Ellan's voice in her mind, echoing down through the ages.

.

Chapter Forty-One

"You cannot stay hidden. Not any more." Os had asked for a meeting and Gerald had taken him to a sizeable room in the farmhouse containing a table, chairs and whiteboard. On one side of the table sat himself, Cathy and Mena, on the other Gerald, Richard and Julia.

"We cannot endanger everything we've worked for all these years." Gerald folded his arms.

"And how would you describe what we have worked for?" Mena asked.

"What do you mean? The farm has been a place of refuge and learning. It's funded support for communities all over the world." He stopped, calming his voice. "Granted, in a small way, comparatively." Gerald sighed, a pleading expression in his eyes, as he focused across the table on his half-sister. "You know, more than any other, the importance of our work as instructed by Avide. We have kept his memory alive, holding a place of tolerance and a spiritual community free from politics and power games."

"I agree with Gerald," Richard said quietly." Our function is to protect and preserve. That is why this monastery was first built."

"No, not entirely." Os stood up, as Cathy gave his hand an encouraging squeeze.

" I was once Osweald, who supervised the construction of the Ord Na Farraige Eisteachta agus an tAigein Faire. I also know what Avide instructed me to do, in that other life, long ago."

His eyes closed for a moment as he recited the words of the Solar:

"Build it the same Osweald. A refuge for those who see beyond the moment.
Build it the same, led by compassion and love for all mankind.
Build it the same, a house of learning and keeper of mysteries.
And build it not the same. For it must serve the times within which it

dwells, free from the iron chains of what has always been."

All was silent for a long minute. Gerald looked directly at Os. "It was never our intention to start some kind of new religion or cult."

"Nor should it be, I am sure," added Richard.

"Nor will it," Cathy joined the discussion. "Let Os explain."

The ex-chaplain had seated himself at the table again. "Tregothan, Bierscath, has been hidden for centuries. He has become so entangled with Jarinbissar that there is barely anything left of the man he once was. Waterman spoke…"

"You can't believe a word that man says," Richard began.

Os gently raised his hand. "Please, hear me out."

Richard nodded, increasingly uncomfortable.

"Waterman spoke with Amy and she is convinced that he told the truth. Bierscath is still immersed in the events of the late seventh century, when he was more subject to human emotion. His hatred of Osweald and Ellan remains paramount. He is also obsessed with finding Sereka."

"Sereka?" Richard was agitated now, Julia put a hand on his arm.

"Let Os finish," she encouraged softly.

"Sereka, his wife in the seventh century, eventually divided herself from him enough to re-enter the normal cycles of birth and rebirth. Gradually, over many lifetimes, she has become untangled from the net of darkness. It is not something of which Bierscath can conceive. He is convinced that she is only waiting for him to find her and then he will return Sereka to the being he corrupted so long ago."

Richard began to speak again, but Julia squeezed his arm more firmly this time.

"Richard," Os looked at him keenly, "Bierscath cannot find her, she doesn't exist."

Richard gave a nod, a gentle smile. "She escaped the constraints of Jarinbissar long ago," he said.

Os gave an almost imperceptible nod. "Yes she did."

"I don't understand," Cathy looked perplexed. " Are you saying this Tregothan guy thinks she's here?"

"According to Waterman, Tregothan believes that she has been reborn in our time. Maria studied her history and Amy found a file of notes about her." Os addressed himself to Richard. " It was Maria's theory, however, that finally and with full knowledge, Sereka would need to face a choice."

"What choice?" asked Julia.

"We can only speculate," answered Os. "We know that Bierscath is aware of the return of Osweald and Ellan. Waterman told Amy that Tregothan greatly fears that Avide has accompanied them. We are the reason he will show himself again. Rather than hide and run, we must draw him towards us and end his influence forever."

Chapter Forty-Two

The memory was swift and near. Just a moment before or fourteen hundred years ago, it did not matter.

She was descending from the Circle of the Unwoven, in which she had laid her brother Osweald. Shortly, she would join him in Tanamaarin. Bierscath, sword raised, obstructed the path, a black hole in the starlit night.
"You betrayed me Ellan. You will pay the price."
His words, like his twisted mind, were meaningless. He lusted for death as once he lusted for her. What he could not own, he would destroy. She turned and ran up the stepped path. He almost fell twice, but she was quick and knew them well. The crunch of his feet on small stones behind her. His hand on her arm, a savage pull on her cloak. She undid the clasp and heard him fall but he quickly recovered. On the edge of the tarn her hair fanned in the wind. The moon swelled to full light as the clouds shifted. His breath misted the air as he reached her. A momentary hesitation, longing in his eyes, eclipsed immediately as he raised his sword. Even as he struck, her arms were stretched outwards. The water of the tarn rose to embrace Ellan of the forest as she fell backwards, her eyes fixed forever upon the stars above.

Amy wondered if the same memory was passing through her adversary's mind. Perhaps she was still awash with the emotion of the day, perhaps it was the presence of Avide's Mark in her pocket, but she was not afraid. Euair had been dark hearted but very human. Tregothan was simply monstrous. She doubted that there was any recognisable vestige of humanity. And yet..
He produced a napoten and a delnome. "You will come with me."
"And why would I do that?"
"As we speak, my men are approaching the farmhouse in Didsbury."

"And?" Instinctively Amy blanked her consciousness, feeling his telepathic reach. Maria had taught her to do this, to use her own power. People like Tregothan were not used to resistance. His temper flared, but Amy held her ground.

"And the lives of your friends are in your hands," he threatened.

" I'm afraid I'm a bit of a loner. I don't have friends. Where was that farmhouse?"

As Tregothan stepped forward, thundering hooves clattered along the road, knocking him to the ground. Amy flung herself upon Choriscuro's back, heading for a river path she had found on her way back from the church. Her pack was still strapped to her side, she shifted it higher, further onto her shoulders to increase her hold on Choriscuro. Without a saddle, on the narrow path in the dark, Amy soon tired. Underneath the wide span of a concrete bridge she dismounted and let Choriscuro go. "Thank you, my friend. Thank you." She patted his flank. "Run a little longer before you leave. They may find the prints tomorrow and I don't want him near me." Choriscuro would follow her instructions.

Amy trudged along an underpass to arrive in a small town, where a sign welcomed her to Haydon Bridge. There was a mini-roundabout leading onto the main street. A brief search showed a railway station within a five-minute walk, a mini-supermarket and a small B&B that advertised vacancies. Amy bought some toiletries and some sandwiches before booking in to the B&B. She paid in cash and was shown to a room that overlooked the intersection between the river, the road and the town. She needed to sleep but her mind refused to be still. How had Tregothan found her? It had to be through the hire car, as she had told no one where she was going. Clearly someone had seen her and picked up her hire car registration number, tracing it back to the name Amy Sullivan. So soon! That meant that her access to money was also compromised. She had taken several individual sums out of various cashpoints on the way back to the farm, as Os had suggested. She still had a few hundred pounds left but it was no longer the safety net Maria had intended it to be. She would have to risk getting the train back. The most disturbing thing of all was the mention of the farmhouse in Didsbury. She felt in her pocket and placed Avide's Mark under the pillow. Amy was asleep in seconds.

The Travel Lodge was clean and functional. Waterman's injuries must have been more profound than Caleb had first thought. He wouldn't eat, he barely drank anything and mumbled continuously about someone called Maria. A pathetic mess, but soon he would be Venmorin's problem. He rang the Asters again, refusing to acknowledge how disturbed he had been by the voice he had heard. Hoping Ava would answer the phone and be alone.

"Where the hell have you been, Miller?"

Typical Bello. No thanks. The use of his surname marked her disapproval.

"I have Waterman!"

"What? He's alive?"

"Barely. You'd best send a wagon." He gave her the address.

One of the private ambulances they used for their trafficking operations arrived within half an hour. To his surprise, Bello arrived in her own car, parking at the back of the vehicle, as two people dressed as paramedics unloaded a stretcher. He unlocked Waterman's room. "He's in a bad way," he warned them.

The door opened revealing an empty bed. Caleb dashed into the bathroom. "He's not there!"

"You idiot!" Bello growled.

"He can't have gone far." Caleb gave instructions to the two men to search the building, enlisting the aid of the reception desk staff, under the guise of looking for his demented father. This almost backfired, as they offered to ring the police when Waterman was nowhere to be found within the building. Mollifying the young woman at the desk, by pretending to take a call about his father's safe return, Caleb finally ushered them all out of the building. Bello joined them.

"Thank God, we didn't tell him." It was a rule between Bello and Venmorin that they never used Tregothan's name out loud when they were with anyone else. Caleb again noted the same fear he had heard in her voice earlier on. Whoever this character was, he had no intention of ever meeting him. He had been shaken by Waterman's deterioration. Maybe it was time for him to exit the company.

"Follow me back, Caleb," instructed Bello. "we need to debrief."

Half an hour later Bello arrived back at the Asters. She expressed her anger at Caleb by debriefing in the garden instead of asking him in, then dismissing him contemptuously to drive back home. Caleb vowed it would be the last time he had any contact with her.

Venmorin was waiting in the sitting room, looking out for the ambulance that was clearly not going to appear. "Well?"

Ava Bello felt the red mist descending but resisted her rage. "He was gone when we got there!"

"What?" His own vicious temper was rising.

"Look," she calmed her voice, " let's have a drink and talk it through."

If either were given the opportunity they would sell the other out to Tregothan, if it meant saving their own life. Waterman, discussing them once with his so-called guardian, gave Ava a slight edge in the art of betrayal. At this point in time however, Ava saw there was nothing to be served by not working together. The grand fireplace was aglow, warmth and colour filling the room in a postcard scene on that cold afternoon. She poured them both a brandy, as they filled ostentatious armchairs on either side of the fireplace, in what she called her small sitting room, that was not small at all.

"The only useful thing Caleb could offer was that Waterman continually mumbled a name, Maria."

Venmorin's hand tightened on the chair. He carefully placed his glass down on a side table. A rattle of the patio doors, before one flew open. "What the….," he said, standing up and going across to close it.

Ava shivered, waiting for him to return to his seat. "What?" She could almost see his mind working, as her own had just been doing. To include her or not.

"Karl," she said softly, "is it something that could help us?"

A slight hesitation, but he turned towards her. "I'm trying to remember."

A shuffle in the shadows. He sat rigid, staring into darkness. "Did you hear something?"

His assistant shook her head, sipped the brandy, mellowing her voice. "Who is she?"

"Was she," he corrected. " Maria Sullivan. About eight years ago I had Caleb run her down on Tregothan's orders."

The door rattled. Venmorin turned sharply.

"You never told me?" continued Ava.

"No."

"Why was she killed?"

" I never knew."

"Nor cared." A rasping whisper from the curtain. Ragged and thinner than ever, the ghostly figure appeared like some apparition, in a hooded top, hands concealed in its pouch. Barely alive, as Caleb had described, yet the contempt in his face was fierce and directly focused upon the pair before him.

"Marcus!" Both shouted together in astonishment, jumping up, moving towards him. Venmorin slowly reached for the knife in his pocket. Two thuds, one bullet in the centre of each head. He had used a silencer, but no real need. Price was the only staff member allowed there during Tregothan's stay and he had left with his master. Taking the seat that Venmorin had vacated, Waterman placed the gun on the table and picked up the brandy.

As Choriscuro's thundering hooves had come charging over the bridge, Tregothan became aware of a significant change in his dark network. Like nerve fibres reaching the medulla, information of those changes impacted his consciousness. In his momentary loss of concentration the horse had knocked him to the ground. Dispassionately, he watched the slight figure of Amy launch herself on to the back of the stallion. Perhaps she still did not know how quickly he could follow. All this in the instant that the lives of Ava Bello and Karl Venmorin were being violently ended. He could not see how or even where, just the fact that their lives were extinguished in this space and time. Earlier, when he had been waiting for the girl, he had become aware of a mistake which finally allowed him access to what he sought most. The phone had pinged with a pre-set alert, showing a breach by the computer expert who had been anonymously tracing Tregothan's operations. His own people had eventually recognised the trace but were unable to hunt down the IP address. Finally they had succeeded. A farmhouse in Didsbury, Manchester. A relatively short distance from the Asters.

He would deal with the girl later, his priorities had changed. Tregothan bowed his head, allowing himself to transform into a creature created in Jarinbissar and rarely seen on the earth. His neck extended into a ridged and darkly mottled skin, ending in a vulture like face. Widening his arms they quickly flapped outwards to form dark sheets of wing. He rose into the night, absorbed into the sky, as the mottled skin changed colour according to its surroundings. A skeletal and grotesque pterodactyl-like predator that would find its way back in the darkness to Manchester and to his oldest enemy.

Chapter Forty-Four

The lights of an early morning truck flashed through flimsy curtains onto the plain wall. Its engine heaved the vehicle noisily uphill rousing Amy from her exhausted sleep. She stepped to the window, pulling back the curtain to reveal the Tyne rippling in the half-light, the roads empty of all other traffic. She slipped the Mark into her pocket and felt a sea-change in her intuition and awareness. Amy was sure she would feel the presence of Tregothan, should he come near. Something was wrong though. Every instinct told her that he could have found her and perhaps some perverse part of herself wished that he would.

A continental breakfast had been left at her request, so that she could make an early start. The first train from Hayden Bridge was on time. She fretted about the items she had left in her car, knowing Tregothan must have found her through hiring the vehicle. Too risky to retrieve them. As the train pulled in to Stocksfield station, a five-minute stay was announced. Impulsively she jumped off the train and ran to her car only a street away. Amy felt like a clay pigeon in a shooting range, all the time looking for someone who might be waiting for her. The street was quiet and empty, as she opened the boot and quickly pulled out the items she had left out of her pack. At four minutes thirty, miraculously, she was back on the train.

Julia's weeping wounded Os far more than Richard's ongoing admonishment and Gerald's 'I told you so' attitude. Mena and James looked at him with sympathy, but he felt their dismay that the trap they had laid had been sprung with disastrous consequences. James had run back the CCTV of the night before, showing Cathy walking out of the patio doors and a tall man placing his jacket around her shoulders. Neither face could be clearly seen.

"Has to be Tregothan," Richard reinforced the point he had been making. "I said he was too powerful for us to take a chance like this."

"Why would Cathy go with him? I don't understand." Julia turned to her husband, her face streaked with tears, expression tortured. "God knows what a man like that will do with her!"

Richard reached out a hand but she turned away.

"He came for her because, in a former life, she was Sereka," Amy's voice reached them from the doorway.

Os' forlorn, but determined, expression as he embraced her, told her that he already knew. Happily Mena and James came over to greet her. Richard, horrified by events, was white. Julia, who had been standing, slumped into a nearby chair. Os took a deep breath.

Amy turned to him. "How long have you known?"

Os looked at Richard. "I remembered a conversation with Avide. He talked about the Custodians of Souls, who often placed themselves alongside particular individuals who had previously been entangled with Jarinbissar. The new lives presented opportunities to be free from the darkness. The custodian would be aware of their previous history and steer that individual towards good. They might be born as a family member, friend, mentor and so on. In this case, a father."

Richard looked towards Julia whose eyes were wide, trying to process all she was hearing.

"Are you one of these Solars?" James asked him.

"Unfortunately not," Richard replied, turning solemn. "I'm all human but I have an enhanced knowledge of the individual with which I have been placed. My lives number a great many here on this planet. Some of us, outside this realm, are given a choice, either to stay and help others or move beyond entirely."

"To Tanamaarin?" Queried Mena.

"Wherever is appropriate," was the enigmatic answer. "Space and time have different parameters when we are not living human lives." Julia had stepped away from her husband. "I'm still me," he told her, his eyes clouding. Immediately, she moved back towards him, taking his outstretched hand.

Mena turned to Os. "You said that Sereka no longer existed."

"That is my belief," he replied. " Sereka's nature is not that of Cathy Austen. How did you find out, Amy?"

"I wondered why the house made her so sick."

"Maria?" Mena asked.

"Yes. Any taint of Jarinbissar would make the person react badly. It took a day or two with Cathy, as it is so remote, but was still somehow there. I suppose I also recognised something in her relationship with Os that resonated through to this time. And Waterman guessed, but I don't think he passed his knowledge on to Bierscath."

"He told you?" Os asked.

She nodded.

"What can we do? We can't just sit here." Julia was becoming more agitated.

Amy walked towards her, placing an arm around her shoulder. We need to put our heads together . I don't think Os and I can do this alone."

"Do what?" asked Julia and Richard together. "What is it you can't do alone?"

Amy turned to include all of the small group.

"Find Avide," she told them.

The morning sky was dimpled with street lights in the damp grey of the Manchester horizon. The roads were uncharacteristically quiet, as the car headed out of the city on the ring road. Cathy sat quiescent, her mind trying to remember something important. Could anything be more vital at that moment than the power that embraced her in the person of Bierscath? The jacket around her shoulders, silk-lined in purple, exuded his scent. An old concoction of time-served earth, mined treasures and blood. She pulled it closer, wrapping herself in its old comfort, its knowledge of her.

The car bumped over gravel, a long drive that wove through parkland. All his movements fascinated her. She relished the beauty of his face, smooth tanned skin, high cheek bones, hair dark as a raven. Eyes, blue as a summer sky. He smiled as he guided her inside. She was so very tired. The bed was fresh, linen caressed her bare arms and legs. She could sleep now, she was home.

Amy's return had brought new hope and a calmness to the farmhouse. She persuaded the others to shower and dress, as most of them were still in nightclothes. She and Mena made a simple meal, working together in the refectory, where the older woman explained how and why James had deliberately given their position away to Bierscath. "We are all distressed, but I think Os most of all. It was his decision to lure Bierscath here. And he must be beside himself with worry for Cathy."

Amy had already heard a hurried version of events from Os and agreed with Mena, he was profoundly distressed but trying hard to keep it together for the others.

Once they had eaten, she asked Os to bring the original scroll which contained Avide's Mark. There were gasps of astonishment as Amy took out the beautiful pyramid she had found in Bywell.

"How did you find it?" Os asked, his fingers stroking each side.

"The night that Waterman came, pretending to be Richard, I had the memory of Avide giving another Mark to Ellan. I felt certain that I needed to go to the site of the Monastery of the Folded Wind. Avide was adamant that Ellan should be on her own, without revealing her purpose to another, when it came time to retrieve it from the place that it was hidden. I decided therefore to go without telling even you Os, knowing that I carried much of the same DNA, into the place where Ellan spent her whole life. I was, as a result, able to become an integral part of the grid she had created to protect the Mark."

"I'm not really getting much of this Aims," James told her.

"These hidden energies were largely visible or, I think, in some way palpable to Ellan. Choriscuro and Nesu use shapes and patterns to link with us in physical form. Maria hypothesised that where consciousness is purposely placed, the patterns created by energies not in our time period, may be revived."

"Nope! Not happening for me!" James shook his head.

Mena reached for his hand. "When you think of your mother James, do you sometimes feel she is with you again?"

James sighed, his mother had died some years ago. He nodded. Amy looked gratefully at Mena.

"And Maria would say that she really is," Amy continued. "The pattern of her energy, the deep personal relationship you shared, is revived by you thinking of her with love. And that love, Maria believed, is the key ingredient of connection. Going alone to the old church in Bywell and concentrating on where Ellan had hidden the Mark, revived the patterns that Ellan had created. Unlike Richard, Os and I haven't lived lots of lives in between our existences as Osweald and Ellan.

I knew, as soon as I was near enough, that the energy of Ellan would manifest itself. And it did."

"It's beautiful and clearly very important to you all, but how does having this Mark help us to find Cathy?" Julia, though she had showered and eaten a little, still looked exhausted and strained.

"It's a good question Julia and one that we need to answer together," Os informed her.

"Both of us have memories of being given these Marks for safe keeping," said Amy, "but neither Os nor I really know what to do with them."

"But you've already used it to heal him," Gerald commented. "How did you know what to do?"

Amy brought the heavy book out of her bag, laying the 'Geometric Patterns of the Spirit', before them. The cover was a mosaic of different shapes that caught the eye, and Maria had inserted pencil notes in many parts.

"She wrote it!" Mena said laughing. " And I never knew." She pointed to the name of the author on the cover. "Livia Ramsnal, an anagram of Maria Sullivan."

"Of course." Os looked reflective. "I think Waterman knew."

"Oh, he knew," confirmed Amy. "He worked on it with her at university, when they were together. No title back then, but he recognised the artwork on the front cover as a conglomeration of the discoveries they had begun to make. He thought she had abandoned it but it seems she simply continued on alone after they split."

"And you think, that in here, we'll find a way to use the Marks?" Os reached for the book.

"Well, not exactly," Amy replied.

The odour of human decay came not only from the hidden cellar but also from his own body. Marcus was propelled chiefly by an iron will and the cocktail of drugs Bello had often used to anaesthetise her conscience. Caleb and Price had repaired the outside door, replacing the oak with solid steel, that opened only from one side using a concealed lever. As soon as Tregothan returned with the girl, he had positioned himself on the bridle path. In less than half an hour, as he had predicted, his old guardian's arrogant tread could be heard on the path above. Marcus waited until the dreadful rage began, when his previous master would enter the hidden space to find the rotting bodies he had left there. He shunned aside the fear evoked by memories of his own beatings, hearing the rasping, cruel utterances, the language of Jarinbissar emitting from inside. A momentary triumph, to lift his waning life force, was all he could now risk. To see Tregothan's utter shock that his pet had turned rabid and dangerous, as he showed himself for that split second before the steel door rang shut between them. A death trap to anyone else, but he knew it would not hold Tregothan for long. As swiftly as he could manage, he made his way back to the house.

Marcus had emptied the cupboards of food, predicting that Price would have the task of replenishing the kitchen. As he arrived at the back of the house, in the deliveries yard, the bodyguard turned with a box of groceries in his arms. His face paled with shock as Marcus approached, barely registering the moment when the bullet tore through his forehead. Marcus left the assassin where he lay and drove the car round to the front door.

The girl was sleeping. She was quite as perfect as Sereka had been in her day. Marcus knew he had spent what strength he had left and was unable to lift her. There was a dark power of suggestibility and manipulation that Tregothan had made an art form, and he had already induced a somnolence of consciousness that Marcus could work with. It wouldn't be the first time he himself had used a lesser form of this method to profit some aspect of his guardian's operations. Very gently he began whispering into her ear; phrases and voices that she most wanted to recognise. Slowly Cathy rose, her eyes open but unseeing, and followed him willingly out to the car. He imagined Tregothan wondering if Marcus intended to kill Cathy Austen, in the same way that his guardian had ordered Maria's murder.

Chapter Forty-Five

"Not exactly?" I repeated Amy's words.

Since she had found the Mark at Bywell there had been a profound change. I think that both these precious objects-only they weren't just objects-allowed us to link more forcibly with our previous lives. As Amy discussed the book Maria had written I saw that it wasn't just a matter of memory, more like bringing the energy of Osweald and Ellan into the present, whilst remaining ourselves. Amy had arrived as I was preparing to go in pursuit of Tregothan. Only she could have stopped me leaving. Even then, I watched the clock, calculating the time before I would set out with Nesu to find the woman who had, once again, become the foundation of my life.

"The Marks are vehicles, at least that's how I see them." Amy reached out her hand to grasp my own. "Os and I are catalysts of a fashion. It is actually you guys that can make this happen."

"Make what happen?" James demanded.

I watched the clock, anxious to leave.

"Please stay for now Os." Amy saw my intention. I felt the war inside me, that every moment lost might mean Cathy was becoming more out of reach. Amy's calm brown eyes told me I had to make the choice to trust her or go. She stood up and walked towards the spiral staircase where she waited for us to follow.

The steel door banged open, scattering the wild life, exposing the dark hole in the earth where so many had cruelly ended their days, well before Inimica had taken possession. One of the reasons that those tainted by Jarinbissar had felt so at home. The spring buds around the bridle path died instantly as the dark shadow of Tregothan passed. Waterman's betrayal brought his mind to that other wound that had never stopped festering. Ellan. The body of Price lay where it had been shot. The unbreakable personal servant, accomplished assassin, caught off guard. From his last brief glimpse of his barely recognisable ward, it was clear to him that this was the only way Marcus could have vanquished the other man. There was little left of Waterman's life now. Tregothan ran up the stairs to the first floor, to the room where he had left Sereka. Gone.

The building trembled, as the power of his rage shook the earth beneath. He reached the window, transforming into the hideous flying creature that reflected far more of his nature than his sleek human form. The chain reaction he had started continued, the home that Bello had so prized, spent years creating, began to implode. In less than twenty minutes, the grounds, of which Ava had been so proud, were reduced to a tumbling mass of fallen trees, dust-choked streams and extinguished growth.

The small group followed Amy down in the lift and along the old passageways to the hidden chapel. She directed them towards Avide's portrait and arranged that they sit in a semi-circle facing herself and Os beneath the vibrant image.

" You are the ones that have held this space and followed the principles taught by Avide so long ago."

She placed the Mark she had been given on the floor between them. Os handed her the scroll but she asked him to transform it in the way she had done, explaining what he must do.

"Use whatever words come to you," she told him.

He placed his middle finger at the centre of the X, feeling the palpable energy vibrating beneath his hand. Gradually the energies swirled visibly into view; blue, streaks of platinum, fiery orange. There were gasps from the rest of the group as it grew to form a pyramid the same size as her own. Without discussion they instinctively held hands.

"I have it," Mena announced. "Look! The shape of the alcove where we found the carving of Os and Ellan." She pointed to the other side of the room.

"It's a perfect octahedron," Richard told them.

"We need to put them together," Amy arranged her own Mark inverted beneath the other.

There was an explosion of different coloured light as the two fused together, a diamond of changing colour, suspended in the air.

They waited expectantly, mesmerised.

"I think that something is missing," Amy decided, about to reach for Maria's book.

"No Amy," Os told her, this isn't written anywhere. "We must find the answer inside ourselves. Try to think with your hearts and not your brains."

Silence.

"There are eight sides," posited Julia, whose eyes had never left the swirling jewel, "but we are only six."

"Two missing," Gerald agreed. He looked around as if he might find the other two somewhere in the chapel.

"Only one," stated Amy, sure. "We need seven."

"Cathy," Os was almost weeping. "I have to go now and find her."

"Together," insisted Mena.

They all stood, the glowing diamond not changing position or form as they moved towards the door of the chapel.

A huge beating of wings sounded outside as they arrived in the refectory. Os and Amy saw the army of Rawdin that covered the fields surrounding the building. Hideously misshapen, their cold mercury stares created a shadowy miasma, a fog of despair that hung, waiting to envelope them. From their midst emerged Elijah Tregothan.

"Bierscath," stated Os.

"Euair," whispered Amy.

"Hold together," Richard said firmly. "Do not be dismayed. Stay inside. Avide's energy still resides here. It will not accept him."

No one had noticed the car crawling into the courtyard. The ghostly figure of Marcus Waterman hobbled out. "Cathy!" shouted Julia.

Richard held her back, running to open the doors but Os got there first. Cathy turned towards him, her eyes distant.

"Hold!" commanded the dark figure, walking unhurriedly across the fields. Cathy stopped a few metres from the building. "Come," the voice instructed.

Marcus, struggling to find his voice, his last breath upon him, somehow made sound pass through his airway and out into the open. "You are released," he said hoarsely, a smile, a real smile, changing his face as he sank to the ground.

Tregothan advanced more quickly. "Sereka, come to me," he repeated.

Cathy turned, struggling to gather her awareness. On the field she saw a dark stain passing quickly over the ground. Threads within threads. Misshapen patterns furrowing into the fields. Turning to Os, she saw the love shining from his eyes, her father and mother close behind.

"I am not Sereka," she said clearly, allowing Os to take her in his arms, swiftly guiding her back to the farmhouse.

Unseen by any of them, Amy had quietly made her way round to the courtyard. She bent over the crumpled figure of Marcus Waterman. She took his hand, as he rasped a final breath, and closed eyes that held the first glimmer of peace she had ever seen in him. Raising herself to stand she shifted her hold on the napoten, walking firmly towards the field. The symbols from the silk cloth found at Croston were now clearly engraved into the awful weapon.

As Os ushered Sereka inside, Tregothan raised his arm in rage to unleash the full power of Jarinbissar. Amy's vision blurred, as she raised the napoten. Like a magnet it drew its maker, his gaze fixing upon her as the Rawdin scattered. The farm, the city, all sank towards the circle of the unwoven as it opened before them. Amy, balanced on a single rock, breathed in the wild air, the visceral force of the land, the touch of infinity. Around her the water remained calm. Tregothan was lifted above her on a black wave, so thick in the texture of his darkness that it formed a platform on the other side of the pool. The sky darkened and howled around the timeless pair. Lightening flashed and ignited the vast net with which he was entangled.

"Ellan," he spat.

"Euair," she said calmly.

"That is an instrument of Jarinbissar. It will not serve you."

"It is your instrument of Jarinbissar and therefore the most powerful of weapons that has served you through the long years you have stolen. Within it I have placed the knowledge of Ellan who loved you, Maria who understood you, and myself, Amy, who stands beside you in the entanglement you have made, with a dimension that no longer possesses purpose on this planet. I have reversed the polarities, Euair."

He laughed. Chilling. Rage turned to madness. Behind him the pool heaved upwards, a black cape of broiling water, from which extended writhing threads of Jarinbissar reaching for Amy.

"Then you will destroy not only me but yourself and those you care for. In a matter of hours you know the ground will no longer hold the city."

In answer, Amy threw the napoten with an accuracy of which Ellan would have been proud. It burned like a flame as it hit his personal magnetic field, finding the black heart of the diseased reality created by Bierscath. Little by little the interconnecting black threads began to disintegrate. In shock and horror, and much too late, he fought the net, becoming more entrapped in its venomous coils. Piece by piece, the napoten swept him into Jarinbissar. Piece by piece, Jarinbissar pulled its dark network from across the planet. The vast coil of water collapsed, swallowing the last moments of the long life of Bierscath, as he descended into the depths of the Circle of the Unwoven.

Amy gasped as the ancient site fell away and left her

standing alone on the empty field. The pain in the arm that had held the napoten was severe, she glanced at the necrotic blemishes across her fingers. The place was now desolate, the fields turned to a scorched, apocalyptic semblance of the former working farm. In order to destroy Bierscath, to exile Jarinbissar, Amy had created the epicentre that would, in a few hours, implode. Wheezing, she dropped to the wasted land, crawling towards the house. Sobbing, she battled with pain and nausea. Os and James were upon her.

"Aims" What the hell just happened?" James looked in horror as the land seemed to be slowly dismantling itself.

"I don't have much time," she gasped. "We need to get to the chapel."

Gently, Os lifted Amy and took her into the building. They shut the doors against the noxious fumes that had begun to permeate the air.

"We need to go down to the Marks," Amy whispered.

The pyramid was still suspended in mid-air, as they filed into the room. Cathy cried out, startled at its beauty.

"Now we are seven," Os counted, as he arranged them in a semi-circle. Amy propped her head onto his shoulder. Once again, without prompting, they all held hands.

The swirling colours glowed inside the compelling diamond shape that the two pyramids had formed. It began to grow in size and then suddenly whizzed across the room . In awe, the seven were mesmerised by the pulsing object, that now filled the back corner of the chapel. It was a perfect fit. No one, until Mena had discovered it that morning, had ever noticed that the area beyond the conference table was a perfect octahedron. Amy saw that the Mark had now become a different kind of space. She could see that the energy was vastly different from that around it. Another pulse of light, a white line across the centre that widened above and below, created an aperture in the diamond. The opening changed shape, moving in and upwards to become vertical. Gasps of astonishment and joy accompanied the appearance of the calm figure of Avide, as he stepped from the centre of the diamond.

"And now we are eight," muttered Amy, raising herself with Os' assistance. All were now standing.

"Dear Amy. Dear Joseph." Avide stepped towards them both. Amy held out her blackened hand, trembling with emotion. He examined it gently, compassionate eyes lifting to hers. At his touch the pain eased to a soft murmur and then ceased as he tenderly embraced her. He raised his hand bringing a chair from the table upon which, with infinite tenderness, he helped her to sit. Os was the only one to see the exchange between them, a silent question answered with the slightest shake of her head. Os found his eyes filling with tears as he felt Avide's arms around him in greeting. The others were too awestruck to speak. Gerald laid himself prostrate on the floor.

"Please, raise yourself Gerald."

"Roderick," embracing Richard and smiling. "My old friend."

Os looked sharply at the man he knew as Cathy's father. "I have lived many custodian lives," Richard told him, his eyes drinking in the serene figure before him.

One by one Avide greeted the others by name, in the same gentle way he had touched the hearts of so many in the Monastery of the Folded Wind. He looked around the chapel, seeing his portrait, taking in each stone as if they told him of the hands that had put them together.

"You did well in your building, Osweald. Thank you all for holding the possibility created by this space," he said cryptically.

Avide was virtually the same as he had been portrayed on the chapel wall. Another small raise of his hand and the table and chairs from one side of the room were now positioned with Amy at its head. He took a seat at the table and indicated that they all gather together around it. A jug of water appeared in the centre with several glasses. Amy saw the energy swirling within and recognised the same liquid she had drunk from the well in the carapace. As each of them refreshed themselves with the water they were gradually calmed.

"Is it drugged?" James felt his agitation and uncertainty

dropping away.

"The water of life," Avide answered. "Your body and mind recognises that this is the essence and gift of the earth."

James carried on, still unsure and bewildered. "Is that like a Tardis?" He pointed to the octahedron. "Are you like Dr Who, floating through time and space, wherever it takes you?"

Avide laughed. It was like hearing the best song ever, he thought. "I am AVIDE," he deliberately pronounced each letter. "Altered Variation of Innate Dense Energy."

"A hologram?" Julia offered.

He reached out his hand to hers. "I am flesh, I am form and I have substance."

" You are a Solar," Richard said softly. "A light being of the dimension of Tanamaarin."

Avide smiled softly. "Part of me exists in Tanamaarin and part of me is here with you. I manifest into form by my will and your love. The Mark is a vehicle that can hold dense particles of light from the dimension of Tanamaarin. The portrait within the chapel helped me to take the form that you recognise from centuries past."

"That's hard to understand," Osweald commented.

"You come when there is a change in possibility," Amy said, somewhat revived by the water. "The heart of the planet, the humans who make it their home, have changed. Possibility has expanded to meet the change. We create our own reality."

"Dear El-lan. Infinite love begets infinite possibility." He reached for her hand. She took and kissed it. "Amy has banished the net of Jarinbissar. In a matter of hours, that deep residue will have left the planet."

"I was just the instrument," she explained. "The world, though it seems hard to see it, has turned against darkness in its heart. What is in our hearts must eventually find expression. Can you make them safe?" she asked, turning directly to Avide, her eyes indicating the dreadful changes above.

"Indeed," he answered.

◆ ◆ ◆

It is hard for me to write these last lines as I watch Cathy sleeping in what was once Amy's cosy sitting room. I took down the picture of Lindisfarne, though her favourite, and replaced it with one I had taken last summer at Simon's Seat. Amy, fresh and smiling, among the heather. I did not know which was more beautiful. The picture of her alive and vibrant or my memory as Avide took her hand and laid her in the carapace in which he had arrived. Only I was able to see inside as she curled on the rug by the well. He kissed her forehead and whispered words for her ears alone. Her face, so childlike, her peace shining, her love as deep as the mysterious well by which she lay.

He went above to the land. At this point none of the others understood that Amy would no longer be with us. A different shock and dismay brought tremors into their voices as they ran out of the monastery. I shouted a warning to remain in the courtyard as the earth shook, gaping craters pock-marked the field where Amy had thrown the napoten. A tornado of swirling darkness coiled over the space that Bierscath had occupied. Avide walked calmly into the centre of it all. As he did so the earth began to settle back to its original shape, the grass reforming across the field. He raised his hand as he reached the wild whirling cone of terrifying blackness, that was preparing to descend. A light, brighter than anything I have ever seen, emitted from his palm. It grew into a magnificent orb that simply swallowed the black malevolence above him. Had it not done so, I had no doubt that in a short time, the city around us would have been destroyed as Jarinbissar retreated. Between them, Avide and Amy had wiped from the planet, the stain of this dark dimension.

And now finally, some months later, Avide remains in the old monastery surrounded by the Order and quietly teaches us all. He no longer wears the robes of a monk and his hair is not so long. He walks even more invisibly amongst us than when we knew him in the Monastery of the Folded Wind. How long that can last I do not know. Just now he lends his presence to those demanding peace and compassion, beyond any rationale for war and hatred. He tells me that, despite the terrible events that pollute our world, in time it will indeed change to reflect the nobility found in the deep heart of humanity. I let the tears come as they will. I feel her arm around my shoulders and her soft kiss upon my cheek and know that Amy's energy is still here. I believe that Avide could have saved her had she wanted it. I knew however, from the silent exchange I witnessed in the carapace, that though it would never be our time to let her go, it was, for Amy, her time to leave.

ACKNOWLEDGEMENTS

My particular thanks to Rachael Shaw for editing this work and bringing Australian sunshine into my Friday mornings. Thanks to Alan Duncan, who not only patiently proofed the manuscript but also accompanied me to so many locations, from underground crypts to elevated moorlands. Special thanks to Veronica Watson who began this journey with me some years ago in Lindisfarne and who has continued to give such valued support for my literary endeavours.

Where would I be without the wonderful advice and feedback from my precious beta readers? Thank you so much Carol Williams, Hilary Evans, Claire Lawton and Bri Hume. I would have been lost without you all. Finally, thank you Conor Watson and Matthew Duncan for your artistic design and production of the cover.

ABOUT THE AUTHOR

Frion Farrell

Frion Farrell is a contemporary fantasy writer living in the North of Engand where unique landscapes have provided much of the inspiration for her novels.

After many years working as a nurse in the NHS, she now spends most of her time writing and travelling.

Printed in Great Britain
by Amazon

48649870R00155